THE ANCESTORS

Also by L.A. Banks (writing as Leslie Esdaile Banks)

No Trust
Shattered Trust
Blind Trust
Betrayal of the Trust
Better Than
Sister Got Game
Keepin' It Real
Take Me There

Also by Brandon Massey

Don't Ever Tell
Whispers in the Night
The Other Brother
Twisted Tales
Voices from the Other Side (with L.A. Banks and Tananarive Due)
Within the Shadows
Dark Dreams (with Tananarive Due)
Dark Corner
Thunderland

Published by Dafina Books

THE ANCESTORS

L.A. Banks
Tananarive Due
Brandon Massey

KENSINGTON PUBLISHING CORP.
www.kensingtonbooks.com

DAFINA BOOKS are published by

Kensington Publishing Corp.
850 Third Avenue
New York, NY 10022

ISBN-13: 978-0-7582-2382-1
ISBN-10: 0-7582-2382-X

First Printing: December 2008
10 9 8 7 6 5 4 3 2 1

Printed in the United States of America

Contents

Ev'ry Shut Eye Ain't Sleep

L.A. Banks

Chapter One

Philadelphia—Early Winter . . .

It was time to get off the street. The darkness was getting darker. Mr. Abe's shop, where he normally slept, didn't have answers for the kind of evil he felt coming. That place had a little light, but he needed the hallowed ground of a church, a mosque, a synagogue, or temple—not just a joint where an old man threw down some herbs and libations.

Too bad he couldn't talk to Abe Morgan about what he was seeing now. But the two had a don't ask, don't tell policy about their lives. Both had done things they clearly didn't want to discuss. Both had seen things they definitely didn't want to see. So as far as him spilling his guts to old man Abe Morgan or vice versa, that was not an option.

Theirs was an uneasy truce and strained living arrangement based on the simple fact that they knew instinctively that they needed each other to survive. Still, that didn't make them friends. It just made them codependent and ornery regarding the unspoken subject. However, something was very different nowadays. He might just have to break down and have a discussion with the old man after all . . . if he could get to him before the darkness finally took his mind.

Slivers of ice clung to the edges of his locks and the new-beard shadow on his face. Bitter wind cut through the layers of sweaters, long johns and sweat pants that he wore beneath his military-green fatigue jacket. But, at least it was morning. His mind always kept the exact time and told him when it was safe. He didn't need a watch.

Rashid Jackson let the tension escape from his spine through a slow exhale as he bent to unload another bundle of newspapers from the stack beside him, the muscles in his arms and legs aching from the exertion. But he had to keep his cover intact, and keep his normal routine, lest he lose the premium lookout post in front of her Rittenhouse Square building. Besides, maybe today would be the day that he could finally work up the nerve to say more than two words to her. If he could just stay awake and sharp until she came down into the lobby, exited the building, and headed off to her job, in keeping with her normal routine. He would ignore the fact that she was good-Gawd fine. That wasn't important. Just interesting. What mattered was the fact that *the shades* were trying to get her. Those vaporous little motherfuckers . . . Vicious.

But would a fine sister like her even listen? Probably not. She didn't even listen to her grandfather who was her last living relative, so why would she ever listen to him? He knew the type: educated, bourgeois, good job, and thought she knew everything. The type that didn't appreciate anything and took everything for granted. The kind that thought that just because he didn't have a so-called good job or a real place to live that he didn't know nothing. Might serve her sidity ass right if he did let *the shades* take her.

Rashid heaved another stack of papers onto the pile he was creating so the police didn't chase him away like a homeless vagrant. That was the thing; he had a place to stay. Mr. Abe saw to that. The old antique dealer was cool peeps and they'd bartered a service arrangement—he was security and kept the young thugs away from the old man's door; Abe Morgan allowed him to sweep up and sleep on a cot in the back. Why the man's granddaughter had such a problem with the transaction was beyond him.

He glimpsed at her building again to be sure she hadn't come out while he was stacking his newspapers. He had a lot to tell her, if she'd believe him. But he also had to wait until the right time to approach a woman like that. Couldn't come out of the blue and seem like he was high on something. He wasn't no druggie, though. With the kinda shit he saw, he didn't need no drugs . . . wasn't trying to alter reality any more than it had already been altered. His mind was all he had, couldn't jack with that. Most days that's where he lived—inside his head. That was the safest place in the world.

Only thing was, how would he convince her that he hadn't had a psychotic break like the Veterans Administration claimed? Demons were chasing him, no matter what the doctors said! Her being a lawyer and all meant that she'd probably dig into his old records or something, and then wouldn't trust him. Would think he was trying to scam the old man out of his old junk in the store, or something equally crazy. But he'd let her know up front that he didn't beg for money—had always earned his. Had worked for over twenty years for the military and had a pension coming . . . had a small disability check that was all he needed. Paid taxes, had given his life to his country, had served well and served hard in the Gulf War. Hell no, he wasn't some parasitic junky that ate out of the garbage; he was a vegan. Rashid looked at his newsprint-smudged hands. His clothes might be old, but he was clean. Kept his body fit; the body was his temple. Did Tai Chi every day. Played dominoes with the old men, the best players, every day to keep his mind sharp.

With the task of arranging papers on his corner turf completed, relief swayed his gait as he sauntered across the park to his favorite bench. All he needed was a few moments to rest and take a load off his feet. It had been a long night of walking the neighborhoods. Three robberies aborted. Not bad. But, it seemed like *the shades* were beginning to gather and get denser each evening. It was as though time was set on fast-forward, and he'd noticed that the crime pace had picked up ever since the real millennium change had taken place.

He glanced back at his pile of papers knowing that he could run back to his territorial spot if someone tried to steal one.

Daylight, praise God. He no longer needed to stand watch for her so close to the apartment building now that the sun would be her shield. *At least we've both lived to see another morning,* he thought. Staying focused on that goal had made him temporarily impervious to the bone-chilling temperatures.

Light was good. Although it was as cold as Hell today, a brilliant full-color spectrum of sunshine washed the streets gold. It had helped to chase all of *the shades* back down into the steam vents and sewers. The buds would soon be out on the branches, along with the quarreling squirrels. Thankfully, it wasn't a normal gray winter day, one that allowed *the shades* more time to slither away into their dark places. The ice was going away, too.

The thought of going to his temporary sanctuary at the antique shop pulled at him, and he stifled a yawn as he looked up at the apartment building before him. He needed to rest, even if for a little while, and just long enough to restore his strength for the upcoming watch.

"Go back to base," he murmured to himself as he walked back toward his newspapers. Rashid cased the streets with a glance. No, he'd rest later. He had a bad feeling about leaving his post. He could stand on one of the steam vents to warm up, then move to another strategic location. As he tailed her later, it would be better to be near the Masonic Temple Grand Lodge by City Hall on Broad Street. There, he'd be spiritually protected, and nothing could try to strangle him in his sleep if he dozed off. Or perhaps he'd go to the hallowed ground surrounding Mother Bethel AME Church in the opposite direction down on Sixth Street.

Again, he peered up toward her window from his position on the sidewalk. How long would it take her to begin her daily routine today? Her schedule seemed off. The weather wore on him, and the city was coming alive.

Usually, the light in the front room of her apartment, which faced the park, went on first. Within an hour, she was normally down on the street saying goodbye to the doorman at The Barclay. Then she'd walk toward Pine Street for a few blocks, and turn left down Pine and cross Broad Street. That's when he could rest—after she got safely into her work building where the law firm lived. On the weekends, he could always count on her to either not show up to her apartment, or to meander around South Street the way he did. No, he wouldn't rest today. He'd follow her as far as Broad Street, make sure she got into her building, and would then find hallowed ground.

He hated the not knowing, the lack of surety about her schedule on the weekends. Those times called for special prayers and exceptional concentration. He fasted on the weekends when she was away, just to be on the safe side. Intervention through prayers.

Chinatown, down on Eighth Street, was a cool place to hang out in order to keep awake. Maybe he'd pick up some sacred incense. The old ones down there knew him and left him be, and he'd do Tai Chi for hours in front of their shops to keep his body ready for the night battles with the unseen. They waved to him, and sometimes fed him to keep him coming back. They also knew, without him having to tell them, he was a sentinel.

However, Mondays were good, predictable, and today was a Monday. She liked the secondhand bookstores and the high-class antique stores. Not her grandfather's, which she dismissed as a junk store. But she was blind to the hidden treasures in it. If she'd give him half a chance, she'd learn that they had similar tastes, styles, and he was sure they shared the same intellectual pursuits. She gravitated to the unusual, and he had glimpsed her through the store windows going toward the hard-to-find book sections.

It was like watching a rare objet d'art that actually moved behind museum exhibit glass. He loved the way she looked, the way she carried herself. Rashid cast his gaze down the street, scanning it for activity, then again toward the windows of the apartment building and tried to imagine what she'd be wearing today.

Usually she had on a simply tailored, shin-length, one-button camel hair coat. He liked her trademark of simplicity. Everything she wore had easy lines that flowed. But, she also always adorned her neck with brightly hued silk scarves, or a large wrap held at the shoulder by an imposing hand-carved, wooden brooch. The colors were good for her, and added to the regal quality of her deep-brown, flawless skin, which seemed to glow from an inner light of its own. His favorite colors that she wore were the purples and gold-tones . . . her complexion seemed to drink them in, only to reflect them out again through her luminescent mahogany skin.

Contrasts . . . Yes, her style was as complex as it was simple and he was sure that no one else could see why. A plain coat, but an unrestricted fusion-of-color scarf. Understated accessories, but a wildly artistic African brooch at her shoulder. Coiled, natural hair—but kept just within Western business standards of acceptability. He chuckled to himself. She was a smart one. Small, business-appropriate earrings, in radical, African art patterns. Short, business-length nails, with only a touch of clear gloss, but bracelets from Zaire about her arms. One definitely had to study her carefully to understand. He was sure that no one else took the time like he did to do so.

He also liked the fact that she seemed to wear only natural things. Tasteful, plain leather shoes adorned her feet, but he could tell that they were made of that expensive fine leather. Plus, her accessories always matched—her briefcase, her big satchel handbag, and her leather gloves. And her hair . . .

Rashid closed his eyes and tried to envision it. Thick, jet-black, velvet ropes of unprocessed hair, coiled and twisted with a natural brilliance. Sometimes she wore it swinging about her shoulders, each coil seeming to have its own life. Other times she wore it pinned up in a tortoise shell comb, and her facial expression seemed to be more serious then. On what he imagined to be her more playful days, she'd have it held away from her heart-shaped face by a bright headband, or would catch it up in a ponytail. He wondered what it might feel like, then immediately censored himself. He was there to protect her—that's all.

He mentally repeated the words "to serve and protect" over and over again like a mantra. Sure he had to know what she looked like, every detail of her dress, where she went, and her patterns of movement. That was a part of his job. It was only coincidental that he happened to like the fact that most of the time she wore amber earrings, sometimes mud-cloth-like sandstone, or cowry shells set in silver, or semiprecious crystals wrapped in copper. Understated, but very classy. Her earrings danced as she talked, just as her eyes seemed to, and the sunlight would strike them and ricochet off of her high cheekbones.

When she'd stop to speak to the guard, she would toss her chin up slightly and offer the older gentleman a wide, light-casting smile. Her lips were full, and warm, and inviting, and were always covered with a sheer hint of berry color.

But her eyes . . . Those rich ebony eyes that sparkled with recognition when she'd give the guard her attention. He always loved the way she stood taller than the average woman and how she held her gloves in one palm and talked as she drew her slender hands inside them.

If only just once she'd lavish a moment of that same attention on him when she bought a newspaper . . . a smile, and deep giggle, followed by a hearty belly laugh and a slap on his arm with her gloves . . . The guard didn't know how much he was taking for granted; to have one's humanity acknowledged daily by such a beautiful woman, was a gift. With a pivot of her hips and the wave of her hands, they'd laugh and exchange a word or two, then she'd be off—walking a full, confident stride on long, athletic legs. A queen. That had been his first impression. A queen who spoke to her subjects and who was in touch with her people.

Maybe it was time for him to strike up a real conversation with her.

He wished the warm weather would hurry up and get there so she'd sit on the benches where he could see more of her. Didn't she know that it was safer outside? Being inside was like being in a cage. Things could find a dark place to hide and might ambush her in there, and nobody would *see* what happened.

She was smart, but why did she seem so oblivious? He could tell that she had a solid mind. It was in her carriage. Tall, proud, straight. Being on the streets had made him a good judge of character. He knew her rhythms.

When she was around and not working, she wore more relaxed clothes, and she always had coffee in a shop outside her apartment, and always ate a very light lunch. Soups, vegetables, salads . . . He'd never seen her eat meat. That was good. Demons lived in the meat. She needed to give up the coffee, though. Teas were better for the temple.

But, he could tell *they* were still after him this morning, even though they'd gone down into the vents—because hunger was clawing at his insides and trying to steal his concentration. The awareness of his physical need made him angry. *They* used anything, every conceivable temptation, to try to get inside of you!

Maybe he would just work his way down South Street where the tiny shops were, but only after he was sure that she was safe. He could keep pushing south to Mother Bethel's pews to sleep. Damn the ass-biting winter. It always made him feel old as he labored to walk against the wind. Today, sub-zero temperatures were turning his feet to stone in his combat boots.

All he had to do was to keep a block or two behind her, or stop occasionally to allow her to pass without noticing him. Who gave a thought to a guy dragging a bundle of newspapers?

It had been that way for over a year, since he'd come to Philly, but he'd sensed in his soul that this was where his next stop should be. When he'd first passed her downtown, he'd seen the aura around her and *knew*. She'd actually led him to her grandfather's shop. Months had gone by before he was able to pick up her trail again. She didn't visit the old man like she should. But where was she today?

Protecting her *was his job.*

Rashid cast a disgusted glance up to the gargoyles that haunted the building facades like giant vultures. He forced enough energy through his limbs to stand, from the top of his head down through each cell in his six-foot four-inch frame.

"Strength, and the light of protection, surrounds me," he whispered with his eyes closed while he gave his muscles a painful stretch, then hunched his body against the elements.

Nobody could see it, or them, or her light, but him. Nobody believed him, or could fathom what crept up from the vents at night, or why he had to pray hard into the steam of the vents. No one but those *that see*, understood. Demons were tricky, if you didn't know how to send them back down into The Pit.

But where was she?

Chapter Two

Aziza threw up her hands and let out a harsh breath in disgust. She'd told the movers that she'd wanted them to be at her apartment by 8:00 AM, which would have given her enough time to get her things over to her grandmother's house before noon. That way, she could unpack, utilize the day efficiently, and perhaps be able to get a good night's sleep. Worry had broken her rest for weeks, and now she just wanted the whole ordeal of changing locations and lifestyles to be over.

For once, the weather was cooperating with her plans. True, it was cold and blustery outside, but at least they didn't have to contend with the sudden ice storm that had hit the Delaware Valley just a few days prior. The storm had blown in from nowhere, followed by unseasonably high temperatures, which melted the ice—only to be followed by sub-zero temperatures. And the last thing she'd wanted to consider was moving what little bit of furniture she still owned down slippery streets and pavements over to the narrow Fitzwater Street. But on the positive side, she thought, the streets were indeed dry and clear now, despite the light precipitation the evening before. All she needed was for the freakin' movers to come! Why couldn't she bring such a simple task to closure?

Getting relocated to Ma Ethel's house felt like a conspiracy had mounted against her. Everything that was supposed to go smoothly had become so unnecessarily complicated that it was positively maddening. Even the smallest effort became a part of a larger domino effect that then triggered another major issue to contend with. It was like being back at the law firm!

Pacing about, she took inventory of her belongings again. A futon, a stereo, her law books, her clothes, photo albums, a laptop and printer . . . her collection of fancy dinner dishes—none of which were real china like her grandmother's treasures. "Pitiful," she whispered to herself in disgust. Where was she going to put her large Oriental rug, or her bed, for that matter, in her grandmother's home? Where would her expensive collection of African Art fit—next to the funeral home calendar with the trio of JFK, Martin Luther King Jr., and Jesus?

Their tastes totally clashed, just as their beliefs had, and there was no way to really blend their styles together. Ma Ethel's place was an overstuffed, turn-of-the-century floral world, filled to the brim with bric-a-brac, knickknacks, and doilies on every conceivable surface. Conversely, her minimalist style demanded space and simple lines. Clutter made her insane. That was the same thing she hated about her estranged grandfather's so-called antique shop. It literally gave her the claustrophobic sensation of being trapped, as did having too many old family pictures around. She hated dark corners skirted by dust ruffles and little porcelain ornaments. Why her grandmother had kept junk from a man she'd divorced decades earlier begged the next question—why couldn't the elderly just let go of the past and throw things away!

Aziza looked around at her once orderly, Swedish modern, less-is-more lifestyle, and winced. The art would have to go into storage, like the rest of it. There was just no place for it at Ethel's, and the recent storms had made the walls treacherous domain for a numbered piece of original artwork. The damp basement was no better. In fact, it seemed as though the whole house was imploding from age, and was dying right before her eyes—just as her grandmother had.

If only she'd had the time before this move, she would have continued her negotiation with the legitimate antique dealers to get them to take the entire contents of the Fitzwater house, lock, stock and barrel. Then it would have simply been a matter of gutting the house, getting the necessary repairs done, and she could have moved in her belongings. But everything was off, timing-wise. Even the sale of her Saab could have waited another month—but she'd needed the cash, and didn't need her insurance to go up just because she was moving home to the old neighborhood, to a house without a garage.

Everything was out of sync and impacted every other ensuing decision. She'd had to get out because of the timing of her lease. She couldn't keep paying her high rent, because of the timing of her severance from the firm. She wasn't able to get her own practice off the ground, because of the timing of the holiday season. She hadn't been able to file for unemployment, because she'd resigned. So even the timing of her temper was bad. She hadn't been able to get a realtor out to look at her grandmother's home in order to sell it because of the timing of the storms, and the housing market had gone soft. Again, bad timing.

Then the storms made showing the house in its present condition, with fallen ceilings and evidence of a bad roof, impossible. With her money dwindling, bringing in a construction crew was ridiculous to consider. Now, even the timetable of her move today was starting off wrong.

She could almost hear her grandmother's voice telling her to stop pacing, and to "Stop wearing a hole in the floor, chile." She needed a cup of coffee in the worst way, but even her coffeemaker was packed. If she unpacked it and plugged it in, the movers would probably show up just as the coffee was starting to brew. The morose thoughts about the way her luck was running also held her captive within the building. If she left the apartment to dash down the block to the little coffee shop, she'd probably miss the movers. Then they'd probably tell her that they couldn't do it today, and when they could, it would probably rain, or snow, or there would be another ice storm . . . maybe a damned hurricane for the second time in Philadelphia history! So instead she'd have to continue to burn up her nervous energy by walking around in circles and double-checking everything again, and again—albeit with a serious attitude.

Refusing to give in to the temptation to weep, Aziza headed toward the telephone. Her objective was to give the moving company a piece of her mind. She was tired of waiting on people . . . the right job, the right man, the right opportunity, the appropriate recognition of her ability.

The movers were forty-five minutes late, and counting. The rest of the stuff she was waiting on was *way overdue*, years late! As she smashed each number on the cordless unit, she began to mentally string together her argument. They were late, which violated her contract with them, thus they should have to offer some level of remuneration for the affront since her time was valuable . . . invaluable. Today, she would not allow herself to be violated. Not today and not any other day from this day hence, she mentally affirmed. When she got voicemail, she hung up.

"Damn! You can't even have a good fight in the morning anymore!"

Aziza glanced around the apartment for something to do that would keep her from jumping out of her skin. She'd obviously been too efficient. If she'd waited until the last minute, then she could have made them wait. But after all, wasn't that what had gotten her nearly fired, then blackballed? Being too efficient, too thorough, and way too apolitical? Instead of being made a partner, she'd been on the wrong side of the argument against a few influentials, and had rooted for the underdogs. Stupid. Her wins and the significant financial spoils she brought to the firm notwithstanding, she was politely ostracized, until her sense of dignity could bear it no longer.

They had gotten rid of her the "Old Boy" way—neat, clean, and without exchanging any words that could come back to haunt them legally from an EEOC perspective. They just made it hell to work there, and she'd been the one to quit, so they weren't liable. Stupid! What had been on her mind?

After it was all said and done, she'd been locked out of anything short of ambulance chasing. And, once again, timing was not on her side. She couldn't just up and leave the woman who had raised her. How was she supposed to look for a job in another city with Ma Ethel at death's door? There had been no one else, and her grandfather would have been useless. What was she supposed to do, leave Ma Ethel in the hands of Abe Morgan . . . the man her grandmother had divorced for reasons that had to be so horrific that the poor woman refused to discuss it?

As far as she was concerned, at that point, they were then the only two left in their family and all they'd had was each other. Now, even that had been taken away . . . Ma Ethel. She'd been the only person in the world who'd really loved her, and she'd loved her grandmother back—just as hard as she'd fought all of her career-breaking cases. Now it was a family of one.

Aziza swallowed hard, tasting tears, and looked out of the window. Maybe it was time to just do nothing for a while, and say, "Peace, be still."

Terror forced the air from his lungs as he watched her get into the large van from his rest post across the street in the park. He'd stood there all day waiting for her to come down and go to work, but that never happened. And he'd only gone across the street again to rest for a moment. Had that van been loaded with her possessions?

It was too late in the afternoon for her to be moving about, too near dusk, and they were taking her away. He wanted to run after the van, but knew that would create a scene—then he'd possibly never find her again. He'd have to ask old man Abe . . . something he dreaded doing . . . because the old man could *see*. Might be able to see what he wasn't yet willing to admit to himself.

Rashid cast his gaze upward to the waning sun and said a prayer. He thanked Heaven that they hadn't taken her away while he was asleep. It might have been days before he suspected she was gone. Besides, no one would have listened to him if he'd asked them to check her apartment to see if she was alive or dead. The last person he wanted to upset, too, was old man Abe, in case his hunch proved right.

Conversely, if they'd found her harmed in any way, they'd have sent him to Death Row for sure. He would have been on the news as the local newspaper vendor who did it—the vet with a thick psychiatric file, who had inquired about the black princess who had had a good job. The whole thing would be an open-and-shut case, with him cast as the stalker-murderer. It was all a part of the grand plot. He knew how those things generally went down. If anything, he was always able to read the newspapers all day long, and could read between the lines.

He tried his best to walk quickly behind the vanishing truck, pretending that the cold weather increased his gait. But, as a black man, he knew better than to run anywhere in the Center City business district, not even if he had on a jogging suit.

When he lost sight of the vehicle, he turned around in circles, trying to sense her direction, all the while praying that she wasn't going outside of the city limits. They'd gone down Locust a block, then headed south. In the distance, he was sure he'd seen it then turn west. He'd walked as fast as he could, until the traffic filled in behind his target and obliterated it from his line of vision. That's when he panicked.

"Southwest, no, no, no, go to higher ground . . . Mother Bethel . . . east, bright light . . . find bright light . . . or, go all the way down to Twenty-third!"

Words tumbled in his brain and then from his lips, and he bit into them to keep from speaking too loudly. He needed to think, but it was getting dark outside. His mouth tasted salty, warm. Strangers were with her, and it was getting dark outside.

"Find hallowed ground, safe haven, hallowed ground."

If she wasn't somewhere safe, then he had to find hallowed ground himself in order to chant protective prayers for her until daylight, when he could resume his search.

His eyes scanned the block ahead of him, and swept the terrain for any sign of a holy place. All of the storefront churches had been closed along the strip, a few bars were open, and the doorways of those buildings seemed like black, bottomless pits. He was too far from Mother Bethel, and too far from Greater St. Matthews. Everything was getting darker before him, and the shadows in the alley entrances began to shift and laugh at him. People seemed to move in slow motion.

Rashid could feel his legs pumping faster and faster. Tonight he had to get to safety before total nightfall. He knew it deep inside his mind's eye. Every sensory perception he had warned him that tonight it was really bad. He needed reinforcements. The darkness in *the shades* was not like it usually was on his normal patrols. This time it was disorienting.

This time, he'd possibly be caught, trapped, and pulled down into the vents or the subway. A low growl came from a dark corner within a small space between two buildings, forcing him to spin, turn, and run in the direction of the higher-numbered blocks.

Cutting across the street without looking, he heard a car screech, a horn blow, and a curse follow him in the distance. Then he saw it. A place familiar, but he couldn't be sure. The opalescent beacon of a haven called him. It was a building wrapped in the pearl-like rainbow light only offered by holy ground, almost as bright as Mother Bethel's. If he could just touch it, he knew that he'd be safe for the night.

Abe Morgan hated vagrants. He was always chasing them away as he locked up for the evening. "Dis ain't no church mission, brother. If you been fightin', you need to move along and go see a doctor 'bout that lip." It was the same thing every night, somebody looking to bring their bad vibes to his door. Abe held his head for a moment. Something was wrong. The hair stood up on his neck. Something evil was near, he could tell and it blurred his thinking.

Rashid whirled around at the sound of the familiar voice behind him, and almost lost his balance. All he could do was blink and stare at the tall, lean figure that occupied the doorway of the South Street building. Still disoriented, he wiped the warmth away from his mouth with the back of his hand, and kept his feet firmly planted in the spectrum of light that flowed onto the sidewalk. "It is too a church! Open up! Mr. Abe, you know I'm no druggie or robber, but I do need to come in and pray." He was back at the shop, but somehow his benefactor didn't know him. The shades had taken him over.

The elderly man standing before him shook his head in sheer disgust, squinting. "My store, and the steps outside my store, is only for people who are my customers. Look at you—bleedin' from the mouth, all dirty and probably drunk, or high—"

"—You're just messin' with me, trying to make me think I'm bleeding when I'm not, and trying to tell me this ain't a church step because I'm not a dressed-up, formal member of your congregation—but I can see good lights here! They're the only ones on the block, now that it's dark outside. You're the Trick-master, Ol' Slew Foot, and you're trying to get me away from the protection of light. I know whatcha tryin' to do. Just like you took her away! But I ain't havin' it! I command you in the name of the Most High to open up this sanctuary to me!"

Rashid could feel his heart racing and slamming against his breastbone as though it would explode through his chest. What the hell was he saying? None of it made sense. *The shades* had to be laughing. When the old man suddenly smiled and stepped behind the door, fear burned the saliva away from his mouth. Pure evil had obviously become so strong that it could stand in a beacon of light on a church step and forbid him entry. Tears stung his eyes and he wiped at them with raw anger. When he tried to speak, he could feel his vocal cords vibrate down in his Adam's apple, but nothing formed in his mouth but a gurgle. Suddenly, it felt like he couldn't breathe, and he opened his lips wide to suck in a large gulp of air. Rashid said a prayer in his mind. It was a silent, urgent plea. Within seconds he felt something release him.

"Dat you, boy? Rashid?" Mr. Abe said, peering closer and opening the door a crack. "Didn't have on my glasses and normally you in here before dark. Wasn't sure—cain't be too sure."

"I have prayed, and prayed for my sins, and the Father has forgiven me! I was in the military and I take responsibility for what I've done. But *you* cannot keep me out of this church tonight! Get thee behind me, Satan! This is my Father's house."

"Dis ain't no church, boy. It's an antique shop . . . some calls it a junk shop. You know that. But you worryin' me wit your crazy talk all of a sudden tonight. My granddaughter told me you might flip out on me one day and go crazy. Said you might be using that funny stuff, too. Said I needed to take care . . . I ain't believe her till I seen you like this. Hmmm . . . not sure I should open the door."

"Let me in! Please, old man, *the shades* is out tonight!"

Rashid's words congealed into pain, until his vision blurred and he found himself leaning against the doorframe of what he knew in his heart to be a church, no matter what old man Abe said. He would not be put out of the light.

Abe Morgan stared at the young man who kept touching parts of the building and looking at the ground. The way his eyes held a mixture of pure terror and conviction . . . the way he reverently touched the air just a fraction above the surface of the concrete, as though there was something palpable there that he couldn't himself see.

"You does have the gift of vision," Abe murmured in awe, changing his position and approaching the strange soul in his doorway. Despite the possibility that the person before him might be lethal, Abe held out his hand. "You know who I am? You remember you sweep for me for some food and a cot in the back? You know I don't keep no money in the store, right?"

"Mister, I don't know nothing except there's lights at your door—healing lights that keep the demons back. This place never had lights like this before."

"Brother, brother, listen to me," the old man's voice soothed.

"You can come into my antique shop that you claim is now a church, for a cup of tea. I'll make you something to eat to fill the hole in your belly—then you gotta go move on. We can't keep up our arrangement if you having mental blackouts. The cold air and an empty stomach done addled your brain. I ain't Lucifer, so I ain't gonna let you die in front of my shop in the street like a dog, dat ain't Christian. But, I ain't the Salvation Army or a mental ward, neither, so you *cannot* stay here all night while you acting crazy. But, I damned sure ain't about to judge a man in uniform for what he had to do. Okay? Peace?"

Rashid peered at the hand that was extended toward him and looked at it hard through squinted eyes. He touched the light on the concrete before accepting the handshake—just in case it was the dark side trying to trick him into going with them. Then he glimpsed into the old man's eyes, briefly, just in case it was the wrong set of eyes that might attempt to hypnotize him. Tonight he couldn't tell who or what to trust. But his body relaxed when he felt the current that ran through the old man's palm into his own. It was strengthening, warm, and in an eerie way the touch drew the pain from his body. The man before him really was Mr. Abe, not an illusion or an entity.

As he moved away from the wall, he still felt it prudent to keep his free hand on the mother-of-pearl-like opalescent light that bathed the building, part of him never losing contact with some portion of the building's structure. He had to stay grounded. The shop, tonight, was lit up like a cathedral. Odd thing was, it always had a little light before, but not like it did tonight. That had to have been what threw him off. Then again, *the shades* were darker too. If evil was denser, maybe places with light were burning brighter? That was the problem—he just didn't know.

Things weren't always what they seemed.

Chapter Three

They'd won. All of the cussing and fussing in the world had not gotten the truck to her apartment any faster. In fact, it seemed as though her theatrical outbursts had actually delayed things to the point where the van showed up at 2:30 PM that day. No amount of threats had got a rise out of them. The whole episode galled her no end.

"People are so inept," Aziza grumbled under her breath, as she walked her tormentors to the front door and thought back upon the myriad of supervisors she'd spoken to that day. Being bounced around an impenetrable voicemail system, then speaking with individuals who were not authorized to make a decision, and finally being told that the truck destined for her apartment had broken down, had been exhausting enough to drain most of the fight out of her.

Aziza slammed the door behind the nonchalant moving men, and fumed as she tried to unpack the disaster of boxes strewn about her grandmother's living-room floor. A good night's sleep was now out of the question, since her evening was obviously going to be devoted to struggling with cardboard, finding the most basic items of her clothing, and trying to cram as much as she could into an already too-small space. Plus, there was no way in the world that she could entertain sleep with things not in their rightful place. Clutter made her nervous, and what lay before her gave her the hives.

Since childhood, shadowy corners and dark closets that didn't click shut with a definitive sound made her recoil and want to bolt toward fresh air. Here, every door was ajar, every table was skirted, all of the chairs, and even the sofa, had an apron—leaving room within one's imagination for what might be under or behind any of it.

The stairs creaked and groaned from age, just as the elderly storm windows rattled from the wind. Childhood memories of shadowy things reaching out to claw at her little legs when she was supposedly asleep put a damp sheen of perspiration on her now adult body. Her mother hadn't believed her; her father hadn't believed her, and something had killed them both.

Fear made her tentative as she ran through every room, switching on all of the overhead lights and table lamps. Why hadn't they moved her during the day like she'd requested? By nightfall, she'd wanted to have things in their proper place. Was it so much to accomplish? Was it too much to expect to have all of the hidden places revealed? She wanted an early start to get all of the closets cleaned out and investigated.

Before she could rest, she still had to get all of the drafts plugged so that the curtains didn't ominously blow, or the papers on the dining room table didn't stir. It was imperative that she feel comfortable enough to simply glance around each dimly lit room in a relaxed fashion, having eradicated any concealed corners where something might lurk. It had always been that way for her . . . ever since she was a child.

Spartan felt much safer than cluttered.

* * *

Rashid eyed his benefactor with unconcealed suspicion while the elderly shopkeeper hummed around in the kitchen at the back of the store. Rashid scratched at the stubble on his face and appraised the dried blood on the back of his hand. He didn't like being indoors.

How was it that for a moment he hadn't been able to tell who this man was—a man he'd lived with for almost a year? Something wasn't right. The old man claimed that his name was Abe Morgan. Rashid turned the name over and over again in his mind. Studying the man, he thought that his name should have been more exotic, because his gaunt face held high cheekbones within its angular form that reminded him of the Masai people. Only Abe Morgan wasn't tall enough.

Now it was time for some tough questions. When he'd first signed on to take a cot in the back and some food in exchange for protecting the shop, he hadn't entered into the bargain to sell his soul. The old man had said he wanted a favor, would ask him for that one day in the future, so they needed to get it straight about what that favor could possibly be. He might have been tricked; the old man might be more than he seemed. Rashid continued to eye the person that now made him unsure.

"How long have you been here?" Rashid asked tensely, still peering around the shop as he continued to touch the wall. The place was jam-packed with expensive-looking clutter, and had too many little alcoves for his liking, even though it provided temporary sanctuary from the shadows that slithered just outside. "Not many African Americans have this type of inventory."

"Oh, so now you've finally opened up your eyes. Is that our new designation, African American? Is that why you came running in here all crazy-acting tonight? You finally decided what I got is worth something and you gonna rob me now, or what?"

Rashid looked at the old man, who didn't seem the least bit afraid. "No. I ain't come back to rob you—told you when we met; I ain't no thief or thug. And, yeah, we're African American these days."

The man named Abe chuckled. "When you get to be my age, you've been called everything from colored, to Negro, to boy, to niggah. African American works for me, I suppose."

Rashid dismissed the comment, but not the man who'd made it. "Are you originally from here, or overseas? Looks like you have a lot of imports."

"We're all originally from overseas, ain't we?" Abe answered with a chuckle, bringing a cup of green tea to the table and sitting down with a grunt. "Where you from, boy? I ain't really never asked. Maybe I should have, seeing as how I've been relying on you to keep drug thugs and robbers from my door. You seemed okay by my gut hunch, at first, but you came in here looking wild in the eye tonight. Needs ta know some facts 'bout who's in my store. Where you from? Wasn't my business, but since you wanna play twenty-questions . . ."

"All over," Rashid replied. He could feel himself growing agitated as the teacup was pushed before him. People didn't do things for others without a reason, as a general rule. What was this guy's deal? Why all of a sudden did he need to dig up the past?

"You said you wanted a favor from me, later. I need to know what that might be." Rashid warmed his hands with the thin china between his palms, smelled the brew within it, and looked up before taking a sip. "How do I know you wouldn't try to poison me, or drug me?"

Abe Morgan shook his head and stood. "Have you ever seen

how a person who's been poisoned dies?" He waited for a moment until Rashid shook his head no. "Well, for one thing, it's too messy. If I was gonna kill you, I'd rather you die and soil your britches outside of my shop. That way, all I'd have to do was to hose down the front steps," he added with a deeper grin. "Now, what's got you out on the lam like this, living like a dog in the streets?"

The young man sitting at his table made Abe oddly want to know more. If he had to guess, he would have pegged the youth to be in his mid-forties, but his eyes seemed much older than that. He'd been watching him for a year, but until tonight only his gut registered a hunch—yet tonight he saw it.

Abe furrowed his brows as he studied the face before him. Something about this person was diametrically opposed to what he was witnessing. The young man before him looked as crazy as a bedbug, but something down deep in Abe's soul screamed out, telling him that he was staring at a warrior. A sentinel. For the first time in his life, curiosity got the better of Abe, and compelled him to take an unplanned risk with the question, in addition to the risk he'd taken by extending the generosity he'd offered to his very unusual guest a year ago.

"We aren't familiar enough yet for me to be going into my life story," Rashid finally replied. "If this turns into a confessional, then I'll pass on the hospitality. Besides, you never answered my question about the favor."

Abe allowed a sly smile to creep out from hiding on his face. "I thought you said that this was a church?" He watched the young man struggle to develop a reply as he appraised him. His guest's hands and face were weathered from the elements, yet there was an inexplicable clarity to his deep mahogany complexion. Living on the streets should have worn off the sheen of any humanity beneath his worn clothes, and should have turned his muscular frame to mere skin and bones if he were a druggie. That's the thing—Rashid was clean as a whistle. His teeth should have been brown stumps, or missing, and his eyes nothing more than jaundiced saucers—if he'd judged his condition of homelessness correctly. Plus, it was too difficult to gauge his age. But, that was just it; his guest had no signs of being remanded to living on the streets, other than surface grime. These questions had gnawed at his gut for the past year, and still the same answer stabbed into the second sight of his mind; this young man was *the one*. But he could not rush their conversation or their trust. Rashid was skittish and could bolt. He needed Rashid to stay of his own free will. Where did this enigma come from, and why?

For a moment, neither man spoke as they silently appraised each other.

Ironically, here this person was, insolent as could be, sitting before Abe with a full head of hair—not infested by lice—with teeth as pearly as those of people privy to regular dental care, and the whites of his eyes were nearly translucent. The contrasts intrigued Abe. It was what had made him curious enough to invite this vagrant in last winter . . . especially when he'd felt the strength of his grip when they'd shaken hands. The entire exchange had been amazing to witness. Six feet four inches' worth of human being had unfurled from a clinging position against his doorframe, straightened, and marched through his store entrance with almost a military stride . . . all the while talking about and touching ancestral beacons of light. Even then, he'd thought him to be touched in the head for a moment until he looked at him hard. Since that first night, Rashid hadn't had another episode. What set him off? Abe wondered. Who was this confused man-child?

"Well?" Abe pressed, trying to appear nonchalant. "What's the good of being in a church, if you can't be honest? You claimed that I was blocking your passage to sanctuary. You was the one who forgot who I was for a minute. I've let you in here, so what's your issue? Who you runnin' from, boy?"

"Not who, *what*. And, for the record, for a minute you couldn't tell who I was, either."

"Okay," Abe said in a weary but amused tone to hide his alarm. "Whatcha runnin' from, and why you think this is a church?"

Rashid took an unsteady sip of tea, then returned the cup to the table. "It's got lights like a church, Merlin. That's all I can tell you."

Abe hesitated and grew serious. "What did you call me?"

Both men kept a steady line of vision locked on each other's faces and Rashid brought the cup slowly to his lips again without losing eye contact with Abe.

"I called you Merlin."

"Why?"

"Because you're tall, thin, and talk in riddles . . . old . . . and have an Ethiopian red tone to your complexion, not muddier brown. Muddier, tree-bark brown, stockier build, that's more like Ghanaian. If your skin was smoother and onyx black, I'd say, Nigerian, maybe. Middle East is in there too. Like I said, I'm from all over, and have seen a lot of people. Your build is almost like a very short Masai, but with Ethiopian features in your face. Many tribes run through you. Plus you've got a little something extra with you, old man—can't put my finger on it, but you're sly."

"That still don't explain why you called me Merlin."

Both men looked at each other hard. Rashid's once-tense expression broke into a sudden, wide grin.

"'Cause you aren't who you say you are. But, it's all good. Elsewise, you wouldn't be able to stay here, either. The light's too bright." Rashid cast a glance around the room and motioned toward a large, ornately detailed, silver-framed mirror in the back of the shop. "Most of it's coming from the altar you set up in here."

"The altar?"

"That mirror."

"What does the light look like?"

Rashid fell quiet. This was the first person in the States, who wasn't a Veterans Administration psychiatrist, who had really asked him what the lights looked like. He considered the question carefully, and again studied the inquisitive man's eyes. They appeared to be trustworthy, and seemed to hold a glimmer of real interest within them.

"Northern lights, but thicker, closer to the edges of things you can touch. Not up in the sky, or on the horizon. Swirling. Stand in it, or put your hand through it, and it fuses with you and covers you in it. Feels like a mild electric current. All pastel colors, some more vibrant. Azure, fuchsia . . . light pinks, lavender, golden. All moving together like they were alive. What can I say? I see what I see."

Abe let out his breath in a rush. "Oh, so now you been to Alaska. Boy, what kinda drugs—"

"Don't do drugs, and don't eat meat. It's bad for the body temple. Been to Alaska, and worked on the pipeline. Been in the service, seen a lot of Asia. Paid my own way to Africa, the Gold Coast . . . saw Mecca and Palestine, too. Seen Stonehenge in Europe, and been all through Central and South America when I was in the Peace Corps. Started my travel from the Midwest, stayed there for a while . . . seen a lot of Native American country. Been so many places, I can't remember 'em all. Now that it's up to me, I only go to the places where I know there'll be those lights."

Growing agitated, Abe pushed himself up from the table and went back to the stove to work on the meal he'd abandoned when chaos came banging on his front door. The kid said he could see lights, but talked like a lunatic. He felt compelled to continue to test this man who could be an imposter. False hope at this juncture could be dangerous. He'd been so disappointed in the past, and refused to give in easily with time no longer on his side. He'd test a little more and keep his identity a secret, hidden behind his slow, bad diction and seemingly uneducated banter.

It was imperative that he know for sure who this person was that sat at his table, a man that possibly lied and who sat before him flagrantly discussing the plausibility of miracles, and appearing so ignorant of their real purpose. The other possibility was that his reluctant guest was a lunatic. But he had indeed seen the lights. And his vocabulary was too strong to be that of an uneducated person. Formal training had been afforded him, somewhere. But the lights . . . that part of the young man's story was irrefutable.

"And in all of these travels, you saw this mysterious light, and the light drew you there?" Abe ventured, not wanting to lose the thread of the conversation, but becoming weary of the cat-and-mouse interrogation process.

"No, I *said*, I *went* to places that had the light. That's the first thing I looked for when I got to wherever I was either sent, or could go on my own volition. Kept me alive . . . too bad it didn't keep the others safe, though."

"Who safe?"

"You've experienced losses, correct?" Rashid stared at Abe.

"Who hasn't?" Abe said in the tense exchange. "So then, since we've all experienced losses, who did you lose? I'm not asking their names, just making conversation about something that I've also experienced. Don't get to be my age and not have to attend a few funerals." Abe nearly held his breath waiting for the answer.

"The women."

"What women?" Abe had responded almost too quickly, it seemed, for both men's liking.

"The ones who all died," Rashid finally replied in an openly suspicious tone.

The old man stopped stirring the pot of rice and beans he was tending, and quickly spun around to face his recalcitrant guest, noting how the young man immediately drew back and clutched the wall, as though he were playing the game of tag with the wall representing base.

"Boy, you awful jumpy for somebody not on drugs, and for somebody that's lookin' for a church home."

"Ain't lookin' for no church home. I'm lookin' for the source of the lights."

"Look in my eyes, if you supposedly can see things," Abe challenged in a low, threatening tone. Their gazes locked and Abe prayed silently for discernment. "If something chased you to my door, then there is a reason beyond what you and I can conceive of, so, where's your faith?"

The two stared at each other in a deadlock for a few moments before Abe began his inquiry again. "If you saw lights here, then maybe I'm not so ready to have anyone of darkness breach my threshold, either. So, cut the games. Why do you have to seek the light?"

Rashid considered the old one's statement and his question. There was a simple truth to both, and somehow because of that, the man's gaze had him transfixed. He could feel sentences forming in his mind as reluctant trust began to build. It had been a very long time since he'd felt a sense of safety envelop him.

"That's where I'm supposed to take her, The One, to be safe. Mother Bethel's looks like it has the brightest spirals in the city. Why?"

Chapter Four

Abe scratched his chin and smiled, deciding to drop the Southern accent and appearance of being a mere simple man. It was perhaps time to allow the young man before him to see a little bit more of who he really was. One of them had to trust, if there was to ever be an accord. They both needed each other, of that he was now convinced. So, he'd answer Rashid's question about why the lights were so bright at a place like Mother Bethel. He'd allow the young man to lead the dance, ask the questions, which would tell him everything he needed to know about the proficiency of Rashid's gifts.

"Because a warrior ancestor is buried in the vault of the church. I take it you've heard of Richard Allen?" Abe said flatly after allowing himself a moment to survey Rashid again. Too excited to address the young man's comment about The One, Abe prayed inwardly for patience and for more clarity.

But his reply about Mother Bethel AME Church did appear to give his guest momentary pause. Abe's comment was acknowledged by a nod in the affirmative. A silent understanding seemed to pass between the two men. Trust was in the offing.

"Down at the Masonic Grand Lodge, theirs is real bright too."

"The beacon will be bright in any place that is devoted to spiritual truths, an understanding of spiritual principles, or where many gather in the same spirit. The Masonic orders incorporate principles based on early Egypt, Kemet . . . creators of the pyramids, and then evolved to incorporate Biblical precepts of giving. Their basic mission is to help the less fortunate through philanthropy . . . in various forms or another. Lodge lights are bright."

"Then why do some places of worship, or even some buildings, have brighter lights than others? Isn't hallowed ground, hallowed ground?"

Abe smiled. "To answer the first part of your question, the light is as bright as the spirit. The light of spirit emanates from the energy of the congregation, or gathering of living souls within the material structure . . . a church, a cathedral, a mosque, temple, a house, et cetera, and their combined spirits are met by, and reinforced by, the Divine in equal measure. Light draws light, darkness draws darkness."

"True," Rashid said quietly, and then nodded, accepting Abe's explanation. "Some places I go into, I don't feel anything. Either I feel real good, or I feel rotten. That's why I like to stay outside with my own vibe and the Creator's vibe."

"Correct," Abe added with growing satisfaction. "And the shape, size, or color of the congregation, or the building structure, or the language used to issue up prayers doesn't matter to the Almighty. It's the vibrations of the people who come together. So, to address the second question you asked, hallowed ground is not necessarily hallowed ground. Where the spiritual barrier is weak, the fortress can be penetrated. Your eyes just so happen to see it in the form of light . . . there are some that call it vibes, others feel it through their skins—just like a dog's hair will bristle when it senses something not quite jakey."

Rashid's expression was one of awe, which quickly became animated. Gesturing wildly with his hands, he leaned forward and spoke in a rapid-fire tempo. "You can see it, too, can't you? Tell the truth!"

He didn't wait for a response from Abe Morgan, and took the elderly man's return smile as a yes. It was the first time in his life that another living soul had even halfway admitted that they could see the lights. Relief and excitement drove his words forward.

"I've gone to temples, churches, mosques, synagogues, prayer mounds—you name it, all over the world, and I've seen just about every religion, and they all had bright light, the kind that not everyone can see. Even on Hopi lands out west, there's that same light. But, I didn't get them to it in time. The women all died. Then again, I've seen *the shades* too. So, which are you?"

"Use your gift of discernment, boy. What do you think?"

Slowly bringing a paring knife into his palm, Abe began cutting the tops off of the beets and carrots that rested on the drainboard near the sink. Adding those vegetables in with the others, he watched the young man watch him use the knife, and rolled the question over and over in his brain. He'd gotten so close, then poof. Back to square one. And before the last question was hurled at him, it seemed that they had both been searching for so long. The silence that now hung in the air between him and his guest was deafening.

Abe allowed the deep melancholy only brief residence in his soul before he steadied his countenance. His seeing the lights and also seeing the shades had made his beloved Ethel finally leave him . . . especially when he'd predicted the death of his daughter at the hands of her husband, and had tried to break up the marriage. His wife hadn't understood.

"You'll eat my food, and drink from my cup, but you don't trust me. That's a dangerous habit, young man." Abe's voice was just above a whisper, but his underlying message was clear.

"If you aren't who you say, just an old antique shop owner," Rashid retorted as he glanced around, "I'll still be protected."

"I never said who I was. Just told you my name."

"Doesn't matter," Rashid murmured. "I'll still do what I'm supposed to do."

"Which is?" Abe asked without looking up, slowly adding the vegetables and a pinch of red curry to his concoction, now working with his back turned to his guest.

"You're an old man, and don't look that strong. Taking in strangers, in this neighborhood, could be a dangerous habit, too."

"And if you ain't who I think you are, I'll be protected until I do what I have to do. Always have been. It's also dangerous to judge a book by its cover. I've survived a lot longer than you have. Think about it."

Abe Morgan turned around slowly and brought the pot of richly spiced food to the table and sat down. He reached in a side drawer, and added several soft rounds of spongy bread to their meal. "You gonna wash your hands, before you give me something that even the light can't cure?"

Rashid looked at the newsprint that had inked his hands and stained his clothing. "Eating out of the same pot is definitely Ethiopian," Rashid remarked sullenly, but obliged his host as he made his way toward the kitchen sink. "You're the first civilian that hasn't been afraid of me since I started living on the streets."

He decided that he'd go with the ruse until it was safe to leave the lights. He hadn't made up his mind yet about how far he would go with his explanations. If this was just an average person, then he could let the old man think he was just a delusional street vagrant. But if his host was from the dark side, then he'd deal with him in time.

The old man behind him kept his head bowed and didn't turn around or reply. Okay, then, that much was safe. He could share a meal with a man who also prayed over his food. Immediately Rashid bowed his head and allowed a prayer to move his lips. The smell of the food was nearly intoxicating, and he returned to his seat so fast once done praying that he almost knocked over his chair.

Offering Rashid a spoon, Abe tore off a section of the bread, and used it like a large scoop to bring a portion of the mixture to his mouth. Without looking at Abe, Rashid began gobbling down large hunks of bread, rice, and vegetables, almost inhaling the entire pot while his host slowly consumed the one morsel he still held in his hand.

"Let's begin with your name, son—since we are eating from the same bowl."

"Rashid. Like I told you when we first got together. I didn't lie. Don't have cause to."

"No last name?"

"Not one that I'm ready to share."

"You were brought up in the Midwest?"

"I said I traveled through there," Rashid replied with a wave of his hand, still engrossed in the aromatic dish. But he was growing wary again. No one needed to know his point of origin.

"You were in the military, Gulf War?"

"Special Forces. *Do not* ask me what I had to do over there. Some of the people I had to ice also had the light around them. That's when I first started seeing it more clearly. That's when I heard her voice." Rashid looked up for the first time since he'd begun decimating the contents of the pot, and stopped chewing. The conversation was not supposed to be going in this direction. Either the fatigue and hunger had weakened him, or this old man had some sort of power source other than the ordinary. He'd given up too much information for no reason.

"Tell me that part," Abe said quietly, "the part when you heard her voice."

Rashid stared at him, and then looked toward the mirror in the back of the room. His gaze felt vacant, distant, and his voice took on a hollow quality even to his own ears. Why was he talking to this old man, and why did he feel like he had to? The burden of the information he'd held for so long now felt like this was the place to lay it down. But why? Rashid prayed silently before speaking, then looked at the mirror.

"Front line, we were getting a lot of heat—catching pure liquid hell. I was praying for protection and mercy and forgiveness the whole time I was shooting. Choppers couldn't get in to get us out. Guys were burning up where they stood. We were hemmed in on one side from machine gun fire, on the other side was nothin' but fire dropping from the sky all around us. Pure chaos. Could smell flesh burning. I don't eat meat. Can't. Not after that. Can't even stand to smell it cooking. Learned it was bad for the body and soul anyway. Can't stand the smell of gasoline neither, too much like napalm."

"When did her voice come?" Abe waited and his breathing became shallow.

"She called my name, which was Gerald, then. But she called me Rashid. By this name I have now. That's the name I heard, and I knew she was calling me—even though it was by another name. All she said was, 'Trust the light.' Then this thin beam of light came from where the machine guns had been mowing my platoon down. I was mesmerized, and followed it. Bullets hit the other guys that ran with me, but never touched me. It was like this weird light covered me, and her voice kept calling my name telling me which way to go. When it was all over, they were all dead, and I was the sole survivor. I kept seeing it for days as I made it back, praying the whole time . . . until I caught up with another unit. That's how I got back stateside. A whole freakin' squad blown away and I get to follow the lights and a voice? Enemy search parties walked right past me like I was invisible. Didn't even go out as a POW." Rashid shrugged his shoulders and let his head drop forward. He shut his eyes tight, then opened them to stare at the table.

"It wasn't your fault. It says in the first epistle of John, chapter one, verse nine, that 'If we confess our sins, He is faithful and just.'"

"Tell that to those guys who burned alive. Did you know that guys on both sides had light swirling around them too, and were good people? But they still bought it. Were toast. Did you know that some of the enemies pointing their guns in our direction had the same thing? Could never figure that part out. That day was insane. Used to think I was dreamin' when I was a kid, but that day I saw it, felt it. Still can't tell anybody why my sorry ass didn't die."

"Maybe destiny had something to do with it? A Master's Plan, larger than your own."

Rashid leaned back in his chair and cast a disparaging glance at Abe. "Destiny, or I was just a lucky mother—"

"If you're going to guard the light, the first thing you need to learn is that words carry manifest energy. Change your adjectives and metaphors, immediately."

Both men stared at each other. Abe repeated himself. "Immediately. Do not question who I am, the question is, who are you?"

"A poor street urchin trying to scam you out of a meal."

"So, you've eaten. But you have not scammed me." Abe held him with his gaze. "What happened to the women?"

"Six of them died."

"How?" Abe forced the tension from of his temples by kneading his knuckles into the offending flesh. "What were they to you?"

"Lovers and fiancées are who they were. They died accidentally." Rashid swallowed hard and looked back at the mirror again. "Found a would-be wife in every country. Wanted to settle down and have a family. First one, Jain-Mei, got a fever. Was gone two days after we were together, even though I'd known her for six months. Understand? After I touched her. As long as I hadn't slept with them . . . do you hear what I'm saying?"

"Yes, unfortunately I do." Abe stood, and cleared the food away from the table and turned on the kettle of water again. His mind whirred although his pace remained slow and fluid. As he prepared another tea ball, he allowed the loose leaves to filter through his fingers. The tragedies became a vision of each woman-child who'd died on his watch while Rashid spoke to his back.

"Second one, I met in Ghana. Wonderful people, family . . . woman. Choked to death at our engagement celebration. With the wedding imminent, we'd just spent the previous night together. The third one, a brilliant Native American woman, engineer, brought me home to meet her parents. We were working on the pipeline together. I was just a blue-collar hack. Her grandfather flipped out, said I brought evil to their door. At the time, I just thought that the old dude was prejudiced and superstitious. The next day she'd slit her own wrists. They found her in a clearing in the woods where we used to meditate together . . . where we'd been together. Do I need to go on?"

"No," Abe murmured, bringing over a steaming pot of tea and two clean cups for them to use. It was difficult to control the urge to hug the young man before him. Tears glistened in Rashid's eyes, and he watched how quickly he forced them to recede and disappear. So many wounds . . .

"Funny thing is, see," Rashid said with a hollow chuckle, "the last one, my Southern church girl, I didn't even have to sleep with for her to die young. Had learned my lesson, kept my hands to myself, and was gonna wait till we tied the knot. Thought that would break the curse, or whatever it was that was following me. But, her old, senile grandma kept talking about *haints* coming out from under the bed . . . dark shadows that slipped up under the covers and held the girl down and raped her. So, her momma took her to see a doctor, and when they put her in the stirrups, and did a pelvic exam, that girl was riddled with tumors. Biopsy told everybody there was nothing they could do. She died ninety days later. Lost two in Europe. Irish girl drowned, my West Indian princess from London went insane and ran out into the street and got herself hit by a car." Rashid dropped his head back and chuckled. "I don't have much luck with women. So, what's your point?"

The pain within Rashid's laughter resonated through Abe's bones. It was tinged with the higher-pitched, dissonant chord of hysteria. Waiting until the outburst ebbed, Abe chose his words as though selecting diamonds. He inhaled slowly through his nose, and let the air seep out through his barely parted lips before he spoke.

"They were tragic casualties of an unholy war. That which has hunted you, has sought to break you through them. Anyone that you love dearly is always at risk, for that loss is what drives us away from the light in such pain that the void must be filled . . . often darkness fills that vacant space. But to love is a requirement of the light. And so, thus is our mortal Achilles' heel. Do you understand?"

Rashid wiped at his eyes with the back of his hand and stood. "I understand what it's like to be a monk, and to have every basic pleasure and any crumb of joy stripped from you. That's why I don't do friends, I don't do close, I don't do chitchat about who I am. That's given on a need-to-know basis."

It was definitely time to go. The old man had tapped an artery of pain, and he needed personal space to cauterize the reopened wound. Rashid cast his gaze toward the door, but remembered the gathering shadows outside, just beyond the light.

Abe shook his head, sending an unspoken message to Rashid that to exit the sanctuary now would not be a wise idea. When he watched the muscles in Rashid's shoulders finally relax, he pressed on.

"Yes, in many cultures sentinels are cloistered because that which they are to love with their whole hearts, or to derive a sense of fulfillment from, cannot be killed, altered, or destroyed. At their level, they are seriously challenged by the dark, and must not have an emotional or material possession that would open them to compromise."

"Sentinel?" Rashid raked his locks with his fingers. Sure, he'd thought of himself as that before, even had said the word in his own mind. But to hear someone else call him that—rather than just a soldier—seemed too freaky. Eerie enough to raise the hair on the back of his neck.

"Yes, whether you realize it or not, you've been honed and obviously groomed to serve as a sentinel." His young charge stood speechless, but seemed to comprehend. Shaking off the dangerous emotion of attachment, Abe Morgan moved to stand before his guest. "Are you ready to begin to learn how to fight them, and to protect yourself and the one you guard?"

"Yeah . . . I guess." Rashid cast a nervous glance around the shop and appraised his newfound mentor. He'd been on his own for so long that this new partnership that seemed to be forming made him nervous. "But, how do I know you're the one to teach me, and how do you know when it's time, anyway? What's all of this about? Been tryin' to figure that out for years! When's it gonna end? And why am I the one that's supposed to guard this voice . . . *who in the hell is she*—am I, for that matter? I'm just some has-been vet. Maybe I heard what I wanted to hear, maybe none of it was real and the doctors were right—could be that I'm just nuts, and stalking some chick because I haven't been laid in years, towing survivor guilt along with the baggage of old childhood displacement trauma."

"When the student is ready, the instructor appears."

"Then why didn't my teacher appear when I was in the Catholic Charities orphanage, or in foster care?"

Abe closed his eyes briefly, chasing away the rising excitement inside of him and forcing his voice to remain calm and steady. He'd found him. It had to be him. "Maybe they did."

"Give me a break."

Each man stood back from the other and surveyed his opponent's countenance.

"Did you get beaten, molested?"

"Yes. Beaten. Molested, no . . . well, they tried, but I held my own against the pervert before he did me, and had to do time in juvenile detention. Really learned how to defend myself in that hole. Maybe that's how I wound up in the Midwest. Only vaguely remember my mom and grandmother before they died. They were the only family I had. Right after juvenile detention, I went into the service. Stayed in the service from there."

Rashid tried to scavenge more memories. The stint at the orphanage was still a murky recollection. He could only seem to remember moving from family to family . . .

Abe forced himself not to visibly cringe, or to reach out to embrace Rashid. "Did you ever consider that you had been sent on a path—taught how to defend yourself, taught how to break ties and survive while focused on a singular goal? Did you ever consider that the prayers and Biblical lessons you learned while in a Christian orphanage prepared you to pray while under siege? Did you ever consider that maybe you'd been allowed to travel around the world in order to learn that all people are God's children? Many people have lived their whole lives and don't know that. Oh, yes, the teachers were always sent—you just didn't know it at the time." Too many missing elements were coming together. Abe could hear the voices within the mirror whispering a warning about getting too close too quickly, which he consciously ignored.

Rashid stared at the old man in front of him, and rubbed his chin. "Okay. But those were some hard lessons, brother."

"Correct. Hard lessons—hard and fast instructions given to someone who had much to accomplish in a short period of time, perhaps. And what did you do? Each time you found yourself under attack . . . in danger?"

"Began praying, then pushed myself harder, focused . . . became a third-degree black belt by the time I was fifteen. At least they let us learn something useful in kiddy prison. You do sound like my martial-arts teacher, come to think about it."

"Then those dark early experiences began your path. At each stage in the journey, a teacher appeared. The Most High will often use the dark to provide a tool that leads to wisdom—like judo. He uses the forces of evil against itself after a tragedy to accomplish something positive. It is your choice whether or not you decide to bring that knowledge into the light. That is what is called, free will."

"And the women?"

"Strengthened your soul to the point where you can endure without one."

"And . . . now?"

"And now, something chased you to my door tonight, just like something Divine led you here a year ago. You will take a salt bath to clean your aura, and then rest. You're safe inside the shop of light, and can sleep without fear."

"I haven't slept without fear since I was five years old."

"Neither has my granddaughter."

"It's her voice," Rashid said quietly.

Abe just stared at the man before him, then swallowed hard and turned away from the eyes that haunted him. "I know."

"This favor . . . tell me now, old man, for real."

"She needs a sentinel. *The shades* chase her."

Rashid stared at Abe without blinking for a moment. "I know," Rashid said quietly. "Today a truck came and took her away, though."

Abe nodded. "A confluence of events has made her move back into my ex-wife's house. Ethel, her grandmother, was a prayed-up woman; could keep *the shades* from her door . . . although our daughter, Aziza's mother, couldn't." He began gathering blankets from a shelf behind the register as he continued to speak, refusing to look at Rashid.

"What happened?" Rashid's question was met with silence.

"Demons came into the house, possessed my daughter's husband—he killed her. Aziza was hiding in a closet when the police found her." Abe drew a shuddering breath. "That's my favor. Don't let them get her. I'm old, ain't got much time left before I have to go back."

Rashid remained stone still. "Is that why she's so angry with you . . . because you divorced her grandmother?"

Abe looked away. "I remind her of the terror. Her grandmother put everything into logical context. Domestic violence, people having mental collapses. I speak of things that haunt her dreams . . . shades and such. It's safer to believe in the logical."

"Been there," Rashid said quietly. "But you said you have to go back."

"I do." Abe rubbed his palms down his weathered face. "Son, I am so much older than you can know . . . I've been places you can never imagine." He let his breath out hard. "Did you ever consider what would happen if one point of history changed? If one fact got altered?"

Rashid simply stared at the old man before him.

"Our family and our people got robbed. Something went back and altered the past, *the shades* slipped through . . . it has taken me years to find the exact change, which fact got transposed and twisted—but I'm going back." Urgency made him speak quickly and come near Rashid, his eyes frantic. "If I go back, you have to be her sentinel on this side to guard her. They're trying to wipe out my line. If they do, all those with the gift to see the lights and *the shades* from Madagascar will be gone. We can't let that happen. This family wasn't supposed to dwindle down to just Aziza then die out! We're the balance keepers!"

"Whoa, whoa," Rashid said gently. "Easy, old dude. First you thought I was the one with issues . . . now hindsight being twenty-twenty, you're the one who needs meds and—"

"We will begin our work in the daylight hours. You will read—*a lot*," Abe announced, walking across the room. "You will exercise your mind, your body, and your spirit to their limits. You will keep this shop clean, you will keep your body temple clean, you will keep your language clean, your thoughts pure, and you'll get to continue to provide me with live-in store security, or find somewhere else to live. That will be your job, and I will pay you with food and shelter and teaching. Period. You must find yourself first, before you can guard The One."

"And why would I do all of that with *you* sounding crazy? You're talking about time travel, old man." Rashid hardened his gaze as he stared at his wanna-be benefactor. "I don't think so," Rashid replied after a moment of consideration. "Not."

"Because you owe her; it was her voice and you know it," Abe said quietly. "Isn't that what's been clawing at your insides . . . to know who she is, and why you feel compelled beyond your own comprehension to protect her? I may have the answer to that riddle."

"Then tell me, and I'll be on my way. I'll watch over her, but you're outta your mind if you think you can go back in time to change the past. If I could, there'd be so many things that would be real different, trust me. But you can't!"

"It's not that simple, and I won't discuss anything with anyone that I don't know well enough to be sure it's safe for her."

"And how do I know you aren't a danger to her or me? You sound nuts. How do I know you're not?"

"You don't, I don't—so we share each other's space until we find out. You have one part of the puzzle, I have another, and I suspect she has the missing third of the trinity of information. So, are you in, or out?"

"I'm out," Rashid said fast, moving quickly toward the door.

"And *the shades*? They aren't real either, I suppose?" Abe just stared at Rashid, slowing his exit until they both understood.

"Why? Why are you doing this, making me stay here and go through all this purification mess? You didn't before—so what's it to you now?"

"Now you know. Now I know. We've gone a layer deeper. The

dance is more complex between us. Every time you leave and come back to the light, there is a risk factor that your spirit has been compromised by the unclean. You must stay in the light, boy, from this point forward. Haven't you seen *the shadows* gathering force, getting stronger, darker, and denser with every day that passes? It used to be easier to send them back into The Pit, wasn't it? Perhaps a week ago, when they gathered at night, you would have walked without fear, am I right? But tonight, there was something that spooked you—because your inner being knows that you were not strong enough alone, this time, to contend with whatever is outside this door. *Your soul knew it needed to go to the next level of training.* Stop fighting His will! If I am wrong, open the door and leave of your own accord, and I will pray that your soul reaches Heaven. But, if there's just the slightest doubt in your mind about your readiness to contend with what's out there, I suggest you stay. Tell me. What is your choice?"

Abe Morgan's words had given Rashid serious pause. There was no way around it. He looked toward the heavily grated plate glass store-front window and had to mentally confess that he'd been terrified of the strength of the gathering darkness.

Until now, if he felt it, or saw it, or encountered it in a person about to commit a crime, he'd been able to pray out loud and stare the evil away from an innocent person he was trying to help. But what he saw tonight was worse than he'd ever seen. What's more, the streets were probably slithering with *the shadows* in search of him tonight. The way the metallic-tasting acid built on his tongue told him all he needed to know. The streets, even in the daylight, might be dangerous.

"But why does it have to be this particular location of light? Why not any of the other points of origin?" Frustration trapped him as he and the old man reached a stalemate.

"We'll discuss this specific source of the light, later—and only when *you* are ready. And that's my call, after being informed of your readiness from On High—not yours."

"I'm ready to discuss it now!"

"No, you are only ready when your spirit has accepted total, not partial, surrender to God. And, at the moment, you have only partially given yourself up to Him. Thy will be done, not your will be done. Peace, be still, Rashid. Listen for once with your soul, not your ears."

Rashid hesitated before speaking, and gazed at the countenance of his host. "What if I don't want to stay in here with you, or to do all of this sh—er, I mean, crap? *I'm a free man*. Got that? What if I just walk out this door?"

"Suit yourself. Let *the shades* chase you all night, then. Your choice. But, if you go out of this door tonight, I remove my offer for good. It's now, or never. Choose, but choose wisely."

Rashid paced to the front door and peeped out of the window, then spun around quickly to face Abe. The rage of the trapped shone in his eyes.

"Why couldn't I have just made it to the church steps! You must have tricked me—"

"No, I kept telling you this wasn't a church, but you were so frantic and intent on getting in here that initially you wouldn't listen to me."

Rashid walked in a circle in front of the door, pacing in agitation. "Aw, maaaan . . ." Why in the world did he have to mistake this *store* for a damned cathedral, and accidentally get caught in it after dark?

Abe smiled. Tonight he finally understood why he'd inconvenienced his life by taking in the most unlikely stranger. He'd move Rashid in closer to the ring of safety inside the store, rather than make him sleep in the back on an old rickety cot. "Because," Abe finally said, nonplussed. Still smoothing out a set of blankets on a sofa that had been on display for sale, and pulling off the tag, he answered the unspoken question in Rashid's mind, much to his guest's apparent surprise. "Rule number one, in God's universe, there are no accidents."

Chapter Five

Dawn lazily stretched through the windows as though in no particular hurry. When the first of its rays turned the room a dusty gray, Aziza shut her eyes and drifted off to sleep. Dozing off and on, her head bobbed almost to the rhythm of her breathing. She remembered her grandmother sitting up all night in that same chair she now occupied, with sewing on her lap and a cup of tea on the small oval table beside her. Funny, but it never occurred to her until now that Ma Ethel might have been as terrified as she had been last night, to close her eyes in her own home.

Fatigue had turned the insides of her eyelids to gritty shutters, which slid across her irises with an uncontrolled weight of their metronome timing. She had to get moving. There was no way she'd make it through another evening without rest. That meant that all that didn't get done the night before, now had to be done while there was still available sunlight.

Aziza allowed her strained line of vision to settle on the closet door. She'd already tucked up and pinned back all of the furniture skirts so that she could see under every chair and sofa in the house. She'd removed all of the tablecloths, remade the twin guest beds, so that the comforters were tucked under the box springs and no longer draped to the floor, and she'd dusted until there was a gleam to every surface. The originally opaque floral shower curtain had been removed and replaced with a clear, more modern version. Old pictures had been removed from the walls, and remanded over to the custody of the damp tomb called the basement. She'd even installed a latch lock for that door, and had moved a small end table in front of it.

Every closet had been gutted of its contents, with an outer latch installed to keep the doors closed. The only closet left for her to deal with was the one she now faced—Ma Ethel's closet.

She sat in the chair and considered her options. The third floor didn't require her attention, as it had been made and kept pristine during her earlier weekly visits while her grandmother was still alive. Plus, it was totally empty, and sealed off from her living quarters by a wall she'd installed for her grandmother. The unsuccessfully implemented plan was that tenants could come in through the front door, collect their mail, and use the sealed-off front staircase to get to the third floor without coming through the rest of the house. The main living room, entire first floor, and the full second floor could be accessed through the back kitchen staircase. Aziza stretched and worked against the kinks in her shoulder blades. Her grandmother had been as stubborn as a mule! Rent from that unit would have supplemented her grandmother's fixed income, and perhaps would have offered her a little added security, if she'd had the right tenant.

When she lived with Ma Ethel, she'd wished that there had been a tenant to occupy the third floor . . . someone within earshot should she need to call out—someone who would make living sounds, and who would give justification for the creaks and groans that the house offered up on its own all night. But, no, Ma Ethel had been steadfast about not wanting anyone to live up there again, ever since Aziza's parents had died. It was a waste of damned real estate, all over superstitions and what not. Tragic though it was, the fact that her mother and a neighbor had died up there was no reason to seal off the place forever.

Bad luck did not simply take up residence in an apartment. Pop Abe had no doubt frightened the good sense out of her otherwise rational grandmother. It was all pretty basic, as tragedies in the black community went. Her father had been diagnosed paranoid schizophrenic. Her mother and a neighbor were just the victims of a troubled man. It had nothing to do with the place; it was the insane individual who'd inhabited it.

Aziza let her breath out in a rush and stared at the closet door . . . the doorway that had called to her as a child . . . the place that told her to hide in it to be safe from the raving man that was hunting her . . . the door that didn't have a lock, but sealed itself shut with her on one side and her father on the other . . . the door that kept her young eyes from seeing, but could not block her from hearing, the gunshots that struck down her mother and an elderly neighbor. It was the same door that Ma Ethel had found her curled up behind . . . the same door that the policemen couldn't wedge open—but that had easily unlatched for her grandmother, who had prayed the door open.

Her insides began to churn at the memory. She'd call a plasterer and seal up that old passageway to the unseen, and have another closet built—one that was long and modernized and mirrored and that opened with sliding doors. But how was she ever going to get rid of the permanent stain on her mind, and what plasterer could ever seal over the place in the middle of that bedroom floor where the police had finally stopped her father's mental pain? There were only two small bedrooms on the second level of the house. One was too tiny to consider; the other one had a history. Trying to live alone on the third floor was out of the question.

A new coat of paint and totally new furnishings, her own, were in order. With the old stuff still in there, with nothing changed in the last thirty years that she could recollect, it was as though she could still see her bloodied father lying sprawled at the foot of that old bed. Boarding schools, then college, then her own apartment had been her salvation until now.

Maybe she would take a colleague's sarcastic advice, and open a community legal clinic. Hell, at Twenty-first and Fitzwater Streets, she lived right in the community again. She was the genuine article—a community-volunteer lawyer! Perhaps she could even turn the third floor into an office, then write off a third of the property on her taxes . . . it would be a practical use of the space.

But then she'd be mired in what the community was still mired in—domestic disputes and divorces, defending criminal activity, and settling accident cases. It was too close to her own past . . . courts, family dramas, gunshots, and dead bodies. That's why she'd thrived on defending people against large corporations . . . she could root for the underdog, get the facts, but it was cleaner.

Puttering as she considered her fate was a way to stave off a case of bad nerves. Okay, so she'd won sexual harassment suits, flagrant EEOC violations, and workers' comp claims against some of the largest firms in the Delaware Valley, and that had gotten her frozen out of corporate law. How did those frightened, out-gunned clients find her behind that protective, bulletproof shield of a prominent white law firm? And, when they sat before her with their gut-wrenching stories of personal violation, how could she turn them away? But, despite the nice settlements for her clients, and the firm, there had been a personal price, a sacrificial cost, for taking on their causes.

All of her colleagues got to work on sizzling, high-profile cases, with lots of resources at their disposal, while she'd had to quietly structure a defense, without assistance, for some poor working mother, or broken down old man, until the corporation in question buckled and surrendered under her meticulous arguments—just to keep it out of the news. The hours, alone, had been the death knell to any social life.

But what had killed her career was her politics, which also meant that her firm couldn't represent the offending corporation until after the case was closed, because it would be a conflict of interest. Even though she'd win, it would always result in a Catch-22: her winning a huge portion of the spoils for the firm, but alienating the firm from future long-term, lucrative retainers from the corporations she'd won against. The firm told her that it was "just business, nothing personal," and that she was just too good for her own good, and had unwisely chosen the wrong side, for the long haul, every time—which had been what killed her long-term career with them . . . "Sparkling young attorney though she was . . . with an amazing skill-set." Aziza shook her head and groaned, closing her eyes tightly as she worked the muscles in her shoulders.

Maybe she could hang her shingle to just tackle that specialty area, "David versus Goliath Law," instead of trying to be all things to all people. She shook her head and allowed tears to drop, then chuckled as she wiped them away.

All of her so-called legal friends and colleagues had mysteriously distanced themselves from her. It was in the best interest of their own careers, and quite understandable given the circumstances. There were no real childhood comrades to call today, since she really hadn't had a childhood. School chums were more competitors than friends, and were certainly not the people with whom to bare one's soul . . . and Ma Ethel was gone . . . a stroke had taken her . . . even though when she was alive, Ma Ethel never could understand her granddaughter's driving ambition. Hers was a different era with different rules . . . none of which Ma Ethel was familiar with. And the fleeting men in her life . . . Aziza let her breath out in a rush of despair. She didn't want to think about that disastrous trail of competition and dysfunctionality she'd left in her wake throughout the years.

At least she'd had a great education to fall back on. Good thing her mother's life insurance money had supplemented her expensive education. It had served its purpose, and she'd done her part by getting scholarships to make the money last longer. She'd been an "A" student, ever mindful of where her education came from, and had become an attorney. Now, there was no one to monitor whether or not she ever fulfilled her own dream to become a judge. Perhaps she'd go back to school and become an artist and use the third floor as a studio for herself. It just wasn't fair.

Melancholy weighed on her. Aziza chuckled quietly, allowing the sad tone of her own voice to echo through the room. There might be a certain crazy freedom to it all, she reasoned, one that she hadn't experienced before. "Maybe God has a plan, huh, Grandma?"

She wondered what it would be like to just hang out in South Street coffee shops—since all she needed to afford were the annual taxes on the house, which were nominal, and to figure out how to hustle up the utilities, and a medical and dental plan. Maybe she'd find an eclectic lover who was a writer, or painter, or a musician . . . and she'd work on erasing her past trail of corporate sharks and fellow attorneys who didn't have a soul, but who felt her ambition was too emasculating to forge a commitment.

Banishing the memories, and the foolish turn her thoughts had taken, she made a mental note to call a realtor later in the day. She'd tell them to find some young couple, or students going to the nearby

University of the Arts, to take the place. That way, she'd be assured that there'd be people in there who stayed up all night long, who also played music and danced and had friends over—though she wasn't sure if she was ready for a young couple to engage in love-making over her head.

Aziza let out another sigh. No, art students would be better. A couple, of any age, would be too depressing.

Again she allowed her tear-blurred vision to sweep the room. She still needed to hook up her stereo, set up her home office, and unpack her kitchen appliances. While Ma Ethel had been a veritable cast-iron-skillet chef, her kitchen didn't host the modern appliances of a microwave, coffeemaker, juicer, food processor, or food dehydrator—standards for a ten-minute, health-conscious, executive working-woman chef of the new millennium.

Pushing herself away from the task of puttering in the dresser drawers, Aziza set her priorities and goals for the day. First a shower, quickly followed by coffee, then she'd connect the technology in the spare bedroom and transform it into an office. Too bad, she mused to herself as she crossed the room, that she didn't think to get the movers to haul the twin beds up to the empty third floor apartment—but they'd really pissed her off so badly yesterday that her decision-making capacity had been severely affected. Pain in the butt though it was, she'd drag each piece upstairs on her own volition, board by freakin' board if necessary.

By then it would be 9:00 AM, and she could call a few realtors and post her ad for an apartment in the local art rags. Then she could unpack her kitchen gadgets and make room in the cabinets for her pseudo-china and flatware. Once that was accomplished, she could then go out to run errands. She needed to get in a total grocery list of fresh vegetables and fruits, which meant going down on Washington Avenue to the Italian Market. But, before that, she'd need to scout out, and pin down, an antique dealer who'd not only pay for, but would also haul and remove, most of the remaining furniture from a bygone era. She'd just have to steer clear of her grandfather's shop. He'd never approve of her selling off Ma Ethel's wares, and would probably go through another tirade about it being bad luck. She'd offered him first choice at taking whatever he wanted when she'd lost her job, and he wouldn't hear of it . . . old people got on her nerves. Practicality never entered into their decisions.

With a cleared-out space, she could effectively decide when to get her furniture and art out of storage, and plan another van-load delivery. But the first order of business was to take a shower.

Chapter Six

On his third round of dousing, Rashid's skin stung and burned beneath the salty mixture that his host had concocted as bath water. None of his arguments had prevailed as old man Morgan required that he thoroughly scrub his body with a bar of some sort of terrible-smelling, homemade brown soap in water treated with, of all things, a capful of laundry bleach. Then, after what the old coot had called *phase one*, he'd been subjected to a steaming cauldron of bath water with eucalyptus and a bunch of twigs floating around in it. After that, his dignity was further offended when the old man burst in on him and demanded that he scrub every inch of his body with what looked like a large, hard-bristled dog brush.

The smell alone had made him want to gag. He couldn't tell which had cleared out his sinuses first, the bleach or the eucalyptus. Not to mention, he was still groggy and disoriented from having slept uninterrupted for a full seven hours, through the night, for the first time since childhood. Now his tormentor required yet another bath, this time with so much rock salt and sea salt in it that his skin was turning ashen.

Rashid allowed his body to slump down under the water's surface, and indulged his full senses in the warmth that surrounded him. Reluctantly, he had to admit that it did feel good to get the newspaper ink and grime off of him more thoroughly than a quick shower, and his scalp had a stinging-clean feeling that he hadn't experienced in a while.

Vapors that smelled like a church swirled around his head, and he peered at the strategically placed pots of incense along the edge of the tub, which hosted white sage leaves, and frankincense and myrrh crystals. As aggravated as he had been by Abe's cleansing process, somehow it also gave him an overall feeling of security, if not safety . . . better stated, peace—which was also a very new sensation.

"You ready for phase two?" Abe said in a low rumble, edging into the small bathroom, clutching a hot-water bottle in one hand that had a long hose attachment clamped shut with a metal seal, and closing the lid on the toilet with the other before taking a seat on it.

"I don't suppose that knocking, or privacy, is a part of the routine around here, either?" Rashid scowled at his new drill sergeant when the old man chuckled.

"You ain't got nothin' I don't have or ain't seen before—and this ain't about getting you ready for no beauty contest. It's about work. Spiritual work. Gotta start fresh and clean in body, mind, and spirit."

Undaunted, Abe Morgan handed him the large hot-water bottle that had been slung over his lap as he'd sat down. "When you're done cleaning off the outside, you've gotta clean out all of that garbage *inside* your system. You might have worms and parasites in general and definitely from eating in restaurants where the other side might have tried to poison you. Always gotta worm a new pup," he added with a sly wink. "The body is the temple. I won't bust in here while you do this part. Guaranteed."

"*Do what*?" Rashid was incredulous as he stared at what looked like an overfilled enema contraption. The long plastic nozzle that dangled at the end gave him the shivers. "I know you don't think—"

"It's what you think, but won't give you as deep a clean as a colonic, though. For now, it'll do. Cleans out your colon, where poisons reside. You'll be on some clear broths, teas, and very light meals for a few days. You gotta take a whole juiced garlic bulb by mouth daily, with unfiltered vinegar, cayenne to get your circulation and resistance back to par, and other internal cleansers like echinacea, golden seal, dandelion root tea, lobelia, burdock root, licorice root, ginger, fennel—clean it out. We fast while we pray."

"Are you *crazy*?" Rashid stood and grabbed his towel, casting the rubber bag into the sink. "First of all, I'll be griping and sick as a dog. You're so worried about the way things smell around here, whaduya think is gonna happen if I do this?" Pure indignity swept through him, and he roughly toweled off his body as he spoke in fits and spurts of anger. "Second of all, I don't eat meat, and don't get a decent meal most of the time anyway, so there shouldn't be a whole lot up there for you to be concerned about. Third of all—"

"Third of all, you're hardheaded and don't know what I know, and ain't lived as long as I've lived. Plus, a good, strong colonic will be rugged enough on the first clean-out to kill that morning boner you've got, too. Although, once your physical system gets fine-tuned, well . . . everything will work better, which might not be easy for you to deal with. We'll just have to address that problem, if your mind can't kill it, with some other herbs I have, like saltpeter. We'll cross that drawbridge when we get to it. For now, stop arguing with me, boy. How old do you think I am?"

Embarrassed, Rashid turned his back to his tormentor, shook his head and continued to towel off his body, refusing to answer. "Where's my clothes?"

"Put this tea tree oil and pine sap on them little cuts and abrasions, and use the jojoba oil and aloe all over, even on your scalp," Abe quipped pleasantly, ignoring his question. "Give your new skin a drink of moisture, and drink that gallon of distilled water I left for you over an hour ago—before you pass out, fool. This routine I'm putting you on requires plenty of hydration. And, by the way, brush your teeth with that baking soda and mint-leaf-oil paste I left you in that cup over there."

Rashid shot Abe a look of disgust, and took the skin treatment items from the rim of the sink and began applying the mixtures.

"Now, again, I ask you, how old do you think I am?"

"Eighty-five," Rashid mumbled, as he haphazardly applied the skin balms, "but you look ninety, if a day."

Abe laughed and walked to the door, motioning toward the hot-water bottle he'd left where Rashid had flung it. "Thanks for the compliment, son, but you ain't even close."

Both men stared at each other for a moment, and Abe's grin widened.

"Once you clean out your body, put on the karate whites and slippers I've left you on the radiator. They should be nice and warm by now, and will feel good on a clean body."

"Where are *my* clothes?"

"Your rags are where they should be. Burned in the trash can in the alley."

"You had no right!"

Abe shrugged and leaned against the doorframe, seeming amused. "No ID, pictures, nothing of note but filth and street grime to claim in them clothes. Mighta brought in some trails for *the shades* to follow, or mighta brought in one through the door with you. Couldn't take chances. Here's your money," Abe said with a smile, tossing a roll of bills to Rashid. "But it's wet. Dipped it in holy water to ensure that it is only used for, and came from, Divine purposes."

Rashid just shook his head and set his bankroll down carefully on the edge of the sink. This old man was worse than a drill sergeant.

"So, I am working on your color chart now," Abe continued. "Spirit needs to move me to decide which colors you'll need to wear daily, and when, for maximum protection. Certain colors are symbolic, and we must pray every step of the way for every action we undertake. I've been praying for guidance on the subject of our next move. We'll pray for clarity, then begin easy today with some basic yoga stretches to get you in shape . . . we do need to keep the body in a state of readiness. You will have some more elimination system cleansing teas, a little broth, and some light whole grains for breakfast, then I'll show you how to clean out your living space properly with prayers of authority to oust anything that doesn't belong where you are."

"My space?"

Abe Morgan sighed. "How to prayer-cleanse-out the four corners of a room, and cast out evil, and how to remove dust that could harbor shadows, with essential purification oils and incense. You must energy-balance the mind, the body, and the spirit, as well as anoint the environment. I will also give you a full meridian foot massage at the end of the day. You have been wounded in the core of each of your centers of balance, and as a warrior of light, we cannot have that."

Rashid just stared at the man before him, speechless.

"Then, after you regain your strength, this old man who is a lot older than you think, will proceed to teach you how to defend yourself using those three centers of body, mind, and spirit—by kicking your butt the first time, to indisputably prove the point."

"You're older than ninety?" Rashid stood before his challenger, no longer as concerned about covering himself, still damp and naked except for his towel. "Now, I was born yesterday. Okay, Mr. Abe.

Whatever you say, but would you let me get dressed without an audience?"

"I'm no liar, and I don't generally provide food, baths, foot massages, a place to sleep, and the finest silk aikido-samurai fighting gear for any passerby urchin that just falls into my door with a long story and no last name. And I'm not some weirdo who likes the company of young men, nor do I enjoy seeing you without your clothes on, so you can stop the unnecessary coyness and modesty around me. Go do what I've told you, and meet me downstairs for lesson number one, and stop wasting time this morning. Like I said before, we've got *work* to do—but you ain't nowhere near ready, and if you might have to travel back in time, you're gonna have to have yourself way past ready."

Each argument with the antique dealers had worn a hole in her brain. By midafternoon, all she could do was sit in the park across from her old apartment and stare at the barren trees. Not one of them would agree to set up an appointment to even come out and look at the treasures in her grandmother's house, let alone agree to haul it out of the place that she'd have to accept as her home.

Strange, but they did this all the time, she thought. Any antique dealer would normally be interested in new finds—why now was she meeting such unnecessary resistance? They'd all given her every standard, noncommittal answer in the book . . . it's the slow season, maybe in the spring; we just got a big shipment in. Everyone had an excuse.

The thought of paying movers again, simply to take away the things she didn't have space for, then to have to just donate all of that history to a salvage joint, made her want to cringe. She couldn't do that, and would have felt a lot better about the decision knowing that someone else would cherish and use the pieces. If her grandfather wasn't so stubborn, she would have felt better if he would have taken it.

Aziza pushed herself up from the bench and looked down at her cooling cappuccino. Okay, so maybe she'd give Pop one more try, even if it caused another row about her sanity. Maybe, if he thought that she was indeed just going to chuck everything, he'd be moved to save it himself. Hell, at this point, she'd pay to have it moved to his shop and would help him tag and catalogue every piece, if he'd just get it out of her living space. Anyway, she could be assured that he'd hang on to it forever, or until someone worthy who'd appreciate it would take it home.

Marching with conviction, she pushed past the wind and strode down to South Street, rehashing her argument over and over again in her head as she walked. She knew what the recalcitrant old man would say, and she knew that she'd have to fully hear him out, and seem to hang on his every word, before she'd be allowed to go on her way.

As she approached the block that housed her grandfather's storefront, Aziza steadied herself and drew in a deep, mind-clearing breath. This was gonna be a tough sell, but she needed closure. When his tiny marquee came into view, she hesitated again, then pushed on, stepping up to the door and ringing the chime.

"Sounds like you've got a customer," Rashid yawned, totally fatigued from staring at the tenth lit match Abe Morgan held before him.

"Close your mind to the outside world. The match is your focus. It is your inner world, and you are the flame that wants to be at peace. I beat you on the mats today because you weren't focused. Remember, mind, body, spirit . . . the trinity. Pray for mental strength, then ask the flame to extinguish itself."

When the chime sounded again, Rashid looked past Abe toward the front of the store, and allowed his vision to settle on the thin shadow that was cast against the drawn door shade.

"How're you gonna stay in business if you don't let customers in during business hours, and you keep the blinds shut?"

"Don't need but a few customers a month to stay in business to pay property taxes. The store is paid for, and I don't eat that much. I've put up the vegetables I grow in the backyard in mason jars for the whole winter, and don't use that many utilities—they can shut off gas and electric, for all I care. Got a wood burning stove and fireplace for heat, and oil lamps for light. My water bill is nominal. Any more questions about my livelihood can wait. Now concentrate!"

Rashid just shook his head when his peevish instructor finished the diatribe, and tried to force his mind to grapple with the flame, to no avail. His nerves suddenly felt on edge, as though an electric current was running through him. He'd felt bouts of that same surge all day. It was like something indefinable was calling him, robbing him of even the slightest level of tranquility.

On the third ring, Abe blew out the match and stood with annoyance. "You are too easily distracted, and don't think that I can't tell when you're just tired. You give in to your physical urges too easily. This ain't about my customer. This is about you not wanting to put in the effort it takes. Now, when I get rid of this person, we will begin where we left off. Take five, and be ready when I come back to this chair."

As Abe paced away from the table in the back of the room, Rashid could feel his muscles relaxing. The old man was a veritable tyrant. Why he was subjecting himself to this insanity made no sense. But curiosity had a stranglehold on him. The old man was talking about traveling through time. So, if he had to endure the absurd for a few days to see if that could actually happen, he was game.

Mental and physical fatigue pulled at him hard, making him want to just curl into a ball like a lazy cat, and take a late afternoon nap in the warm sun coming through the edges of the window shades.

True to his word, Abe Morgan had worked him like a mule all day . . . cleaning, and stretching, and praying, and making every surface in the place gleam with new energy. Odd, but even in the daytime, he could still see muted swirls of opalescent light dancing off the polished surfaces and playing cheerful tricks with his vision. He'd never been able to see them during the day before, nor had he ever experienced being bodily tossed to the floor so easily by an elderly man, which had a lot to do with his decision to endure Abe Morgan's lessons.

If nothing else, he wanted to know how he'd done that, and perhaps more importantly, he was now curious about the old man's true age. He'd stay and take this unnecessary abuse only until he found out, then he'd be gone, he told himself. Abe had promised him that he'd get the answer only when he could beat him on the mats. That seemed fair enough, and probably wouldn't take him that long. All he needed to do was to regain his strength after being in the cold for so long . . . a day or two, at best. Maybe *the shades* had weakened him? It was all too odd. But if he was weakened somehow, it certainly didn't make sense to go back out on the streets, so vulnerable that an old man could best him. So, for showing him that, he did owe the old buzzard a bit of gratitude. But the mats and this new match trick had become a man-to-man challenge that he wanted to meet. Abe Morgan could light a match and just by staring at it he could make it go out. He *had to* learn what was behind that.

Ignoring the sound of the locks being turned, Rashid struck another match and stared at the tiny flame, determined to make it go out as simply as Abe had done with his demonstration of sheer will of conviction backed up by prayer. Heat began to permeate his fingertips, but he kept his vision on the base of the flame, which crept down the stem of the matchstick.

The collision in his skull of a familiar female voice with Abe's connected simultaneously with the flame and his peripheral vision. The match went out. Rashid stood, still holding the half-burned matchstick between his fingers as his vision swept the front of the store. He didn't move, not sure which sensory perception held him most in awe—the sight of the extinguished match, or the sound of the woman's voice.

"Aw c'mon, Pop," the female voice at the front of the store pleaded, "we've been through this a hundred times, if once. Grandma's house is only a few blocks around the corner on Twenty-first and Fitzwater, and—"

"I know where Ethel lived, and, for the one hundredth time, you don't need to be selling off her life. Y'all young people don't have no appreciation for history, time, or what's good for you."

"But I can't live in there with her stuff *and* my stuff. Nobody else will take it."

"Nobody else is *supposed* to take it. Belongs in there! Protects you."

Rashid watched the two dicker about the merits of keeping or discarding possessions, totally oblivious to their words . . . captivated by the young woman drenched with sunlight in the doorway. The way the light hit her, and Mr. Morgan's body blocked her, he couldn't be sure—but the voice was immediately recognizable. When she looked past Abe, into the shop, Rashid's perception was confirmed. Her tense expression melted into a half smile.

"Okay, Pop," she said begrudgingly. Her shoulders sagged a bit with the defeat. "I'm sorry, sir," she added, looking in Rashid's direction, "if I interrupted your conversation. I'll come back another time when you don't have a customer, Pop."

Then she waved at Rashid.

Abe Morgan cast his gaze between the two and scoffed. "Oh, Rashid ain't no customer. He's my, er, new help. Well, new and old—was helping me just sweep before and was good on security, but I'ma teach him more. I'm getting on in years, don't have to tell you that, and need somebody around here to help me tend the store. Was just training him on how things go." Abe glanced at the unlit match that Rashid held between his fingers, then looked Aziza over thoroughly. "At least come in and have a seat," he said without facing her. "Shouldn't discuss business out on the street."

Aziza paused and tilted her head to the side, studying Rashid hard. "*This* is the same guy who used to sweep up for you, Pop?" She looked from Rashid to her grandfather. "The same guy who sells papers outside my building, right?"

"Yeah," Rashid said flatly and oddly hating that she'd made the connection. He also hated the way she looked at him like he was a different person, now that he was squeaky clean, and it pissed him off that she had the audacity to openly speak of it. Previous conversations between her and her grandfather about him being in the shop had been strained. Today he didn't want things to go in that direction. She left him conflicted—pissed off and mesmerized at the same time.

"Rashid is good people," Abe Morgan said with a sly half smile. "Told you that, but you stubborn like your grandma was. He cleans up real good, like I said. Been real consistent for about a year and I'm showing him some of the business of antiquing, if that's all right with you, Miss Lawyer."

Rashid's gaze locked with the older man's for a moment before he stepped away from the table to offer the young woman a seat. A knot had formed in his throat that only allowed him to nod at the woman who had just referred to him as "sir." Never in his wildest dreams would he have imagined that she gave a second thought to the person she bought her morning newspapers from on the street.

As she neared the table, her smile opened to full brilliance and she extended her hand easily. "Aziza. Guess we got off on the wrong foot the few times I was here . . . have to be protective of family. Nice to see you again, and glad Pop has someone trustworthy in here to help him. Now, if you can just convince him to take a look at my grandmother's furniture, I'll be indebted to you for life."

Rashid allowed the smooth warmth of her hand to connect with his. Just as he'd always imagined. Her palm was like rich buttercream against his before it ignited the rest of his senses. Still too stunned to speak, he stifled a shudder of pleasure, smiled and nodded again before looking down at the table.

"Let me get this mess out of your way, so your coat sleeves don't get dirty," he managed to rasp out, refusing to look in her direction, or at Abe Morgan. Just like that, he'd learned her name . . . after serious prayer about it . . . after being cleaned up and cleaned out . . . just like Abe Morgan told him.

"It's fine," she insisted, plopping herself down and smiling broader. "Don't make a fuss for me. I'm just here on a quick visit and trying to plead my case with my very stubborn grandfather—it runs in our family."

It hadn't been lost on him that his usually opinionated instructor had become very quiet, and had walked toward the stove without turning around. However, instinct told him that every move he made now, and every thought he had, Abe Morgan was watching from a curious spectator's position. Continuing to over-clean the table area, Rashid allowed the delicate scent of her perfume to intoxicate him as he worked around her.

Aziza watched the two men share the space as though in a prerehearsed waltz. But she couldn't force her gaze away from the younger of them . . . something about his voice . . . and the brief encounter with his eyes . . . there was something electric that she'd never fully experienced until this moment—it had occurred when she shook his hand. And he was absolutely breathtaking . . . tall, dark, finely sculpted chocolate, reeking with a quiet magnetism that almost made her forget why she'd stopped by the store. None of that had been visible to her before.

Clearing her throat to regain her poise, she wrenched her attention from the younger man to her grandfather. "Well, can we at least discuss it?"

"You still drinking that poison, coffee, or can I make you some herbal tea?"

Aziza chuckled and shrugged her shoulders. "Tea will be fine, Pop."

"Don'tchu know that caffeine is bad for your skin?" he grumbled without turning around. "Not to mention the strain it puts on your other vital organs."

"Yes, sir," she laughed easily, "but I got hooked on it in college. So, what's a girl to do?"

"Try some of them cleansers I tol' ya about. Get control of your urges and master your fate."

Aziza cut a half glance toward Rashid and let a sly smile create a lopsided expression on her face to make him chuckle. "Has he been on you too, or is it just me that he harasses?"

Feeling more at ease in her presence, Rashid shook his head no and let out a long breath in a way that seemed to amuse her, and took the seat across from her. "Oh, believe me, you are not alone."

For a moment they stared at each other, glimpsed Abe Morgan's back, then let out a peal of laughter at the table. Her mirth covered him, seeped inside of him, and fused with her voice down into the marrow in his bones. It had been so long since he'd laughed, deep belly-laughed, that he found the corners of his eyes becoming moist from the sheer release of emotion.

As Abe made his way to the table with two cups of a nasty brew that he claimed to be tea, Rashid breathed deeply through his nose to stifle his response. But as soon as he and Aziza looked at each other again, they burst out laughing.

"Okay, okay," she giggled, waving her hand in Rashid's direction, her self-composure out of reach, "I'll try some of your tea."

Her hands shook with repressed giggles as she brought the cup to her mouth. Rashid watched her lips caress the side of the china, and he briefly closed his eyes to ward off the new awareness that she was causing him to experience. Abe Morgan did not appear to be amused, and simply folded his arms over his chest, which threatened to make them both laugh again. When the bridge of her nose wrinkled at the taste of the dark liquid in her cup, that was it, Rashid doubled over and howled outright with laughter.

"Pop," she apologized, still giggling, "I'm sorry, but this tastes like that stuff Ma Ethel used to make me drink when I was little and had a cold. How do you do this every day?"

"It'll clean you out," the old man said in a huff, sitting down heavily on a tall stool next to the chair Rashid had taken. "And will keep you healthy and alive."

Seeming to lose patience, the elderly man turned his attention to Rashid. "And you could use another dose yourself. Once you get the toxins out, you can move from medicinals to better flavors."

Again, the two young people stared at each other for a moment and tried their best not to laugh. Aziza gave up first, closely followed by Rashid.

"For real, Pop," she said, trying to squelch her laughter, "I appreciate your herbal remedies. But I really need your help with moving Ma's furniture. Can you use any of it?"

"Nope," the old man said plainly, looking her dead in the eyes. "Ethel is all in that house, keepin' things static-free. She polished and anointed every stick of that furniture almost every day she was alive. She kept the place swept out, and after all that bad business was over, there wasn't no more problems in that place. You go to movin' her energy and prayers out, and it'll leave room for somethin' else to come in. I won't be a party to it. Hear? Won't have her haunting me for leaving her grandbaby unprotected."

"Then I guess I'm going to have to just give it away to the Salvation Army," she said with a sigh. "I hate to do it, but I can't live in there with those memories. You of all people should understand that, Pop."

Rashid glanced at Abe Morgan then back to Aziza, only to watch a slow sadness eclipse her once joyous expression, and his mouth formed words without asking his brain for consent. "Maybe you're supposed to keep your grandma around you, Princess."

As soon as the words had tumbled from his lips, he regretted the comment, because she stared at him for a moment, almost shook off his statement with a physical shrug, then just nodded, stood, and extended her hand. Rashid immediately stood and accepted her palm into his, holding it for a moment longer than necessary before allowing it to withdraw.

"I can't," was all that she said, hugging her grandfather while still staring at Rashid. "But thanks a lot for the good company, good cheer, and the tea," she added as she walked toward the door. "I understand."

Again, words stopped in his throat. He could only nod.

When she paused and walked back toward them, he nearly held his breath.

"I've always admired this piece," she said quietly, passing them and approaching the large, silver-framed mirror next to their table. "Pop, if you ever decide to part with it, promise me, you'll call me first."

An opalescent light from within the center of the object seemed to reach out and caress the outer edges of her body, merging with the light that she already emanated on her own. Rashid blinked to try to clear his vision, but he saw what he saw, and the spectacle of dancing lights wouldn't go away.

"Tol' ya a long time ago, it ain't for sale, and won't never be for sale and you gotta wait till I die to get it, baby," her grandfather huffed, standing and walking toward the mirror to throw a cover over it. "Was passed down through generations. But I, unlike you, appreciate the history of things."

Rashid watched her carefully as her hand hovered just over the surface of the cover as the lights receded. Her eyes seemed distant, and her voice took on a mesmerizing vacant quality.

"What did you say?" she asked, not turning in their direction.

"I said—" her grandfather began, then stopped as she waved her hand.

"No, I was talking to Rashid," she nearly whispered. "He asked me a question. Do I know you, other than from your newspaper post . . . we've met before that . . . before you came to help Pop in this shop, haven't we?"

Again, both men looked at each other and remained silent for a moment.

"I didn't say anything," Rashid said awkwardly, his eyes darting between Abe Morgan and Aziza. "And I don't think we've ever met . . . I would have remembered."

Turning to face them, her expression was puzzled. "But you did say my name, then something else I couldn't hear. What did you say?"

"Uh, I forgot what I was going to say," Rashid lied, not looking at her, but reading the warning expression in Mr. Abe's eyes. "Wasn't important."

Aziza let out her breath in a long sigh and shrugged, then walked toward the door, telling them to have a nice day as she opened it.

All he could do was to watch her slip through the entrance and out into the dimming sunlight. Rashid sat down and looked at his tea, then lit a match and turned his attention on it without saying anything to Abe Morgan.

"I'ma let you be for the rest of the day," his instructor said quietly, moving the tea away from him. "But, maybe we've been approaching this the wrong way . . . why don't you take one that hasn't been struck, pray, then try to light it?"

Rashid didn't look in Abe Morgan's direction, but blew out the match he was holding and picked up a new, unlit one. He closed his eyes, said a prayer, and thought of how her hand had ignited the senses within him. Immediately he heard a small pop and felt an intense heat.

"Open your eyes, son," his instructor murmured. "It's lit. Very good."

Staring at the flame between his fingers until it nearly reached his skin, Rashid allowed himself to become the blue light at the base of the fire. When the heat threatened to burn him, he willed it to self-extinguish.

Abe Morgan smiled. "Later, I'll sleep down here in the back of the store tonight, you take the second floor. You'll most likely be needing your privacy. Just change my sheets in the morning, is all I ask . . . don't dream too hard."

Rashid glanced away from the old man. Embarrassment singed him, but he would not give Abe Morgan the satisfaction of being so totally right about his thoughts.

"She's gonna keep on trying to sell the furniture until she finds a buyer, then *the shades* are going to come into that house for her."

"I know," Abe whispered, sitting down beside his student and taking the burned matchstick from his trembling fingers. "And that's why you have to be ready to help her. That's why I put you through all that purification . . . I knew she'd recognize you once you was back to yourself."

"Who am I to her?" Rashid whispered, his gaze locked with his mentor's.

"That's enough exercise for one day. Rest . . . if you can. You're too wired for further study today. Pray on it, if you can't rest. And let the physical urge she creates in you pass. I may be old, but I also know what a long time can do to a young man. If you want to really help her, relieve the urge, alone, gather your focus, and do not let it be a future distraction. Mind over matter. Spirit over mind. Right now the body is weak, and the mind is confused, so use spirit to shore you up. Don't make love with anything that comes to you in a dream, it might not be her—understand that," Abe warned.

Both men stared at each other for a long time before Rashid cast his gaze in the direction of the door.

"She hears things, and I see things," Rashid murmured, carefully watching his mentor's face for any signs of agreement. "Now, I'm starting to *feel* things . . . I wonder if she can too?"

"What did you ask her in your mind?"

Rashid ignored Abe's question, and kept his gaze away from the old man's prying eyes.

"Maybe I should go over to her new location and keep watch?"

"She'll be all right as long as Ethel's spirit permeates that house. Do not try to go after her yet. You're not ready, and neither is she. Understood?" Abe warned.

"What is going on?" Rashid insisted. "Tell me the truth, all at once, not in these cryptic bits and pieces of information."

A sudden tightness gripped his throat, and Rashid swallowed hard to force it away. He stood and paced to the stove and lit a fire under the kettle. "Tell me what I've gotta do to get cleaned out, and stronger—to be ready. Today I wasn't an anonymous vendor on the streets that she just passed by, and I felt good about her seeing me all cleaned up . . . I was somebody that she called trustworthy, and I had a job that she didn't look down on—even if it was just selling papers, or providing security for your store. There was respect. She never even knew where I came from, but gave me that much due anyway. Thank you, for showing me who she really is, and for allowing her to see me in a better light."

"Thank the Father, not me," Abe murmured. "I was just the vessel. You were the one who prayed for it to happen like this. Did I not tell you the power of prayer to change things, circumstances, even the physical, in ways that may initially appear impossible? That's why we were practicing with the match."

Abe Morgan stood and walked over to the cabinets beside Rashid, producing a bag of dried leaves that he began to sift into a tea ball in preparation for the boiling water. He took his time, speaking slowly and deliberately, in the same manner that his hands were working the tea leaves. "You're welcome for the small part I played in this, and I thank you too—for being an excellent student. You're a natural. A quick study, which is fortunate, because we don't have a lot of time. Every day, our position gets compromised. The signs are all around us. And I need to be able to close my eyes on this wretched earth, knowing someone will care about my baby girl."

"I'd give my life for her."

His benefactor stopped his tea-making process and looked directly at Rashid, without a smile. "Son, don't you understand that's why she knows you—'cause you already have?"

Chapter Seven

Abe Morgan looked up at the ceiling and walked over to the mirror to uncover it. The sound of Rashid pacing overhead made him nearly grind his teeth. His vision slid to the wall clock, and he reverently touched the edges of the mirror then returned to his seat at the table, waiting for Rashid to come downstairs. Eight o'clock at night and the boy had to make it till sunrise, Abe mused. He'll never make it.

"I thought you were supposed to be resting, and if not, praying," he commented in a tired voice, as Rashid entered the room.

"Yeah, well, I was praying while I was walking and thinking," Rashid retorted, taking a bit of bread from the table and eating it where he stood.

Abe sighed and brought another slow spoonful of his stew into his mouth. "Not tonight," he murmured without looking up from his bowl. "Sit. Eat. Then, go to sleep. Tomorrow is another day."

He watched the young man wrestle with his order before reluctantly taking a seat. "I know how you feel, but—"

"You *do not* know how I feel!" Rashid countered, slamming his fist on the table. "Something's happened. I'm getting a bad vibe."

Abe looked up and sat back from his meal. "What kind of bad vibe?"

For a moment Rashid didn't answer, and he began fiddling with the teacup and dishes on his side of the table.

"I can't explain it. But I know I need to go by her spot tonight."

Abe waved his hand and sighed, and dismissed the comment, returning to his meal.

"This isn't stir-craziness, or just a random thought," Rashid persisted, "It's—"

"Pure lust," Abe chuckled, and took another healthy spoonful of stew. "Outright lust."

"Bullshit!" Rashid yelled, standing again and pacing toward the mirror.

"Watch your language," Abe warned, no longer finding the exchange humorous.

"She's in trouble. The light's too dim around the damned mirror. It's been dim all day. We're losing light!"

For the first time since he entered the room, Rashid had Abe's full attention.

Slowly pushing the bowl away from him, Abe Morgan wiped his mouth with the cloth napkin that had been on his lap, and stared at Rashid directly in the eyes.

"I know."

"Then, why are you playing with me—*like you don't know*? We ain't got time for this cat and mouse game, Abe!"

"Because," the old man said slowly, "I had to know that you knew which urge was more important, to protect her, or to have her—well before I could tell you what I know. There's two elements surging within you that I'm dealing with here, and only one of them is important at the moment."

Rashid whirled in a circle and plopped down in his chair. "You can see the lights dimming, too, can't you?"

Abe only nodded.

"You can read thoughts? Predict shit."

"Events. Human feces is easily predictable. Anybody can read that."

"And move objects."

"How many times did you hit the mat?"

Rashid sat quietly for a moment. "Then you can throw at least two to three times your own weight, right, old man?"

"Modestly speaking, about eight to ten. After I saw how pitiful an opponent you'd be, I eased up so as not to hurt you."

"Get the hell outta here . . ."

"I've already told you about the language."

"Okay, okay," Rashid apologized, "but you've gotta admit that you don't run across that every day."

"True," Abe admitted casually, "and you don't see someone with your spirit, and attendant skill-set every day, either. By the way, for your expanding vocabulary's sake, they're called *fruits of the spirit.* They are gifts, and not to be played with, got it?"

"Yeah," Rashid remarked quietly. "That's deep."

"I told you not to judge a book by its cover. That you must trust in a Higher Power to make the seemingly impossible possible, didn't I?"

Rashid simply nodded.

"That's what today was all about . . . to help you believe that there is an Authority so awesome, so powerful, that it can allow you to walk through fire without getting burned, it can transport you to places without the use of conventional contraptions, and it can allow you to defeat an opponent that appears to be much stronger than you. We will go back to our spiritual studies, as the examples of such miracles are our evidence. Prisoners of war had been remanded to furnaces, but they walked out alive while their captors were consumed in the flames. A prophet was transported to another country and yet had no recollection of how he arrived there. And, of course, David slew Goliath, and there's the witness of how lions in the Roman Coliseum did not kill and eat one of God's chosen when he was thrown in amongst them. Yes, I beat you on the mats today—not because I am stronger than you in body, but because I am much stronger than you, at this point, in mind and spirit."

Rashid could only stare at the old man who had handily bested him in physical contest after physical contest, all day long.

"You actually did quite well with the matches." Abe smiled. "Ah, yes, you thought I didn't see when it first happened. I see a lot more than you can imagine."

"You knew I was coming to your door, didn't you? And you knew I had stumbled onto something when I called you Merlin—that's why you freaked, and kept asking me why I'd called you that. Right? I can see things, too."

Abe smiled wider and stood, taking Rashid's bowl to the stove to fill it with vegetable stew. "I had hoped, but couldn't be sure until the signs were there."

"You also knew about her, too . . . that she was the one I was talking about?"

"I knew," Abe said carefully, dishing the stew, "that there were two of you left."

"Left? What's that supposed to mean?"

"Left generally means remaining, unless used as a directional term."

"Okay, don't start down some long, windy path to get me off track. You knew about us, that—"

"But, I wasn't sure *which* two would come together, and what time you'd appear. Some things are not to be predicted. But to answer your initial question, yes, I knew."

"But that's the whole thing I can't figure out. Left for what? To do what? And, more importantly, how did I lock onto her as somebody to protect? I've never met your granddaughter before in my life, and she said she's never met me, but she knew me! You saw the look on her face."

Rashid tentatively accepted the bowl of food from his host, and spooned down a few big mouthfuls before asking more questions. His brain felt like it was on fire, and he needed to absorb what he'd just heard before finding out anything else. Only two left . . . what was that all about?

"It was in the prophecy."

"Okay, I guess I'm not supposed to know about this prophecy yet, huh?"

"Not yet, but soon."

"So," Rashid finally added, never losing eye contact with Abe Morgan, "since you knew somebody was coming, you prepared yourself to have a person in boot camp living with you."

"Correct."

"And," he pressed on, feeling annoyed by the simplicity of the old man's response, "you knew that person would probably lead you to the female counterpart—the other half of this dynamic duo you were looking for."

Abe Morgan just nodded as he returned his attention to his own bowl.

"You've known it was probably your granddaughter all of her life, right? You just needed me as confirmation, as a bird dog, to be sure. And you knew that was who I was talking about when I first showed up, right?"

"I suspected that it was her. Yes, I've known all that child's life that she was different, but I wasn't totally sure until I saw the effect she had on you, and vice versa. At first she was totally repelled—when you weren't the spirit she knew. I would look at how she looked at you with distrust and venom in her eyes as though seeing you in your previous condition literally offended some distant memory she had . . . one that she couldn't even articulate. Then I cleaned you up and presented you to her the way you'd been before, and she took an immediate shine to you. Recognized you, right off. That couldn't have been a coincidence—but I had to know, first. It's a complementary pair of gifts that we're searching for."

"We?"

"The Ancestors," Abe replied simply. "They're all in the spirit realm now. I'm the last one on this side."

"Dead? You have been consulting a committee of dead people?"

"Dead is a strong word, one that connotes the lack of everlasting life. Death comes only to nonbelievers. The Ancestors are made up of those given the promise of everlasting life. Don't say dead. They've just gone home."

"All right," Rashid sighed. "We won't debate semantics. Crossed over, gone home . . . whatever. But then, why in the hell did you act like I was crazy, and that I was nuts to be seeing the lights coming out of your store that you could already see? Huh? Answer me that one. Is it me?"

"Confused, yes. Crazy, no. And I never show who I am, or what I know, to people I don't know or trust yet. Basic rules of engagement and of camouflage. Now, is that crazy?" Abe waited for a moment, took another spoonful of his stew, and stood to go to the sink with his empty bowl. "I didn't think that security measure would sound crazy to a man who trusts no one. For all I knew, you could have just been some poor soul, foaming at the mouth and taken over during a drug-induced delirium, and sent by *them* to scout me out. Ever consider that?" He stared over his shoulder at his young pupil until Rashid briefly looked away. "Or the fact that the same source that wants you two just might have been after me for a *very* long time? But, judging by my age, I must know how to handle my business, as you young folks would say."

"Yeah, I'll give you that," Rashid begrudgingly admitted. "Just like I wouldn't stop touching the lights until I felt like you were okay . . . just in case." Before continuing, Rashid waited for the customary nod that he was now used to Abe giving him when he was making progress. "Okay. Then why didn't you just tell her—sit your granddaughter down and explain everything?"

"First of all, I said that *I suspected* it was her. Wasn't sure if she was The One, or had the right spiritual core. One can never be totally sure about anybody, when free will comes into the equation—just like I suspected you, but wasn't totally convinced at first. Life, filled with experiences, temptations, ambitions, tragedies, disappointments, other people . . . all of these things are a constantly changing series of obstacles—or blessings, depending on your viewpoint—strewn along your path and designed to sway a person—via their own free will, of course—to either lean left, or right. Plus, that child is hardheaded. Doesn't believe in this stuff and is scared to death of anything remotely spiritual . . . her grandmother was that way, too—God rest Ethel's soul. I loved that woman, that's what nobody understands, especially not Aziza. I told Ethel she couldn't run from fate by sending that girl off to fancy boarding schools and whatnot."

"Seems like maybe your ex was running from something or trying to spare Aziza from *the shades*, is all?"

"Yeah. Ethel was scared to death, that's for sure—and I can't blame her."

Rashid waited until Abe looked at him again, ignoring that Abe had removed his half-eaten bowl from the table to wash it out. "Is that why you don't want her to sell her grandmom's furniture? I saw it in your eyes, so you might as well admit it. That house is a safe house, as long as her grandmother's light is in there, and it's connected to every stick of furniture in there. Right?"

"You're improving," Abe said with a somber expression, then turned back to the chore of washing out their bowls and putting the food away. "I anointed every piece in there when Ethel wasn't home."

Okay. Progress. Rashid looked at Abe Morgan hard. "Talk to me. You want honesty, then you've gotta give honesty. You want help, then let me know what I'm up against for real."

Abe Morgan nodded and released a weary breath. "Ethel never left Fitzwater Street, but her spirit was definitely on the run," his host admitted with another sigh of resignation. "Hid that poor girl all over, and kept a prayer vigil going for her from her safe house. You can't imagine how many times I tried to tell Ethel that, if Aziza is The One, she could run, but she couldn't hide. She eventually has to face what is chasing her, and win. Just like you do."

"Hide from what?" Rashid nearly shouted. "What are either one of us running from, or being protected against? Huh? A curse?"

"Hardly," Abe Morgan scoffed, clearing away their spoons and napkins. "Fate."

"Okay!" Rashid yelled. "Quit the riddles and say it plain. What am I supposed to protect her from? What's been hunting us down?"

"The same thing that chased you into my store like a madman."

Rashid tried his best to regain his composure, recognizing that the more he yelled and fussed, the more cryptic the old man's responses became.

"Let me try it this way," Rashid sighed, standing to walk in a circle again. "You've also known for all your granddaughter's life that she might just be in some kinda danger. I've looked for someone that has her exact voice all of my life, then I found her here in Philly. I was even standing out in sub-zero temperatures on the streets because I *knew* she'd somehow come to me in a vision that saved my life, and I *knew* I had to save hers—but from what, I don't know. That's all I do know for sure."

Abe began running water from the sink again to wash the silverware, without commenting or turning around.

"I know I can see lights," Rashid pressed on, "and I'm pretty sure, after what happened to her in front of the mirror today, that she can hear thoughts. I know this, as crazy as it sounds, is some kinda safe house. I also know that there are things we cannot see, that are not of the light—things that can take your life, if not your soul. I call 'em *the shades*, 'cause they move in the darkness and suck up any available light. You believe in negative forces?"

"Where there's light, there's dark. Seen both. But the light has always been stronger . . . always before."

"You said the last part of that kinda quietly, my good brother. Is there some reason why all of a sudden the light wouldn't be stronger? Something I should know about?" Rashid stared at his teacher, who avoided direct eye contact.

"And," Abe said quietly, as he continued to clear away the remnants of their dinner, "*the shades* are now returning to where they last felt her presence to be the strongest, and the most vulnerable, in Ethel's house—where you saved her the first time."

"*I've never been to Ethel's house;* I never knew Aziza a long time ago, and you haven't answered—"

"Your sentinel spirit has been there," Abe said quietly, turning his back to Rashid again as he worked. "And she took a little bit of it home with her again today. The combined force has now created the beacon they were looking for . . ."

With his back still turned to his student, Abe caught Rashid's arm in midair as his student reached for Abe's shoulder in an attempt to spin him around. "Like radar."

"Damn," Rashid whispered, removing his hand from the elderly man's grip, and assessing his strength in the process. "I hear you."

Facing him, Abe leveled his gaze at Rashid and let out a long breath before continuing. "The more contact you have with her, the more energy you both exchange, and the more you'll tip off both of your positions. That's why you need to keep your distance, and if you can, shake her out of your mind and dreams. Right now, they just don't know for sure where, or who, either of you are—yet. However, now they have their suspicions. Being in constant motion, and living from pillar to post, has kept you both alive. I can also finally see that Ethel was right, moving that child around, too, was in the child's best interest."

"She lived just like me, albeit a little better. But we had the same deal." Rashid reached out slowly and placed his hand squarely on Abe's shoulder. When his teacher didn't stop him, Rashid offered his question in a near whisper. "What happened in that house that would make the woman want to sell off every stick of furniture in there?"

"Ain't for me to tell you," Abe sighed, "no more than I'd break your confidence by telling her anything deep to the personal about you."

"Okay, that's fair," Rashid conceded, removing his hand from the old man's shoulder and allowing it to fall to his side. "Then tell me what you can," he added, rolling his neck to relax the muscles in his shoulders, "whatever will help me help her—us. Like you said, time is running out. I may not be honed to perfection yet, but maybe having a willing enough spirit to help her is gonna have to suffice—given the time issue."

The honesty of Rashid's statement gave Abe pause. He leaned back against the sink and looked at the floor before he spoke. *Okay, progress,* Rashid thought. Maybe he'd finally gotten through to the old man.

"Ethel told me Aziza was The One, but I didn't want to accept it at first. Ethel had the gift of prophecy through dreams, and she said this magnificent room filled with finely dressed people of royal stature had come to her and shown her Aziza and named her before she was even conceived. Ethel didn't know it then, but The Ancestors had sent her the sign she'd been praying for."

"Why wouldn't you want Aziza to be The One? She's beautiful, and seems nice, and genuine, and—"

"Because she is so dear to me," Abe whispered. "That's why. And this mission is dangerous. There are no guarantees. Ethel was dear to me, too, and I knew that her grandchild would be in harm's way. If something had happened to Aziza before Ethel crossed over, it would have broken that poor woman's heart—and so, yes, I do know how it feels to be in the cloister, my boy. Oh, *I know*. Trust me on that."

"So, we could never . . ." Rashid let the question trail off, answering it in his own mind.

"Sleep with her—only with profound love for her in your heart, merge your bodies, minds, and spirits, and you'll effectively be offering both of yourselves up to them on a silver platter. That's why lovemaking is a sacred act," Abe said in a low murmur, answering the question that Rashid had never completed. "It is something not to be entered into unadvisedly, or without the proper hallowed rituals, prayers of commitment, and community protection involved. You need a village. Trust me on this."

Rashid looked toward the mirror and rubbed his sore wrist, still feeling Abe's grasp. "Tell me this, old man," he said quietly, but in a more reverent tone, "why are they after me and her?" Tears filled his eyes as he thought back on the number of people that had mysteriously died in his midst. "I was the one at fault, wasn't I . . . for the ones . . ."

Gathering him into an embrace, Abe held him for a moment before speaking. "*You did not kill those women.* Something definitely evil has been after you for a long time, boy. And you, by your very nature, picked decent, good mates whom you loved with your full heart. When you connected with those good people, you gave up body, mind, and spirit. *The shades* went after those young women, initially following your joyous light, thinking they were The One, Aziza. Then they realized those women weren't her, and they needed to keep you on the hunt looking for her."

"They had me walking point . . . taking them all into a trap," Rashid's voice rasped. His shoulders heaved from the deep breaths he took to stifle the agony of those memories. "Why didn't they just kill me?"

Abe held him more tightly, and tried to find soothing words for the inexplicable. "They couldn't just kill your body to win, son, because your spirit would have still been good—eternally. You'd come back time, after time, after time . . . just like she could, and therefore you both represent an eternal risk factor for them. They needed to crush your spirits too, not just your physical bodies. Their goal was to enter your mind, fracture it, make you kill yourself, then draw you from the light. There were no limits to what they'd use to blind you to it, or to break your spirit, in order to keep you from going through The Veil with her—once they discovered who your previous lovers were not. But, even still, it *was not* your fault. How would you have known, and what healthy young person would shun love?"

"Innocent people died," Rashid argued, tensing against the embrace as his voice broke. "And for what? Because I have a spiritual hit on me? She has a spiritual hit on her? Why? What veil . . . what the hell has this all been about?"

A mixture of anger and sorrow collected within Abe's soul as he allowed Rashid to yank himself away. He could only watch helplessly as the young man straightened and refused to give in to the sobs he knew Rashid needed so badly to release. *Damn them, how could they have tortured this young man this way?*

"When you first came to me a year ago," Abe said in a gentle but firm tone, "they'd almost taken your mind over the edge. My granddaughter is the same way now . . . frightened, paranoid, joyless, urge-driven, physically exhausted, light starved, and spiritually confused. They're taking everything away from her, cornering her till she breaks. But I have something you must see." Abe walked across the room and then stared over his shoulder at Rashid. "Something to ease your pain and to let you know who you are . . . something to give you hope and purpose and renewed strength."

Motioning with his arm, he bade Rashid to come closer, leading the young man to stand before the mirror. He flung off the thick dust cover and then returned his attention to Rashid. "Look at your image, and tell me what you see."

"The walking dead. A man who goes through the streets at night helping the helpless, with no life of his own. A man, who killed men in war," Rashid muttered without lifting his head. "Someone now cursed . . . who still gets innocent people killed."

"Look harder," the old man urged, "and it will also tell you who I am—how old I am."

Rashid drew a deep breath and expelled it quickly with exasperation. He stared at the mirror and shrugged his shoulders.

"Pain is blocking your amazing gift of vision. Look at it, and think of nothing hurtful."

Again, Rashid stared at his own battered reflection. He noted how his eyes had reddened, and how he stood next to an elderly man within a tiny shop. But he could see compassion in the old man's expression. There was definitely friendship, a sort of indefinable caring . . . if not an unlikely bond. . . . something almost near a resemblance. "Yeah, it's me and you, Mr. Abe. I guess that's cool. I trust you, and I owe you. I try to look out for those who look out for me, so I'll check on you from time to time—you know, to make sure you're all right. I'll look out for her, but . . . this spiritual stuff just ain't for me."

"Your eyes are still not seeing what they should," Abe Morgan whispered, then waved his hand before the glass. "Perhaps you are too tired. So much at once, and so unprepared. Too much, too soon . . . with hurts so deep. This time, I will step in, and help guide you in prayer." Then the old man's lips began to move as though in fervent prayer. "Let God's truth be revealed. May God's truth set you free."

The once still lights began to dance again in the room. Rashid glanced back at the mirror, squinted, and rubbed at his eyes. Their two motionless images in the mirror seemed to liquefy and move within a new color spectrum bordered by the huge, pure silver frame. His depth perception seemed off, and the three-dimensional quality of the lights splintered any logical explanation within his mind. The store in the background appeared to be replaced by something he couldn't quite make out or fathom. Transfixed by the slow transformation, he took in shallow breaths as the images came into clear view.

Then he saw it all, understood it for the first time in his life, and openly wept.

Chapter Eight

Music blared through the house as she slipped under the warmth of the scented bubbles that covered her. Smooth jazz notes filtered into the bathroom, mingling with the lavender aroma and fresh paint smell that made her heady. God, it was so good to be able to relax . . .

Scrubbing at a stubborn fleck of paint that refused to be dislodged from her forearm, Aziza gave up and tossed her loofa sponge back into the bubbles, and sank down lower to soak off the offending particle. With her eyes closed, she drifted lazily, pleased with her accomplishments of the day. She didn't even open them as she reached for the nearby glass of Zinfandel that rested next to her steaming tub. The chilled liquid slid down her throat easily, and the contrast of heat and coolness made her sigh with pleasure. Today had been an excellent day!

After all, she'd not only made a hefty sum that would keep her from having to immediately panic about employment, which meant that she would be financially stable until spring, but she had also finally rearranged the house to her liking. True to their word, the movers had returned and placed all of her most necessary furniture where she'd wanted it. The living room and dining room now had clean Danish-modern lines, the kitchen looked like an updated chef's haven, her home office was organized and technologically proficient, but most importantly, she could finally sleep in the bedroom.

With her large stereo wall unit blocking Ma Ethel's emptied-out closet, a fresh coat of paint, and just a wisp of sheer curtains to cover the more modern mini-blinds she'd hung, the room took on a new life of its own. No more haunting crevices, bed skirts, or dust ruffles. Old, giant-flowered-print curtains had been trashed. An old, worn hook rug had given way to a brighter, expensive Oriental one, and bookshelves and modern art would grace the walls as soon as the paint dried.

Now, *that* was a room she could sleep in, she mused. Although the transformation had been an eclectic compromise, with antiques dotting the otherwise totally new-millennium look, it worked. An old vanity here, a country basket there, against a background of technology, seemed to be an appropriate mix for who she was . . . a little of the old interspersed with a mostly new-age Aziza.

She giggled to herself, thinking of the panic attack she'd experienced when the antique dealer had come to the house. That had been too crazy, totally silly. The man must have thought she was a lunatic! And her few distant friends did have a point. She was centrally located within walking distance to Center City, and all of the hottest little hideaway restaurants and shops on South Street. She could walk to Penn's Landing, on a nice day, or walk to the Italian Market, and the third floor of her home could either be turned into an office, or could become income-bearing property.

Either way, she sleepily mused, at her age—with no mortgage on the large brownstone she inhabited, no credit card bills, and no car note, and no one to care for but herself, she was literally set. Her options were vast. Indeed, it was all a matter of perspective—a point of view that had suddenly shifted with her change of luck. Why hadn't she been able to see it all before, and what had made her give in to unnecessary depression? Stupid!

She could retire, or go back to school, travel, or even work as a coffee-shop waitress, if she wanted to, just to pay her minimal annual real estate taxes and monthly utilities.

As the sense of peace totally surrounded her, it suddenly dawned on her that she'd found herself in an unheard of, comfortable position for a young black woman. Just like Ma Ethel used to tell her, "Peace, be still." One had to get still enough to count one's blessings.

Reaching up to the spigots, she turned the knob to add more hot water to the cooling tub, and finished her glass of wine. She gently returned the glass to the floor and shook her head in amazement as she eased herself back into her previous lounging position. Wow, everything had a domino effect, triggering the next event as each piece fell into place. It was like a grand design on an enormous swath of fabric, where one couldn't see the entire intricate pattern up close, and full understanding required an aerial view.

Aware that the tub was about to overflow, she used her toes to pull the plug, still allowing the hot water to run. "Yep," she whispered with her eyes still closed, "you were right, Ma."

She let the comforting thoughts join the escaping water. If her parents hadn't died early, and the way they did, maybe she wouldn't have hidden her pain behind the books, and been as driven to go into the field of justice. If she hadn't been so terrified of the house, she wouldn't have spread her wings early on to experience schools and internships around the country, which gave her an excellent foundation.

Without that foundation, she would never have been able to get a plum position so young. And, at that firm, she was not only able to help a lot of people in need, but she was also able to acquire exquisite art and still pay off her bills. If any of her relationships had culminated in marriage, hindsight being 20/20, she'd probably be in divorce court now, she laughed to herself, or perhaps involved in a custody battle with one of those jerks! Plus, they probably would have done the perfectly acceptable yuppie thing, and bought a big house . . . somewhere far away . . . had kids, and been locked into a certain lifestyle. At her age, without a potential lover on the horizon, she reminded herself to keep that reality in front of her to chase away any looming blues.

"It's all good . . ." she whispered. Had Ma Ethel not taken ill, and had she not left her job, perhaps she would never have trimmed down her lifestyle, which now gave her unsurpassed freedom, nor would she have ever considered moving back into this wonderful old house. And, she reasoned, if she had not witnessed how short and unpredictable life could be she would probably be in credit-card hell now.

Aziza laughed at her own stubborn temperament, as she began to draw herself out of the bath. Her muscles still hurt from attempting to get it all done in one night. But, she mused, that was her way. Just like with the credit cards. She'd put things on credit for a few months, then pay off the entire bill when her cases settled. She'd buy things that she liked, but only after striking a deal, or meticulously watching for them to go on sale. The old farts at the law firm had taught her one basic rule: never buy retail.

She chuckled again as she toweled herself dry, and thought of those fairly wealthy gentlemen who stood around the office each morning with coffee mugs in hand, bragging about how much they'd saved over this insignificant item, or that. While she'd witnessed and endured with excruciating anguish their attempts to out-cheap each other, there had been a method to their madness. Like Ma Ethel had instructed her, she'd watched them, picking up little contacts, tidbits, and knowledge from everyone she encountered. Yes, it was all good, she reasoned. You could learn anything from anybody. And, like the harvester ant that her grandmother often compared her to, she'd worked hard, lifting ten times her load, had run around frenetically working, and now it was time to be still. Thank God she hadn't had a heart attack in the process!

Sitting on the edge of the tub, she stretched and began applying moisturizing cream to her skin. She'd stayed in the bath so long that the water had wrinkled the tips of her fingers and the bottoms of her toes. The smell of fresh paint from the bedroom filtered under the door. Grabbing her heavy flannel robe, she steeled her senses to the cold blast of air she expected to greet her from the bedroom's half-opened windows as she opened the bathroom door.

"See," she told herself with a chuckle, "if you'd had a lover in here waiting for you, flannel wouldn't be acceptable."

As she made her way across the bedroom to the vanity, additional warmth soaked into her feet when she stepped onto the bedroom rug. But there was something wrong with the sensation. It felt wet.

"Oh, please, not a leak," she moaned, looking up toward the ceiling. "There's eight of my ten thousand dollars right there, in a roofing job!"

Upon inspection of the freshly painted ceiling, there was no evidence to suggest where the dampness at her feet had come from. Aziza ran her fingers through her wet hair, thinking about the tub. "A plumbing job is just as bad," she groaned, pacing back into the bathroom and throwing on the light switch. Kneeling down at the head of the huge, old claw-footed tub, she inspected the spigots, the drain, and then looked back over the floor for source evidence of a trickle of water. Then she froze.

Her own incoming footprints were crimson, not clear.

Slowly she brought her hand to her mouth to repress the scream that bubbled in her chest. Her vision darted around the room and down at her feet. Nauseated, she kept her hand over her mouth as she balanced herself first on one foot, looking at the sole, then the other.

Terror slammed into her brain and her heart kept pace with it until elevated blood pressure and adrenaline made her ears ring. There was no evidence of a cut on either foot.

"Okay, okay, okay, think, and be calm," she warned herself out loud. "There's a logical explanation." Again, she carefully inspected the floor. Damp, clear footprints went out of the bathroom, and crimson ones facing her came into it. That had to mean that she'd obviously sustained a cut, one that she didn't feel, when she stepped on the rug.

Although she still stood in the same mid-room position, unable to move, her heart rate began to normalize as she thought about possible, logical explanations. After all, the rug had been in storage, moved twice in old trucks—where a stray nail, splinter, or shard of glass could have been hiding in the dense fabric. Also, she'd just taken a bath, and her feet were as soft as a baby's butt. So, one little prick could have caused them the bleed . . . then she'd obviously tracked around in it with both feet.

Aziza forced herself to laugh at her own silliness as she moved to the medicine cabinet. Relief swept through her as she took out a bottle of peroxide, and walked over to the tub. Rinsing her feet off, she sat down on the toilet and looked for the offending scrape. But her heart rate returned to its previous threatening level as no evidence of a wound could be found.

"Yuck!" she yelled, creating an echo. "A dead mouse? Eeeew! That's why you need a man in the house, *Jesus*!" After slathering peroxide on her feet and then scrubbing them hard with soap, she washed her hands with soap and antiseptic. Refusing to acknowledge that the amount of blood on the floor couldn't have possibly come from a small rodent, she continued to douse her limbs, feeling faint. Then she found the liquid Lysol bathroom cleaner, dumped it full-strength on the floor, and gingerly stepped around the cleaning agent and the bloody footprints.

"City life," she grumbled, carefully avoiding the rug, and finding her clothes and shoes. That's all she needed tonight, to find a fresh dead mouse in the rug, take it out into the trash in the alley, and have to then get her rug cleaned before turning in.

"So much for peace," she fussed, pulling her sweater over her head, and slipping on her socks and loafers. Fully dressed, she paced into the office, yanked a coat hanger from the closet, snatched the plastic liner from the wastebasket, and returned to the master bedroom. Squinting in dread, she shakily extended her arm, using the wire instrument as a hook. Prepared to see the gruesome remains of some unfortunate small animal, she flipped back the edge of the rug and held out the plastic bag in front of her, expecting to find the smashed rodent that was the only reasonable source of the blood.

This time her scream would not be stifled as she edged her way out of the bedroom, dropped the hanger and plastic bag, fled down the hallway, turned, and almost fell down the stairs. Without looking back, she grabbed her coat, purse, and keys in one deft sweeping motion, hurling her body through the front door. After clumsily managing the locks, she kept running.

The cold air slapped her face, seized the moisture in her hair and cut through her coat and sweater, but her body was on fire. Heat and sweat fused her clothing to her, and her legs pumped without consulting her mind. She could hear shrieks coming from the house and she briefly glanced over her shoulder to see long shadows playing out a macabre scene in the third-floor windows, which were now mysteriously lit.

Tears blurred her vision while she ran until she couldn't breathe. When she came to a stop, both of her fists pounded on the locked door in front of her as her own screams for help deafened her.

She could feel hands pulling at her, assisting her, voices urging her to stop screaming, then came the darkness.

"Give her some lukewarm tea," Abe Morgan instructed quietly. "Bring it to her lips slow, gentle . . . and keep that compress on her forehead."

Rashid's hands shook as he followed Abe's directions and knelt beside the stricken woman he now held in his arms.

"I knew something was wrong," he faltered. "Jesus Christ, what could have driven her out of the house like that?"

"Something went wrong," Abe whispered. "Let her lie back on the sofa, and rest. I need to prepare an anointment . . ."

"But I thought you said she'd be safe for the night." Rashid searched Abe's face for an explanation that wasn't forthcoming. "I thought you said that you and Ethel had already anointed the entire house, and that she'd be all right there."

"Ethel did and so did I," Abe remarked, "but there's been a disturbance to the protection. When she wakes up, we'll find out what happened. Right now, you and I have work to do."

Time passed in painful increments. Never too far from Aziza's side, Rashid followed his instructor's orders, reading Psalms over the young woman lying prone on the couch within a protective ring of white holy candles. He kept returning to one psalm in particular, the one to protect the embattled, ". . . a thousand may fall at your side, and ten thousand at your right hand; but it shall not come near you . . ." Rashid repeated the Ninety-first Psalm quietly, until his voice began to escalate with his own increasing alarm.

Thick clouds of church incense burned and stung his eyes, as he watched Abe work on Aziza's body, sprinkling holy water and prayer oils on her head, chest, wrists, and feet. Following directions, he took the cup of sea salt Abe had prepared, and made a circle around where she lay on the sofa.

"We stay in vigil till sunrise," Abe murmured. "I'll take first watch, you relieve me at three AM," he added, lowering a tiny burlap bag filled with odd leaves, dirt, and a vial of holy water over her head. The bag was held together by a long leather cord with a small silver cross attached on it. He positioned the bag over her heart and stood back from her.

As Rashid reached to accept a similar necklace from his instructor, the old man answered his unspoken question.

"The burlap casement is from royal Ghanaian mud cloth and Egyptian linen, seeds from Madagascar, earth from Ethiopia, the cord is from the ropes used at the original Crucifixion of our Savior. The protective herbal contents and hallowed Ethiopian earth from the monasteries at Axum have been treated and soaked with holy water from the Vatican baptismal font, and the small crosses are from the first Pope's rosary. Needless to say, I've been holding on to these items, for just such a crisis, for a long time."

Awe consumed Rashid as he bowed his head to accept the amulet over his head.

"That's all we can do, for now. The rest is in the Father's hands."

Her skull felt like a giant claw held and crushed it. When she tried to sit up, she saw Rashid huddled at her feet, and her grandfather dozing in a chair. The smell of incense and burned tallow made her cough slightly and then she felt like she had to throw up.

"Give her some ginger tea," the old man rasped as he stirred from his chair. "It's passed over us."

Rashid touched her hand and gazed at her briefly, then went to turn on the kettle. Dropping her face into her palms, she quietly wept.

"It was horrible," she choked out, drawing Rashid and her grandfather to her side. "You should have seen it . . . bubbling up from the floorboards . . . blood everywhere, like a faucet had been turned on." Looking up at both of them, she searched their faces for answers. "It came up from the same spot where Daddy fell."

Both men exchanged a glance, and Abe Morgan stooped down and reached for his granddaughter's hand. His eyes cautioned Rashid not to ask about what had happened to Aziza's father. "Baby-girl," he began quietly, "what did you move in the house?"

Aziza looked at Abe Morgan, then at Rashid, her eyes filling with new tears that she didn't try to wipe away. "I'm having a nervous breakdown, aren't I, Pop? Schizophrenia is hereditary, isn't it? I have what Daddy had, don't I? First the walls almost seemed to be whispering my name, things are never where I've put them in Ma Ethel's house . . . *now this*?"

Rashid sat down beside her on the sofa and clutched her other hand to his chest. "Princess, what did you do when you left us yesterday?"

Her eyes searched their faces again as she began to speak very slowly. Confusion swept her piteous expression, and her bewilderment made him want to pull her to him. But a warning glare from Abe Morgan reminded him not to.

"I just walked home," she stammered, "then returned some business phone calls, then had Delaware Antiques & Collectibles come in, and—"

"Stop!" her grandfather shouted, standing quickly and pacing in front of her. "You defied my direct order not to sell anything in the house, didn't you?"

Rashid dropped his head and shook it slowly from side to side, "Oh, Princess . . . tell us you didn't."

"I told you both that I had to sell at least some of the things to make room for my own," she exclaimed, snatching her hand from Rashid's hold. "What does that have to do with blood bubbling up from my floor? I don't want to talk about the furniture. You guys aren't listening to me!"

Abe Morgan let out his breath and walked in a circle, speaking to her without looking directly at her. "Did you accept money from them?"

"Of course I did," she said, sounding totally perplexed, "I didn't *give* it away."

Abe stopped his pacing and stood above her with his arms folded over his chest. "Give the money back. Immediately. You have seventy-two hours, in any contract, to change your mind."

Aziza raised herself from the sofa slowly, and Rashid flanked her, helping her up.

"Okay, I know you didn't want me to remove Ma Ethel's furniture from the house, and as an attorney, I know how to get them to give me my furniture back, but I really don't see—"

"That's the point!" her grandfather yelled. "*You don't see.*"

"Don't take him there, Princess," Rashid murmured. "Give the people back the money, and—"

"Why?" she demanded, reaching for the check that was still in her jeans pocket. Brandishing it in front of both men, her voice escalated. "It was a good deal, and more importantly, I'll need it now to move—since I'm not setting foot back in that haunted house!"

Abe Morgan carefully took the check from her hand and inspected it, then handed it back to Aziza and Rashid for them to view. "Do you know who you did a deal with?"

"Of course I do," she snapped. "They are a reputable firm whom I found over the Internet, and checked up on. They've been in business for over a hundred years."

"Yes, they have," Abe muttered. "A lot longer than that."

"So, it's not like it was some fly-by-night folks who robbed me. What does this have to do with blood on the floor?"

Rashid's eyes posed the question that his mouth wasn't ready to ask.

"Rashid, tell her what that crest is on the check."

"It's, er, uh . . . a demonic pentagram, Princess. A very old one."

When Aziza's jaw went slack, her grandfather pressed on. "Did you invite the person who offered you this check into your house?"

"Of course I did," she nearly whispered, her gaze still fastened on the check, and her mind instantly recalling the antique dealer's ring, and the identical crest on his business cards. "I had to let him in so he could see what I was selling."

Abe Morgan frowned and his glare narrowed on Aziza. "Think back, and answer me very specifically. Did he just walk in behind you, or did he ask you for your permission to enter?"

She hesitated, and again her eyes darted between both men. "He asked me, and waited until I did so," she murmured. "But he acted weird, and he didn't want to go through the house," she added in a more audible tone. "He stopped just inside the front door. We did the deal, and he left."

"Uhmmm, hmmm," the older of the two men grunted with a wave of his hand. "That's because our Ethel had salted-out, saged, and anointed the place so good, he *couldn't* come further into the house. That's what I have been trying to get through your too-educated-for-your-own-good, stubborn head!"

Aziza covered her mouth with her hand and new tears brimmed in her eyes. "And," she admitted in a muffled voice, "he made me clear out all of her little Psalm scraps and herb leaves from everything . . ."

"Before they touched it," Rashid said quietly, finishing the sentence for her.

"No doubt, the room that suffered the greatest loss was the bedroom," Abe remarked flatly, then turned and walked to the back of the store to turn off the flame under the boiling kettle. "That's why the bedroom was the epicenter. Tell me the name on the check," he demanded from across the room. "Then tell me whom you've entered into an agreement in principle with."

Both Aziza and Rashid looked down at the check, then up at Abe Morgan and shrugged.

"Some foreigner, obviously into the dark side . . ." Rashid's voice trailed off.

Aziza just nodded in agreement.

"Read me the name!" Abe Morgan demanded, fury singeing his tone.

"Bezel Robere," Aziza answered, shrugging again, and glancing at Rashid.

Abe Morgan just shook his head as he prepared three cups of tea. "He goes by many names, and is always the reverse of what you think is good. Unfortunately, he's been around a lot longer than a mere hundred years," Abe sighed, bringing their cups to the table. "Robere can be translated into Robert, which can be contracted into Bob. Conjunct the names, and you have Bezelbob."

"Okay, so?" Aziza quipped, growing impatient.

"And, a bezel is also known as a cutting edge of a chisel, or as something that holds, or *captures,* if you will, a jewel in place—which you are. You have been cut off from your source of protection, chiseled, and you have been captured by a bezel, my Princess. Or, in plain English, chiseled by a robber—and the best chiseling robber in the damned universe at that, child!" Abe sat down and sipped his tea, motioning for them to join him. When they continued to stand there motionless, he smiled. "Ah, now I have your attention, perhaps even a little respect. Give Bezelbub, otherwise known as Satan, back his offer, and kill your deal with the Devil." He ignored the audible gasp his comment drew from the young woman before him. "Like I said earlier, you just didn't listen."

"What I saw in the mirror with you last night," Rashid whispered.

Abe looked up from the rim of his cup, and set it down carefully. "Ask Rashid one day about listening, seeing. He saw that you both have a purpose. I pray that you haven't destroyed her items in her sugar chest?"

Aziza shook her head no, and allowed her hand to reach up and fondle the little bag around her neck.

"Good," Abe snorted, then folded his arms. "At least some of your gut instinct is intact. Because first of all, in material terms, a Virginia sugar chest alone would bring four to five thousand dollars at auction. Check it out with Sotheby's in New York, if you don't believe this old man. Every item in the house, all total, would be worth more like fifteen thousand dollars per room, since Ethel kept every piece in mint condition. It originated from the spoils of Southern estates and was willed to her by her grandparents, who stayed in the South during and after the Civil War."

Both men watched the young woman before them tighten her grip on the bag around her neck. Rashid sighed and took a seat at the table and began to sip his tea.

"So," Abe Morgan railed on, "you were indeed *also robbed* in broad daylight, by a man named Robere—which, not so coincidentally, also sounds like robber, all because you didn't do your research, counselor. That alone is reason enough to get your grandmother's furniture back. But there are higher stakes involved, like your personal safety, to consider. Now what did you do with Ethel's protections?"

"Oh, my God . . ." Aziza whispered, and then closed her eyes briefly before edging to the table. "I threw it all out in the trash can in the alley, but trash day isn't until Wednesday. I can get it back."

"But I'm not finished," the older man croaked. "All of that notwithstanding, the sugar chest holds her anointing oils, remnants of church vestments, purification salts, everything you need to spiritually cleanse her house. Today, we retrieve everything out of the trash, re-purify it, and get it back in the house. Then we'll have to go through the entire house, stem to stern, and re-cleanse it. Your job will be to work on getting your furniture back, Miss Attorney know-it-all."

"But, I can't stay in there alone," she whispered, pleading with her eyes for them to understand.

Rashid and Aziza glimpsed at each other, then turned away to stare at Abe Morgan, who had begun pacing.

"I might have to go back early before they come for her again," Abe said quietly, staring at Rashid.

"Or maybe I'm the one who's supposed to go," Rashid said quietly, his gaze slipping from Abe's to the mirror. "Before they try to hurt her again."

"Who?" Aziza whispered. "Who is after me, and why? What have I ever done to anybody?" Her eyes darted between them, and Rashid simply cleared her cup away. "I deserve to know!" she shrieked, standing with them and grabbing her grandfather's arm. "And what does an old mirror have to do with anything? What are you two talking about? Demons and whatever after me for some antiques in the house? They can have it all!"

"Ah," her grandfather said calmly, "but you wouldn't listen to any of us old souls before. We just spoke of superstition and wives' tales. Until you increase your faith, learn to control your urges, strengthen your mind—"

"But Mr. Abe," Rashid protested, "just like me, in the beginning she didn't know. Once she *sees*—"

"It's not time!" Spinning to face his male pupil, Abe remained steadfast. "She's willful, arrogant, hardheaded, recalcitrant, obstinate, and questions everything!"

"Yeah, because she's been trained to think for herself, which means she has a strong mind already, she has faith in her gut judgments—which is the start, the core of listening to one's spiritual directives—and takes nothing on face value, which will come in handy when she goes up against those that twist the truth! I say, let her stay here, under our protection, until we can get everything back in order over on Fitzwater Street, or," Rashid hedged, "I'll take the risk, and stay in the house with her. Your choice, but she's not going it alone. Under your roof, or hers, I'm staying with her! And you, old man, will have to learn to trust us, and have some faith in human nature, yourself."

Aziza watched the two men take an opposing stance from each other in the small kitchen area before her, as a strained silence engulfed the room. Never had anyone so thoroughly defended her, and the new awareness gave her pause.

Glancing between Rashid and Aziza, Abe Morgan rubbed his chin. "Well," he muttered, as a smile crept out of hiding. "We finally have a real knight in shining armor. Now, all we need is a real princess."

Chapter Nine

Nothing in all her educated years prepared her for what she saw as she stood beside Rashid and her grandfather, staring into the mercury-like surface of the mirror she'd always admired. Reality suspended right before her very eyes as an antebellum scene came alive. Aziza covered her mouth with one hand as Rashid steadied her lest she topple over from shock.

She could hear them, everything—people talking, birds in the trees, literally feel the heat wafting off the cotton fields. The stench of manure fused with rich soil and summer grasses. She saw her people laboring, and almost turned away.

Then she saw someone who looked similar enough to Rashid to be his next of kin. The man smiled at a young woman, which made her gasp, but he kept walking to not alert the watchful eyes of the overseer who rode down the rows.

In awe, Aziza extended her arm away from her body, her fingers trembling with electric excitement. "She looks just like me," she said in a faraway tone.

Those were the last words she murmured before her grandfather yelled out, "No!"

Tumbling, moving faster than her mind could comprehend, colors swirled in her head until her ears began to ring. Centrifugal force crushed the air from her lungs and deafened her. Then all of a sudden she came to a thud on a soft, grassy surface. The young woman that could have been her body double rushed over and helped her up.

"Be quick, be quick—don't let 'em sees you slackin'."

"I'm going in behind her!" Rashid yelled. "You know what happened to Theodora! They raped her and—"

"And they strung up her man," Abe said, holding Rashid's arms, blocking him from the mirror. "Why do you think I've been trying to get you ready! She'll survive that horrific attack—and yes, she'll have that child of the plantation owner's son—but if you interfere, if you or he dies on that side of the mirror again, the second baby won't be born . . . that's the child we're waiting on. That's the one that will make decisions that will ripple forward!"

"I'm not leaving her over there, old man. Don't even ask me to do that!"

Abe caught Rashid by the arm. "*That's my granddaughter.* Do you think I, of all people, would want to leave her *there* in some hellhole to be raped and enslaved? Aziza was never supposed to go—her mind could buckle and snap over there! You two were supposed to be on *this side* protecting the mirror," Abe said between clenched teeth. "This is a portal. A veil between worlds. That's why *the shades* want it . . . do you know what they could do with access like this to the past? They've already altered history once, by making sure your ancestor was killed before he ever sired an heir. That cannot happen again. It's my job to go back to the time I came from to stop it."

Rashid stared at Abe for a moment. "You're stronger than me in mind and spirit—so you guard the mirror from this side," he said quietly. "But this time, you can't beat me on the mats . . . because that's my wife."

Rashid landed hard behind a stand of trees. Spanish moss swayed and every instinct in him told him that he was so far and so Deep South that even a prayer wouldn't get him North whole.

Squinting, he scanned the rows of workers in the distance, trying to see a way clear to join them without being noticed by the overseer. Rashid glanced down at his white karate pants and took off his top, balling it up and stashing it in the bushes, and then dirtied up his pants in an effort to blend in. He just prayed that somehow Aziza would be able to figure out how to get something to cover her jeans . . . maybe an old sheet from a clothes line, or maybe his shirt could be dirtied and tied some type of way to camouflage her. If they saw her cashmere sweater, fine leather loafers, or even her strange jeans, she'd be beaten for theft, for sure. Maybe worse.

But twenty-plus years of stealth training, including how to kill a man with his bare hands, fought to the forefront of his mind. This is what he'd been trained to do—never leave his own, go in and extract his team from behind enemy lines.

Rashid scoped the landscape, noting where the barn was, the main house, the smaller outcropping of shacks, approximate number of overseers to contend with . . . the number of able-bodied men that might fight against him or with him. That part was the gamble that left him unsure—the variable of people so broken that they'd rather fight against a potential source of freedom than risk the wrath of their captors. Happened in POW camps all the time, and the people working down field from him weren't trained military personnel.

Nightfall, for the first time in his life, would be his friend. Booby traps could be set, firearms located. If Aziza would just lie low and could hide until the darkness covered them.

A crash on the second floor made Abe look up. He already knew what it was. *The shades* had found him, they'd confirmed his location, knew the mirror was here. He smelled the sulfur before he smelled the smoke. They'd burn him out . . .

The grates went down on the windows as the stifling heat began to cause sweat to run down his face, locking him in. Lamps and glass cases exploded around him as his voice belted out the refrains of the Twenty-third Psalm.

Walls moaned, and floorboards began to buckle as though something were coming up from the depths of the basement. Entities slithered from beneath every conceivable surface, their claws extended, swiping at him. He looked up and saw embers coming through the ceiling above and then in a fit of madness, he laughed.

"Burn the place down and the mirror is lost forever!" he shouted. "Kill me and I'm more dangerous to you dead than alive—because I will become an Ancestor! Ev'ry shut eye ain't sleep—I know who you are and you will never make me give up!" He spun around and then rushed to a shattered glass case that contained a World War II German Lugar pistol and ammunition, as demons positioned themselves to leap at him with bared fangs.

"Bullets don't work on them, my friend," a smooth, melodic voice said in the din. "Oh, trust me; I'll stop the fire before the mirror is ruined . . . but not before your human breath expires. So blast away. You'll only amuse my pets."

Abe smiled and sauntered over to the mirror, his gaze on the tall shadowy figure in the corner of his burning shop. "So, as in every era . . . we meet again, Lucifer. And this time, like always, even after all you've done to us, you've forgotten about the power of love." Before the black bolt could hit him, Abe Morgan flung the gun and ammunition through the mirror. He dropped to the ground, his chest smoldering from the charge that had blown him across the room, and smiled. "I love them, I don't care about me."

"Fool!" the entity shouted and rushed forward to grab the mirror, but then recoiled, hissing, as a brilliant white glow left Abe's body to fuse around the silver frame. Scorching white-light heat made the tormentor and every dark entity in the room cover its hideous face and disappear.

Fifteen years later . . . Walnut Street, Center City—Philadelphia

"*Mom*, why do we *always* have to go visit that old antique shop where Great-grand started, and why do we have to be there to hand out meals to the homeless *every year* right before Christmas? I mean it's like you and Dad act like it's your fault people are homeless and like you've gotta do all this give back stuff because you're guilty that you own a chain of antique dealerships. I don't get it—we know the history already, we know you've gotta care about your fellow man, blah, blah, blah . . . geeze! But it's not your fault that you guys have money. Can't we ever just go straight to the mall?" The teen flopped back in her chair and yanked her cell phone away from her ear, pouting.

"Yeah, and Dad be trippin' with all that spiritual commando stuff . . . man!" her brother said. "I thought we were going up to King of Prussia after we got Dad from the store. And why can't I drive?"

"One day you and your brother will finally figure out that you stand on a lot of people's shoulders," Aziza said calmly. "And until your spoiled little bourgeois behinds get it, we'll be there . . . in fact, we'll be there whether you get it or not. You know how your father feels about that first store and about people who have to live on the streets."

"It's so not fair," the teen fussed, applying lip gloss. "Donna and Suzie's mom and dad do not even go there. I don't know anybody's parents who really—"

"Yeah, and Robert got to drive his dad's Lexus—so why can't I even spin the Beemer around the block?"

"Oh, right, like Mom and Dad are putting you behind the wheel of their car, puhlease."

Aziza peered in the rearview mirror, wondering what planet her children had come from. A part of her smiled knowing that Pop and Ma Ethel were probably laughing at her and Rashid's struggle, but in context and perspective, dealing with spoiled, willful, upper-middle-class teens was the better end of the time continuum for sure.

"You know it's a family tradition to honor the ancestors," Aziza said quietly but firmly, navigating the sedan through gridlock. "It's important to know your history . . . how things could have turned out. If it weren't for one man's courageous vision—you might not even be here."

The Patriarch

Brandon Massey

Prologue

Before I begin to tell you how I learned the truth about my family, there's one thing you must understand and accept here and now.

Every word is true.

You may know my reputation, of course, and assume otherwise. My name is Daniel Booker. I write crime novels—fast-paced, blood-soaked stories about an Atlanta private investigator. I've written seven of them so far at the relatively tender age of thirty-four, and they've won a couple of prestigious awards in the mystery fiction field, been reprinted in a half-dozen foreign countries, and sold enough copies to keep food on the table.

But just because I earn my living telling lies doesn't mean I'm lying about this. As my Grandma Ruth likes to say: "Some things you don't fool around with." In my mind, family is one of those things. To be frank, I don't think I ever could have made up anything as . . . well, shocking as what I'm about to relate to you.

Are we cool? Okay, good. Prologue over.

Here's what happened.

Chapter One

Now this is what it's all about, I thought with a smile.

We were rolling along at seventy-five miles an hour in my Ford Expedition, cutting a blazing path up the middle of Mississippi on I-55. The brilliant August sun created quicksilver heat mirages on the highway, boundless fields of cotton and soybeans blurring into the hazy horizon. It was probably ninety degrees in the shade, but with air conditioning, a cooler full of bottled water and turkey sandwiches, my beautiful girlfriend at my side, and John Legend crooning "Ordinary People" on satellite radio, all was right in my world.

I'd wanted to make this trip for years. Finally, it was happening, and I was so hyped I could hardly believe it.

"Can you pull over at the next rest stop, baby?" Asha said. "I need to wipe the dew off the lily pad."

I glanced away from the interstate and caught her eye. "That's why I love you."

Her brown eyes narrowed. "Because I need to pee?"

"Because you're an original. You and your odd euphemisms."

"I didn't think telling you I need to piss would sound very ladylike."

I smiled. "Not very MDish, either. What would your parents think after all the money they spent toward your education, Doctor Cook?"

"Hmph. You should know by now that I don't care what my folks think about what I do. We're living together, aren't we?"

I winced. "Ouch."

Asha's lips twisted into a satisfied smirk. She had a sly way of pricking you with those little needles when you least expected them. In this case, I probably deserved it.

We'd been dating for slightly over two years, and living together for five months. Her parents, devout church-going folk born and raised in Georgia, condemned our living arrangement. *Y'all playing house, living in sin.* The pride of the family, who'd studied abroad and gone to medical school at Columbia, Asha claimed to be above their sanctimonious judgments about her lifestyle.

But I knew her better than that. Like most children, grown or not, she wanted her parents' approval. She wanted us to get married.

But I wasn't ready—and it had nothing to do with her.

A sign announcing a rest area soon came into view. I took the exit and veered into the big parking lot, eased into a space in the cool shade of a magnolia.

Asha grabbed her purse and turned to me. "I love you, too, you know," she said. She leaned in close and kissed me, and I got a chocolaty taste of the Snickers bar she'd nibbled on earlier. "Be back in five, baby."

"Your limo will be waiting."

I watched her stroll inside the squat brick building. The handful of men filtering in and out of the restrooms watched her, too. In white Bermuda shorts, a pink halter top, and wedge sandals, Asha was a striking sight—five feet five inches of sweet and shapely cinnamon loveliness. I was lucky to be with her, which made it all the more perplexing to family and friends, on both sides, as to why I'd yet to pop the question.

I sipped a bottle of water and checked the GPS unit on the dashboard. We'd left Atlanta at ten o'clock that morning and entered Mississippi around two that afternoon. We were a couple of hours from our destination in Senatobia, a small town in the northwest region, right above the Delta.

A more direct route would have shaved hours off our drive, but I'd wanted to take in the sights. Admittedly, there hadn't been all that much to see thus far. Maple and pine trees dressed in kudzu. Run-down motels advertising rooms for thirty dollars a night. Hole-in-the-wall diners offering all-you-can-eat fried chicken dinners. Mud-splashed pickups grumbling past with Confederate flags proudly plastered to their bumpers.

But excitement crackled through my veins. This was the land of my ancestors, and merely inhabiting the soil of the state they had called home made me feel closer to them.

After all, that was the purpose of the trip: to plumb my family's background. I'd been raised in a loving, two-parent household, but my father's people were few, so I knew them and their history well. Conversely, my mom's kinfolk were like some fabled tribe—*hundreds* of aunts, uncles, and cousins, a colorful stew of relatives both dead and alive, so many that no one could cite all their names and exploits. I'd long dreamt of digging into our genealogy, of talking to the elders, of writing down everything they remembered of our roots, of creating a book exclusively for our family. Building a bridge to my ancestors, for my own self-knowledge and the benefit of generations yet to come.

Since I was between novels and Asha had a break in her residency, we'd decided, why not do it? Although I suspected that Asha's motive for tagging along was much different than mine.

I thumbed on my digital voice recorder and brought it near my lips. "It's three-seventeen in the afternoon on Friday, August fifteenth. We're in a rest area about an hour north of Jackson, and well . . . it's a rest area. They seem to be the same no matter where you go.

"We have a couple of hours ahead of us before we reach Senatobia. I can't remember the last time I've been so hyped. I feel as if I'm standing on the brink of a big discovery—it's a gut feeling I've had ever since we crossed into Mississippi. Somehow, delving into my family history is going to teach me more about myself. That vacancy I've felt in the back of my mind for so long, like there's a chunk of me missing . . . I think—I *feel*—this trip will finally fill it in."

Chapter Two

At half-past five, we arrived in Senatobia.

Senatobia was one of those "blink, and you miss it" towns that you could find all across the South. On the main thoroughfare, there were a couple of budget-priced chain hotels, a sad string of fast-food restaurants, and that was it. There might have been more to the place, but we wouldn't see it; we were staying there for only one night. Tomorrow morning, one of my cousins would lead us to the family home in nearby Coldwater.

We parked at our hotel. Getting out of the air-conditioned SUV was like entering a steam bath. The sun bore down savagely, and the cloying humidity robbed the lungs of air.

As we carried our luggage across the parking lot to the entrance, I turned to Asha. "Do you hear that?" I asked. "Like a soft humming, sort of buzzing noise?"

Dragging her carry-on piece, she shook her head.

"I guess my ears are ringing from being cooped up in the car all day," I said.

"Possibly." She released a sigh of exhaustion, perspiration beading her brow. Although I was saddled with two other pieces of luggage, I took her bag from her, and she thanked me with a grateful smile.

We checked in and squared away our luggage. Our room was standard issue: lumpy king-size bed, faded brown carpet, rattling A/C, generic landscape prints on the walls, a window that offered an uninspiring view of the interstate. Asha made a beeline to the shower, and I went out alone to grab dinner.

That soft buzzing sound followed me, as if some old television on the fritz were just beyond my range of vision. I decided I needed to sleep, clear my head. Six hours of continuous engine noise had settled like sediment into my brain.

When I got back to the hotel with two fried chicken dinners, Asha had changed into an oversize tank top and was dozing in bed. She came awake to eat a piece of chicken and a biscuit, and promptly burrowed back underneath the sheets.

All the driving and energy-sapping heat had worn me down, too. I showered, threw on a pair of boxers, and joined her under the covers. Although it was early evening, with the Levolor blinds shut and the A/C pumping out cold air, the room was so comfortable I thought I might well sleep through tomorrow morning.

As I lay there, Asha turned toward me. She placed her palm against my chest, feeling my heartbeat. Her face was a dusky oval in the shadows.

"I'm glad we're making this trip together, Danny," she said, voice hushed.

"So am I." I placed my hand over hers, knitted her fingers in mine. "The journey to the family roots. Could be a movie."

"I want to know about your family, too. I want to see what they're like, see the kind of people you've come from. I'm sure they're fascinating."

"You can't know where you're going until you know where you've been," I said.

"So true."

We were quiet for several heartbeats. I listened to the rattle of the air conditioner, the distant rumble of trucks hauling past on the highway, and farther away yet somehow close, the whispery buzzing.

"After this trip," she said, "are you finally going to be ready for us to go to the next level?"

My hand tightened over hers. "You think that's why I've been waiting?"

"You just said that you can't know where you're going until you know where you've been. Right?"

Warm blood flushed my cheeks. She knew me so well that it was scary.

But in the timeless, bumbling male manner, I said, "I wasn't talking about us getting married, Asha. I was talking in, you know, general terms about life, that's all."

"General terms," she said.

"That's all."

"So, in *general terms*, can you tell me if you'll be ready?"

"Honestly, I don't know."

She rolled away from me, muttering under her breath. I'd been giving her that *I don't know* response for several months now, and she was obviously beginning to lose her patience.

I touched her shoulder. Her skin was warm and smooth. I pressed myself against her firm hips, and felt lust stirring.

What man on earth wouldn't have wanted to go to bed next to a woman like her for the rest of his life? I wanted to marry her. I really did. But—and this was difficult for me to explain even to myself—I felt hampered by my inadequate knowledge of my family. My maternal grandmother, Grandma Ruth, was eighty-three years old and as mentally sharp as a razor, and she had shared much with me about growing up in Mississippi, had recounted the family lineage of which she was aware . . . but I still had a nagging sense that something was missing. Some crucial piece of knowledge. Maybe a family secret. I didn't know. Logically, it didn't make much sense. But I had a gut instinct that would not go away, and it had driven me to make this trip.

When I had satisfied my thirst for that hidden insight I knew was out there, then I would marry Asha. I'd privately made that vow to myself as I was planning the trip, but I didn't dare tell her. I mean, what if I never tumbled to the big secret? What if it proved to be all in my head? I couldn't expect her to wait on me forever. A woman like her, with her beauty, brains, and career prospects, would not have to wait on any one man for very long.

If I wanted to keep her, I had to be right about this. Although I suppose I could have married her anyway, family secret discovered or not, something deep inside me would not allow that to happen, as if I would be crossing some inviolable moral fence. Like withholding from your would-be fiancée that you had a criminal record or had been recently diagnosed with a brain tumor. I didn't think that the mystery awaiting me was anything so world-ending . . . but what if it was?

Beside me, Asha surely felt my growing rigidness against her hips, but she didn't respond. I kissed the back of her neck. She bristled.

"Let's table this talk until we get home," I said. "Okay, sweetheart?"

She rolled over to face me, her shadowed gaze probing mine. "Do you love me?"

"Of course, I love you. I love you more than anything."

I lifted her hand to my lips, kissed it. She traced a finger along the curve of my jaw.

"Because I love you, too," she said. "I want us to build a life together."

"That's what I want, too. It'll happen in time."

"I'll be thirty next month, Danny," she said.

"I know."

"I want to enjoy being married for two or three years, do some traveling together, and then have a baby or two. *Our* babies."

"I know. That's what I want, too, exactly."

"But the older I get, the harder it will be for me to conceive, the greater the likelihood that I'll experience issues. I'm not being an alarmist—it's a medical fact."

"We love each other, we're living together. We're practically married already. Marriage is just a piece—"

She pulled her hand away. "Don't even fix your mouth to say that, 'cause you know I can't stand that nonsense. Marriage is *not* just a piece of paper. It's a binding commitment we make before God and our families and friends."

I yawned and laid my head against the pillow. This was one argument I couldn't have, because I knew she was right, and debating the issue wore me out.

"We'll talk about this after the trip," I said.

"We sure will," she said, a note of finality in her tone.

Chapter Three

In my dream, the air was buzzing.

The night was black, deep as the ocean. I walked through a forest full of pine trees so tall the crowns seemed to poke against the starry firmament. I was alone, but I was aware of eyes on me. The creatures of the night, watching expectantly.

The buzzing came from somewhere ahead. It was not loud, but it was distinct, utterly real. The warm, damp air thrummed in concert with the sound, and the hairs at the nape of my neck rose on end, and tingled.

I threaded through a grove of oak trees, and entered a clearing. A shotgun house stood ahead. It had a red door the color of fresh blood, white wood siding, and dark shutters, and looked as if it had been constructed decades ago. Orange light flickered in the front window, like candle flames, and shadows danced on the surrounding stubbly grass.

The buzzing originated from inside the house. I was compelled to go in.

I climbed the short flight of wooden porch steps. The door was ajar. I pushed it open, and stepped forward.

And found there was no floor.

With a yelp, I plummeted forward into a pitch-black abyss . . .

I came awake with a strangled shout, the sensation of falling grabbing my stomach. I clutched fistfuls of the bed sheets in my sweaty hands.

Asha braced her arm across my chest as if to keep me from dropping away. "Shhh, baby. It's okay. Only a dream."

I sucked in air, my chest heaving. "Jesus . . . that was so damned real."

"Only a dream, Danny. It's over."

I swallowed, glanced at the clock on the nightstand. The numerals flashed 2:17 AM. We'd been asleep for at least seven hours.

The buzzing was still in my ears, softer than in the dream, but audible, as it had been before I'd fallen asleep.

I was certain that I'd never seen the shotgun shack before, in real life . . . yet there was something disconcertingly familiar about it. As if the image of it had been buried deep in my head, years ago, and it had finally tumbled into my conscious mind like a faded quarter from an old jacket.

Murmuring words of reassurance, Asha slid one of her legs across mine. She ran gentle fingers down my abdomen, and then lower, found me half-erect, and worked me to firm readiness with the casual skill that only a longtime lover possessed.

I reached for her, suddenly needing her more than I'd ever needed her before, my desire so urgent it was like a gnawing in my stomach. She straddled me, guided my length inside her, and enveloped me like a warm mitten. A gasp of pleasure escaped my lips. I ran my hands up the smooth, flat plane of her stomach and caressed her firm breasts, and above me, she slowly began to rock, drawing me deeper inside with each sinuous gyration, softly calling my name.

It was as if she'd felt me slipping away to somewhere dangerous, and wanted to bring me back home to her, to ground me in our world.

I gave myself over to her.

Chapter Four

When I was twelve, I was struck by a car.

I'd been riding my Huffy bicycle through our neighborhood one summer afternoon, zooming down one of the steep hills in our subdivision, feet pumping the pedals, cool wind clipping my ears. I was about to pass through an intersection that was pretty much a blind turn for anyone turning onto the road—when a yellow Mustang thundered around the corner in a wild trajectory and crashed into me head-on.

The collision sent me flying high into the air, as if I'd bounced off a trampoline. I came down and smashed against the car's roof. I tumbled like a crash-test dummy over the trunk, and finally dropped to the pavement.

I didn't feel any pain—I didn't feel anything. I lay there, body contorted like a broken action figure, and gazed blankly at the puffy clouds sailing across the cerulean sky.

One of the clouds looked like a giraffe, I thought. Another resembled an elephant. And didn't that one over there look like a big fish?

I heard doors open and slam, shouts, cursing. Then a young and scared-looking brown face blocked my view of the heavenly menagerie. He had a thumbtack-size mole underneath his right eye.

"Hey, little man," Mole said, his voice coming to me as if from the end of a long tube. "You aaight? Can you . . . move or anything?"

I slid my tongue across my lips. I tasted blood, my blood, and in spite of my dazed state, I felt a jolt of excitement. For some reason, tasting my own blood always gave me that jittery feeling.

Another face joined Mole, this one darker, with a goatee.

"We better call an ambulance, man," Goatee said. "Kid's fucked up. I told you to slow down comin' 'round that corner!"

"Goddamn." Mole nervously wiped greasy sweat off his brow. "I don't need this shit right now, I only been on parole a motherfuckin' month! We should just bounce."

"You can't leave the little man here, what the fuck's wrong with you?" Goatee looked around, licked his lips. "People startin' to come over here. Nosy bitches. Shit."

"I'm okay," I said.

Both of the men stared at me as if I'd risen from the dead. I wondered if they had heard me clearly. My throat felt raw, as if it had been scrubbed with sandpaper.

"Did he say somethin'?" Goatee said, looking from me, to Mole.

"I said, I'm okay," I said, in what I hoped was a louder voice.

"Holy shit," Mole said, eye wide with awe.

I started to sit up. Pain burned through my limbs, but not enough to keep me down. It really wasn't all that bad.

Looking dazed and more than a little apprehensive, the men helped me to my feet. I was a little woozy, but kept my balance. My knees were skinned and smeared with blood and grit, one arm was scraped bloody around the elbow, and I felt a knot throbbing at the back of my head.

But I was basically fine.

"You sure you aaight, little man?" Goatee asked.

"Yeah," I said. "I'm good."

"You need us to call an ambulance or somethin'?" Mole said.

I shook my head. "I'm going home. My mom'll take care of me."

While they gaped at me, I shuffled to my bike. The Huffy was in worse shape than I was: the front tire was warped and missing several spokes, the frame was bent in half, and the seat had been ripped off and had landed in the grass about ten feet away.

Anyone who'd been riding that bike should have been broken up bad, I thought. I guessed I was just lucky.

I picked up the bike and hefted it over my shoulder, wincing a bit at a dull ache in my wrist, and walked home.

Chapter Five

The next morning, my cousin came to our hotel. Her name was LaToya, but she was known in the family as Cousin Tee.

We met up with Cousin Tee in the lobby. I'd last seen her at a family reunion in Atlanta about five years ago. She owned a hair salon in nearby Southaven. I knew she was in her mid-forties and was the mother of two teenage boys, but with her burnished caramel complexion, thick dark hair, and trim figure, she didn't look a day past thirty.

That was one thing I'd long noticed about my people on my mom's side: they tended to age extremely well. Whenever my mom and I went to a restaurant together, the waiters, embarrassingly, assumed we were a couple. I was thirty-four, but I could hardly ever order a drink without getting carded; Asha liked to call me "Babyface," a moniker I'd born for much of my life.

When Cousin Tee saw us, she squealed with joy.

"I'm so glad y'all made it!" she said, and hugged Asha and me both. She was flamboyantly dressed in a bright yellow blouse, a flower-patterned skirt, open-toe sandals, and at least five pounds of jewelry—gold hoop earrings, a couple of gold necklaces, sparkling rings on every manicured finger, bracelets on each delicate wrist, an anklet, and even a couple rings on her pedicured toes. She'd have no chance of ever passing through an airport metal detector.

Grinning, showcasing a gold-capped front tooth, Cousin Tee looked Asha up and down appreciatively. She winked at me, and spoke in a syrupy accent that was pure Mississippi: "Gotta tell you, Cousin Danny, this one here's a whole lot prettier than that one I saw you with at the reunion."

"I've moved up in the world," I said, and Asha blushed.

"When y'all gettin' married?" she asked. "'Cause I just *know* you gonna marry this woman. Y'all would have some beautiful babies!"

It was my turn to blush. "You know, I suddenly realized that I'm starving. How about we go for breakfast?"

"All right, guess I wasn't s'pposed to say that." Cousin Tee laughed, and even Asha chuckled.

We followed Cousin Tee's silver Lincoln Navigator to a Huddle House down the street from the hotel. It was another scorching day; at nine o'clock in the morning, the sun was hot enough to raise heat blisters, and the air was thickening into another warm, lung-blocking stew.

The low-volume buzzing was with me, too. I was beginning to visualize it as a beehive buried deep within the core of my brain, and theorized that perhaps it was a symptom of some kind of developing auditory problem. But I was reluctant to mention it to Asha, the internal medicine resident. Maybe it would go away in time.

"Everybody's so excited about y'all coming," Cousin Tee said as we settled into a booth. "We gonna have us a big family dinner after church tomorrow. You'll get to meet *everybody*."

"How many people will that be?" Asha asked.

Cousin Tee drummed the table with her colorful acrylic nails, lips drawn thoughtfully. "Hmm, maybe 'bout sixty, seventy folks."

"Wow," Asha said. "That's all family in Coldwater?"

"Uh huh." Cousin Tee grinned. "We got a whole clan down here, girl. I know Cousin Danny told you he had a lot of kinfolk."

"He did," she said, glancing at me with a soft smile. "I come from a relatively small family, so this is going to be an experience for me."

"Oh, you'll fit right in, don't worry," Cousin Tee said, as if our marriage was a foregone conclusion. "Everybody's gonna love you, honey."

Asha found my hand under the table, squeezed. No doubt, she loved the idea of what lay ahead that weekend: everyone in my family naturally assuming that we were due to be wed, or were already married. Little wonder that she'd wanted to come along.

Clever girl. I had to smile back at her.

A waitress stopped by, poured coffee for us, and took our orders.

"So, Cousin Tee." I added cream and sugar to my coffee, stirred it with a spoon. "What's been going on down at the home place?"

"The home place?" Asha asked, eyebrows arched.

"Where most of our folks live, honey, you'll see," Cousin Tee said. She lifted her coffee mug to her lips, a shadow flitting over her eyes. "There've been some home invasions over the past month."

"Home invasions?" I set down my cup. "Are you kidding me?"

"Wish I was," she said.

I frowned. "But the family lives in a rural area, right? I haven't been to Coldwater since I was maybe ten years old, but from what I recall, there's like, nothing at all back there."

Cousin Tee shrugged. "Our people ain't been hit yet, but our neighbors have. Last week, they busted into Miss Lula's place, pistol whipped her, took all her things. She's still in the hospital up in Southaven in critical condition."

"My God, that's awful," Asha said, clutching her mug. "How old is she?"

"Miss Lula's gotta be pushing ninety." Cousin Tee shook her head sadly. "Such a sweet, sweet lady. If she pulls out of this, she probably gonna have to stay in a nursing home. So sad."

I made my living writing about crime, but Atlanta was the setting of all my books, and as anyone who lived in Atlanta knew, the city had its share of crime problems, like most big cities. I couldn't wrap my mind around brutal home invasions occurring in some backwater Mississippi town.

"How many other times has this happened?" I asked.

"Miss Lula was the third time," Cousin Tee said. "Wish it would be the last, but I don't think so. They ain't caught nobody yet."

"Do the police have any suspects?" I asked.

"Ain't nothing but maybe three police officers in the whole town, Cousin Danny," she said. "It ain't like Atlanta."

"Actually, it sounds more like Mayberry," Asha said.

"Folks are scared," Cousin Tee said. "We've ain't never seen anything like this here. You'd expect that kind of stuff to happen somewhere like up in Memphis, but here?" She sipped her coffee, grimaced sourly.

"I guess nowhere is safe anymore," I said.

"Sure ain't," Cousin Tee said. She touched one of the many rings she wore on her right hand; it was a brilliant oval-cut ruby in a gold setting, and I thought I'd seen Grandma Ruth and other relatives wearing similar rings. Rubbing the gemstone as if for luck, she uttered under her breath, "If it keeps up . . . somebody 'round here gonna have to go 'head and take care of it on his own."

"Excuse me?" I asked.

But Cousin Tee's attention shifted to Asha. "Girl, those is the cutest earrings! Where you get 'em from? You know I love me some jewelry—can't you tell?" She cackled, and Asha went on to relate where she'd found them.

I gazed into my coffee, frowning. I suspected that Cousin Tee had purposely ignored my question. I decided to let it go.

But her remark lingered in my mind.

If it keeps up . . . somebody 'round here gonna have to go 'head and take care of it on his own.

Who was she talking about?

Chapter Six

After breakfast, we followed Cousin Tee's Navigator along a bumpy, two-lane highway bordered on both sides alternately by dense woods, and swampland. Leaving the diner, Cousin Tee had promised that Coldwater was only a ten-minute drive from Senatobia, but we appeared to be in the middle of nowhere.

A few times as we wove through patches of forest, I spotted shanties nestled within the trees: lean-to homes that looked a stiff wind away from blowing down and collapsing in a heap. They brought to mind the strangely familiar shotgun house from last night's hyper-vivid dream.

Would I find that house somewhere out here? I wondered. *Or had it been merely a figment of my imagination?*

Finally, we passed a sign: *"Welcome to Coldwater, Pop 1,674."*

"Your family is close to five percent of the town's population," Asha said.

"You know, you're right. Amazing, huh? We're not in Kansas anymore, Doc."

About a mile ahead, there was a traffic light. We made a left turn, and found ourselves on a four-way thoroughfare that was a fair approximation of civilization. It had a couple of fast-food joints. A Laundromat. A thrift shop, gas station, grocery store, car wash, and People's Bank. Everyone moving about the town was black, and in light of Asha's comment, I wondered if I was related to any of them.

After driving a few blocks, we left the main road and entered a residential neighborhood. All of the homes appeared to have been built decades ago: modest ranch models with carports. There was not a new subdivision or a McMansion in sight.

As we neared a stop sign, a mobile home park came up on our right. A group of young brothers clad in sagging jeans and white T-shirts as long as dresses milled around a black Oldsmobile Ninety-Eight. The car had supersized chrome wheels and tinted windows, the stereo booming the bass line of a popular hip-hop song.

"Looks like home," I said, thinking of the number of times I'd seen similar scenes in Atlanta, young men with nothing to do hanging outside a car.

The men turned as one to examine us.

"Damn, that bitch up in there fine as hell," one of them crowed to his partners. He tugged his crotch and shouted: "Yo, ma, you want some of this? I got somethin' for ya!"

"Classy," Asha hissed between tightly clenched teeth. "Can we hurry it up, Danny?"

"Yeah, sorry."

"Some men are pigs. What else is new?"

I pushed through the intersection, and we left the leering posse behind.

We trailed Cousin Tee onto another road that carried us deeper into a rural area. Back there, the small, old houses sat farther apart on expansive plots of wooded land. Although the surroundings were remote, the twisty road was newly paved.

Cousin Tee swung into a long gravel driveway that led to a brick, ranch-style home that stood on a grassy crest. The lush, well-trimmed yard was at least three acres, dotted with pines and maples, and ringed with a wire fence.

I hadn't visited the home place in over twenty years, and with the exception of a few minor cosmetic enhancements, it looked as if it hadn't changed at all. My heart swelled, and that sense of certainty that I'd had since yesterday, that I was finally going to unearth new wrinkles in my understanding of my family, was stronger than ever.

A silver Cadillac was parked underneath a carport at the end of the drive. Cousin Tee parked behind the sedan, and we nosed in alongside her car. The driveway was large enough to accommodate half a dozen more vehicles.

I cut the engine. "Well, here we are."

"The home place." Asha took it all in, smiled. "Wow, I just realized how much of a city girl I am. This feels like a different country to me."

"The land of my ancestors," I said, my chest tight with emotion. On impulse, I kissed her. "Thanks for coming on this trip with me. It means a lot to have you here."

"Of course. There's nowhere else I'd rather be."

When we climbed out of the SUV, the first thing I noticed was the air. It was heavy with the mingled fragrances of flowers, grass, and trees, a stark contrast to the grimy urban fumes I'd gotten accustomed to in Atlanta.

The second thing was that the buzzing noise was louder. Not quite loud enough to be intrusive. But I could feel the hairs in my ears vibrating.

"Do you hear that?" I asked Asha. "That buzzing?"

Her eyes narrowed. "I hear birds chirping, but no buzzing. Is it the same noise you heard yesterday?"

I nodded. "Louder here, though."

She examined me with what I recognized as her physician's look, and I regretted that I had said anything. Asha was, not surprisingly, a stickler for physical health. In the two years we'd been together, thanks to her prodding, I'd gone for twice-a-year physical exams, whereas before she had come along, nothing short of unbearable agony would have convinced me to visit a doctor's office.

"I may need to examine you, baby," she said. "This could be a symptom of something."

I shrugged. "Never mind, I'm sure it's nothing."

"That's what I would expect you to say. I'll arrive at my own conclusion."

Cousin Tee came around the car and rescued me from further probing.

"Welcome to the home place, y'all," she said. "Let's head on in. Aunt Lillie's waiting on us."

Chapter Seven

Inside, we found a neatly kept home full of comfortable furniture, polished hardwood floors, live plants, and clusters of family photos. Two tall, lean teenage boys lounged in the living room watching a wide-screen TV. They unfolded themselves from their chairs and rose to greet us. I realized that they were twins.

"These are my boys, Trey and Jomarion," Cousin Tee said. "Boys, say hello to Cousin Danny and his fiancée, Asha."

His fiancée, Asha. I decided to let it slide, but in my peripheral vision I saw Asha smirk.

"Wassup, cousins," one of them said, and the other one tilted his head in greeting and shook our hands. I'd already forgotten who was who. "You the one that wrote all them books?"

"That's me," I said.

"When you gonna make them into a movie, cuz?" Trey/Jomarion asked.

Asha chuckled. I'd fielded certain questions about my books so frequently she could have answered on my behalf.

"As soon as Will Smith returns my calls," I said, my standard answer.

Their eyes widened. "For real? You gonna get Will Smith to be in your movies?"

I was about to say that I was kidding, that there was no movie in the works yet, when I heard footsteps approaching behind us.

"Who's that I hear up there?" a woman's voice said from the shadowed hallway. "Is that my nephew visitin' from 'Lanta?"

It was Aunt Lillie, my grandma's eldest sibling at ninety-two. Aunt Lillie was slender and almost as tall as I was, with a thick head of silver hair, eyes like shiny pennies, straight white teeth—real teeth, not dentures—and a healthy, cocoa-brown complexion. Attired in a gaily colored sun dress, she moved down the hall with the sure-footed gait of a much younger lady. I remembered meeting her at the reunion five years ago, and she hadn't lost a step.

I was relieved to see that she was still spry. Since she was the eldest surviving member of the family, she was the main person I was planning to question for information about our clan's past.

"How're you doing, Aunt Lillie?" I said.

"Come here and give your auntie some sugar, baby!" She clasped me to her bosom and kissed me on the cheek. "So glad you could make it here to see us, uh huh. How my baby sister doin'?"

"Grandma's doing well," I said. "She sends her love."

Grinning, Aunt Lillie whirled to Asha. "Oh, my Lord. Now who's this pretty young thang here? This your wife?"

"Fiancée, ma'am," Asha said, and grinned at both of us.

"She sure is pretty, my, my, y'all gonna have some beautiful babies," Aunt Lillie said. She pulled Asha into a hug. "Nice meetin' you, sugar. You with family now, so make yourself at home, you hear?"

Around Aunt Lillie's shoulder, Asha winked at me. I could only shake my head.

Cousin Tee ordered her sons to return outside with me to help bring in our luggage. When we got outdoors, we found three big, muscular, mixed-breed dogs gathered around my SUV, sniffing at the doors.

I stopped in my tracks. "Whose dogs are those?"

"They the family's dogs, cuz," Trey/Jomarion said. "They ain't gonna bite. Just let 'em smell you, you'll be cool."

As if on cue, the dogs trotted to me, tails wagging. They sniffed intently at my shoes and legs. One of them stuck his snout against my crotch. I massaged the dog behind the ears, and he licked my fingers.

I noted that none of the canines wore collars or tags.

"What're their names?" I asked.

Both of the boys shrugged. "They ain't got no names, really, man."

Dogs without names? All righty, then.

"Do they stay in dog houses somewhere around here?" I asked.

"Naw, cuz," Trey/Jomarion said. He swept his long arm around. "They just, like, roam 'round here. They watchdogs, you know."

"They seem awfully friendly to be watchdogs," I said.

One of the boys fixed me with a stern look. "That's 'cause they know you family," he said.

Chapter Eight

Aunt Lillie offered to cook us breakfast, but we told her that we'd already eaten. She seemed offended that Cousin Tee had allowed us to dine at, in her words, "some greasy spoon when they got family here they coulda ate with." We assured her that it was no big deal. She insisted on feeding us, though, and dug out a sweet potato pie she'd baked last night, and a tall pitcher of sweet iced tea.

Cousin Tee left with her sons to take them to a football camp, and promised to return later. Asha and I sat on the fabric sofa in the living room, balancing plates of pie on our laps, while Aunt Lillie got on her knees and dug out one photo album after another from a cabinet underneath the coffee table. They were humongous, thick albums packed with a dizzying array of pictures, some sepia-toned, others in full color.

Grandma Ruth had a good number of snapshots at her home in Atlanta, but Aunt Lillie's collection was much larger. Paging through the album, I discovered photos of relatives whom I had never seen or heard of before. Whenever I came across such a picture, I would ask Aunt Lillie about it, and she would relate with her steel-trap memory exactly who the individual was, how he or she fit in the family lineage, and colorful anecdotes about the person's life. She was a walking and breathing history book.

"Who is this, Aunt Lillie?" Asha asked, index finger tapping a black-and-white portrait of a tall, regal, mustached man dressed in a dark suit. She glanced at me. "Danny strongly favors him. He has to be family."

There was, I had to admit, a striking resemblance. It was almost like viewing a photo of myself, if I'd lived in another era.

Sitting in a nearby upholstered chair, Aunt Lillie leaned over Asha's shoulder, squinted. "Ah, that there's your Grandpa Orin."

"Grandpa Orin?" I flipped to the family tree that I was sketching on my pad. "I don't think I've ever heard of him. Where does he fit in, Aunt Lillie?"

Aunt Lillie took a sip of tea, gazed out the window. She seemed to be gathering her thoughts, remembering, perhaps.

I waited for her to continue. I'd already filled in the names of Grandma Ruth's and Aunt Lillie's parents, and their grandparents, too. It confused me that Aunt Lillie had called this man Grandpa Orin, because I didn't have any entries that went back further in time than their grandparents. Could this Grandpa Orin person perhaps have been Aunt Lillie's *great* grandfather?

But if that were true, I reasoned, doing quick math in my head, the man would've lived in the mid eighteen hundreds, if not a bit earlier. The photo didn't appear to be that old. It had the look of a portrait that had been taken no more than a hundred years ago, if that.

"We'll come back to that, child," Aunt Lillie said, and reached over and turned the page. "I gotta think on it, gotta get things straight in my mind first."

Up until then, Aunt Lillie had been able to narrate minute details of family history with great precision and quickness. Her hesitation seemed out of character, but I merely shrugged.

"Okay," I said. "We'll do this at your pace. You're the oldest surviving relative I have. I'm just grateful for the opportunity to spend time with you and soak up whatever you can tell me about our roots."

"The child wanna know 'bout our roots," Aunt Lillie said, as if speaking to an unseen presence in the living room. There was a gleam in her eyes. "You come to the right place for that, sugar. Uh huh . . . done come back home to where it all started for the family."

I was suddenly convinced that Aunt Lillie knew something key to my project. What hidden knowledge she harbored, I had no idea, but secrets danced in her bright eyes.

I suspected that they had something to do with this new person, this Grandpa Orin.

But as I'd learned from talking to my grandma, you couldn't rush old folk. They would tell you what they wanted, but in their own sweet time and fashion. If I could keep Aunt Lillie talking, perhaps she eventually would reveal her secrets.

I reached inside my leather satchel in which I kept my laptop and research materials, and withdrew my digital voice recorder. "Mind if I turn this on, ma'am? It's a recorder."

She gave the device a suspicious look. "Don't be recording me, child. You apt to get me in some kinda trouble."

"Sorry, my mistake." I started to put it away, but she stopped me with a wave of her hand and a laugh.

"Go 'head, sugar," Aunt Lillie said. "Somebody need to set all this down for us."

"That's right," Asha said. "It'll be helpful for the next generation."

I switched on the recorder and placed it on the coffee table, close enough to capture our voices.

"I'll tell you most of what I know 'bout our roots," Aunt Lillie said. That secretive shine came into her eyes again. "Anything I leave out, you'll learn in God's time."

"That's good enough for me," I said, though my curiosity had become like an ache in my gut.

Aunt Lillie laced her long, spindly fingers across her stomach. Sunlight streaming through the blinds caught the ruby-encrusted ring on her right hand. It was an exact replica of the ruby that Cousin Tee wore, and that my grandma wore, too. I wondered if the gem-stone was a family heirloom of some kind.

Quietly, Aunt Lillie looked from Asha, to me. And then, she started talking.

Chapter Nine

Bruno Jackson wanted to kill me.

I had committed the unpardonable sin of embarrassing him during a flag football game in our PE class. I'd repeatedly and easily blown past him to catch several throws downfield while he struggled in vain to keep up with me—during one play, he'd actually fallen on his butt as I raced past him—and in his mind, the only way to even the score and reassert his dominance over most every kid in the eleventh grade was for him to rearrange my face in front of the locker-room crowd.

Bruno was the stereotypical school bully: bigger than everyone, strong as an ox, and about as dumb as one. I'd managed to avoid a confrontation with him simply because we'd never had a class together—I was in College Prep level courses; he was in Liberal Arts—but every student got thrown together in gym class, a combustible mishmash of braniacs and academic bottom-feeders like Bruno. Bruno was such a poor student and had so many disciplinary problems that he couldn't remain academically eligible for any school sports. Gym class was his stage to shine, and I had stolen his glory.

He showed up beside me in the locker room after the game was over. I was about five-ten, slender. Bruno was six-two and reputed to bench press four hundred pounds.

"Thought you were the man out there, huh, Danny Booger?" he said, purposely butchering my last name. He had a habit of making up demeaning names for kids he didn't respect, which was half the student body.

Sudden electricity buzzed through the musty locker room air. The other boys nearby immediately sensed a fight brewing, and gathered around us in a loose circle.

"I don't have a problem with you, man," I said, my voice a little shaky as I reached for my shirt inside the locker. "It was only a game. Who cares?"

"I care!" Bruno hammered his big fist against my locker door, slamming it shut in my face. "I fuckin' care, you fuckin' cheater."

Don't take the bait, I thought. Walk away, and go to your next class. It's not worth a suspension.

But this was a matter of respect, and in school, respect was worth more than money. I saw what happened to the kids who'd failed to take a stand for their own dignity. They scurried like field mice through the hallways, unable to garner respect from even the teachers.

"I didn't cheat," I said.

"Bullshit! You were takin' off before the goddamn ball was hiked! That's the only reason you kept gettin' past me, man."

Everyone, of course, knew Bruno was lying. They knew he was strong as hell, but brick-footed. The only way he could salvage a shred of self-respect was to make up a story about why he'd failed to catch me.

"You can say whatever you want," I said, wondering where I was getting the balls to talk back like this, "but I wasn't cheating, and you know it."

I think I felt the punch coming the instant that Bruno had made up his mind to unleash it. I often had a feeling for things like that, almost a sixth sense for what would happen, and I never doubted it—my need to listen to it was hardwired into me, as primal as the need to breathe.

I dipped sideways. Bruno's fist sailed through emptiness. He lost his balance and tumbled across the bench in the middle of the aisle.

The crowd around us exploded in shouts of, "Damn!" and "Oh, shit!"

"You fuckin' tripped me!" Bruno roared, leaping to his feet. Blood leaked from one nostril. He blinked, dazed.

"I don't want to fight you," I said.

He charged me. I nimbly slipped aside again. He smashed like a tank into the lockers.

I took a step backward. Screaming, he swung a wild fist at me.

And missed. He spun off balance, drunkenly.

I easily captured his hand. I got a grip on his middle finger, and bent it back. He yelped like a child and sank to his knees on the concrete floor.

"Don't ever bother me again," I whispered.

"All right!" Fat tears spilled down his cheeks. "I'm sorry, man! Fuckin' let me go!"

I relinquished his finger. He cradled his hand against his chest, wincing in pain, and scooted away.

I realized the room had fallen silent. The faces in the crowd regarded me with something approaching awe, and maybe a measure of fear, too.

I wasn't sure what I had done to deserve those looks from them. It wasn't as though I was a karate expert. I'd done only what had come naturally to me to defend myself.

"What are you guys looking at?" I asked. "Leave me alone, okay?"

They promptly scattered.

I turned back to my locker, finished dressing, and left for my next class.

For the rest of my high school career, Bruno Jackson never bothered me again . . . and neither did anyone else.

Chapter Ten

Aunt Lillie spoke for over two hours. She recounted her childhood growing up on the home place, back in the days of Jim Crow segregation. She spoke of running off as a hot-tailed teenager and marrying a man who dragged her to Chicago, gave her five kids, and then went off and died on foreign soil in World War II, a tragedy that brought her back to the home place to raise her children, in the warm, protective circle of family and friends.

She spoke of her parents, and how they'd also lived there on the home place; and her grandparents, too. Although many of the children produced by each generation had migrated from Mississippi to other parts of the country, several always remained behind to raise their respective families. The family's property had never been abandoned.

In her narrative, Aunt Lillie echoed something remarkable that my grandma had told me, too. Unlike many other black folks in the pre-Civil Rights South, they had somehow avoided falling victim to the notoriously unfair sharecropper economy: an arrangement where farmers, usually former slaves, were loaned a plot of land to work, and owed a hefty portion of their crop earnings to the landowner. It was a system that virtually guaranteed blacks would never accumulate significant property, would forever be steeped in debt.

"We done always owned this land outright, and everything we grew on it," Aunt Lillie said. "All three hundred acres here. Belongs to our people, and always will, God willing."

"Three hundred acres?" Asha whistled. "That's incredible."

"No kidding," I said. "I didn't know we owned that much land back here."

"Done had plenty offers to sell out," Aunt Lillie said. She laughed. "Shiny-head white man came through here 'bout a month ago, wanted to mow down all God's green beauty and build some new houses. Ha, I 'bout to laughed him outta the door! Told that man he ain't gonna never have enough money to buy this from us."

"Good for you," I said. "Good for us."

"I needs to stretch these old legs of mine now." Aunt Lillie got to her feet and smoothed down the front of her dress. "Come on out back, y'all."

We followed Aunt Lillie into the kitchen and through the back door, onto a large pinewood deck that looked newly built. At midday, it was hot and sticky outdoors, the air a fragrant haze.

"I don't know how you can stand this heat, Aunt Lillie," Asha said. She blotted perspiration from her brow with a napkin. "It makes me want to faint."

"You get used to it, child," Aunt Lillie said.

The grassy yard beyond the deck was flat as a football field, and about as long as one, extending to an immense cathedral of pines, oaks, and maples that seemed to go on for infinity.

Perhaps it was imagination, but when I looked toward those woods, and the impenetrable shadows within, the buzzing I'd been hearing got louder. I flashed back to my dream: a shotgun house with a blood-red door nestled deep in the forest . . .

I pointed. "What's back there in the woods?"

"That back there is ancestor land," Aunt Lillie said softly, eyes glimmering.

"Ancestor land?" Asha asked.

But the grumble of approaching car engines drew Aunt Lillie's attention away. "Sound like more kinfolk comin'. Come on, y'all. Everyone wanna see you."

I gazed into the forest for a moment, the buzz in my ears and that red door in my mind, and reluctantly turned away.

Chapter Eleven

That night, Asha and I lodged in a guest bedroom at the back of the house. It had two neatly made twin beds placed on opposite sides, and I figured that Cousin Tee's sons often slept there when they spent the night with Aunt Lillie.

There was another room that had a queen-size bed, but Aunt Lillie said she couldn't sanction me and Asha sharing the same bed in her house since we weren't yet married. It was such an old-fashioned notion that I could only chuckle.

Freshly showered, Asha came in from the adjoining bath, a bright orange towel wrapped around her. She stood in front of me—I was sitting on the bed in my boxers, reviewing the genealogy notes I'd written that day—and snatched the towel away from her body with a dramatic flourish.

Desire rippled through me. I set aside my pencil and pad and reached for her. She eased onto my lap, kissed me tenderly, and then got up and moved away.

"Not tonight, baby," she said. "You know what Aunt Lillie said. We can't disrespect the house rules."

"You know you're wrong," I said.

"Sorry, rules are rules." Bending over in front of me, she took a tube of lotion out of her suitcase. She glanced at me over her shoulder with a mischievous gleam in her eyes. "Mind lathering some on my back?"

"You're such a tease." I took the lotion from her, squeezed some into my palm, and began to rub it across her shoulders, trying and completely failing to keep my gaze off her lovely derriere. "You must not want me to get any sleep tonight."

"You might get lucky," she said with a giggle. "On a serious note, though, we learned a lot today, don't you think?"

A virtual caravan of relatives had stopped by that afternoon. Aunts, uncles, and cousins. Everyone was eager to meet us and tell their stories. I'd compiled so much information in my notebook and recorder that it would take me weeks to sort through it all.

"I'd sure like to learn about Grandpa Orin, though," I said. I slid my hands down to Asha's hips, though I had run out of lotion.

She lightly swatted my hands away and stretched across the bed. "I was thinking about that, too. You look so much like him it's amazing."

"It's in the blood, I guess."

"But Aunt Lillie was vague about where he fits into the family tree. Maybe he was the black sheep of the clan. Every family has someone like that, you know."

"We've got a couple more days here, so maybe she'll open up, or maybe we'll get the scoop from someone else."

"Maybe we can find out about ancestor land, too," she said.

I thought about the forest, and how the buzzing had grown louder when I'd peered into its depths. "I hope so."

On the bed, Asha turned onto her back, her smooth brown skin oiled and smelling sweetly of strawberry-scented lotion. She extended one delicate foot toward me and rubbed it gently across my crotch, where things immediately perked up nicely.

"What about the house rules?" I asked.

She smiled. "What about turning off the lights, Babyface?"

I cut off the lamp sitting on the nightstand between the beds. She reached out in the darkness and grabbed my hand, pulled me onto the narrow mattress with her.

"You're being disrespectful," I said.

She responded by smothering my face with feather-light kisses.

Back in Atlanta, though we made love frequently and passionately, since we'd been in Mississippi it seemed we were hornier than usual, as if the fresh country air were an aphrodisiac.

"Aunt Lillie might hear," I whispered. "You know old folks sleep light."

"Then you better keep it down," she said, her minty breath hot against my face. "I know how you like to shout . . ."

Afterward, I dragged myself to my own bed, and collapsed atop the sheets.

I dreamed, again, of the shotgun shack with the red door. The buzzing coming from inside. Candlelight flickering in the windows, shadows writhing on the grass. Climbing the steps, pushing open the door, stepping inside . . . and falling into unimaginable black depths . . .

I came awake with a gasp, cold sweat saturating my face. In her bed, Asha snored softly.

I pushed out of bed and padded to the window on the other side of the room. I parted the curtains.

The window faced the woods, but I couldn't make out the trees at all. In the inky-black night, the forest was only a hulking blur.

On impulse, I dressed in shorts and a T-shirt, and slipped on my sneakers. I quietly left the bedroom.

The house was dark, the only sound the hum of the air conditioner. Aunt Lillie's room was on the other side of the hall, and the door was shut.

I left the house through the back door. I thought of looking for a flashlight to take with me, and decided against it. I felt strangely confident here, as if I'd spent all my life on this land. No harm could befall me while I was here.

I walked off the deck and into the warm night. Toward the woods.

Chapter Twelve

Walking toward the forest, I encountered the most perfect darkness that I had ever seen in my life. There were no bright city lights to alleviate the blackness, no streetlamps. No silver moon.

This was pure night, fathoms deep, and in it, I felt at home.

Swishing through the crisp grass, I became aware of three dark shapes converging around me, and I heard soft panting. The nameless family dogs. One dog took the lead; the other two flanked me on opposite sides.

It was as though they were escorting me.

I've gotta be dreaming. Ordinary dogs don't behave like this.

But I knew I was wide awake. The warm air against my skin, the crunch of the grass beneath my shoes, and the buzzing in my ears were all too real to be just another dream.

We reached the forest wall. The point dog plunged ahead, breaking through shrubs and branches, and I followed, twigs skidding across my arms and legs and leaves caressing my face.

The buzzing grew louder, and with it, so did my pounding heartbeat. Was I really going to find the shotgun house nestled in here? On ancestor land?

The trees around me were as thick and tall as steel columns that might have been erected by some ancient master race. The woods had a heady, primeval smell, and I wondered how long it had been since anyone had ventured back here. My eyes had adjusted somewhat to the darkness, and I didn't see any signs of human habitation: no worn trails, no discarded wrappers, no forgotten soda cans or beer bottles. The land was pristine.

I pushed ahead. I saw a glimmer of light through the dense undergrowth, and tightness gripped my chest.

Trailing the lead canine, I stepped through a grove of trees, and emerged in a clearing.

"My God," I said in a whisper.

The shotgun house was ahead, just as I had seen it in my dream: the blood-red door, white shingles, dark shutters. Candlelight danced in the front windows, and shadows wriggled on the grass.

The buzzing was so loud that I felt it in my chest.

How can this place be real? Who the heck lives here?

A shadow as tall as a man floated past a window.

Terror exploded up my throat like hot oil. I spun around and ran pell-mell through the forest.

The dogs didn't accompany me, and as I raced away, I wondered if they had remained behind, the hounds of whoever lived in that house.

Sprinting, I heard Asha calling for me in an anguished voice. In the humid air, it almost sounded as if she were underwater.

Legs pumping hard, I broke out of the forest, weeds snatching at my shoes. I saw Asha on the back deck. She had switched on the flood light, the yellow glow leaking across the yard.

When she saw me, I slowed to a brisk walk, not wanting to frighten her more than she already was. She ran off the deck and came to me.

"Baby, where were you?" she said. "I woke up and saw you'd left! I was so worried, I was thinking about the home invasions and thought something had happened to you!"

"I'm okay," I said, breathing hard. "I . . . went for a walk."

"At two o'clock in the morning? Why? It's not safe out here."

I couldn't tell her why. Something told me not to mention what I had seen; something told me to keep it secret.

"I couldn't sleep," I said, which was only half true. "I felt safe walking out here. It's my family's land, remember, and we're in the middle of nowhere."

"Tell that to the old lady down the road who got pistol whipped and robbed the other night. Crime is here, too. You've got to be careful, Danny."

"You're right," I said, just to end it. "I should be more careful. Won't happen again."

We went back inside. Aunt Lillie never came from her room to ask about all the commotion, and I wondered about that. I wondered if she knew that I'd gone to find the home in the forest—and was secretly pleased.

Lying in bed again, I crossed my hands behind my head and gazed at the dark ceiling. I couldn't understand how I had initially dreamed of a house that I'd learned was actually real. I wasn't psychic, had never received visions before, either in dreams or outside of them. How had that happened?

When I thought also about the buzzing that originated from inside my head, I began to think, irrationally, that whoever lived in the house was summoning me. But how could that be possible? I wasn't telepathic, either.

I was angry at myself for running away. Temporary fear had taken hold of me, and to find the answers that I'd gone there for, I needed to be stronger.

Next time, I promised myself, I would not run away.

I would go inside.

Chapter Thirteen

The next morning, we went to church. Cousin Tee came by with her sons, all of them dressed in their Sunday best, and we followed her off the home place to a small, faded red brick church about three miles away called Evergreen First Baptist.

Tucked away from the road, it was a world removed from the Baptist church that Asha and I attended in Atlanta, a mega-sanctuary that routinely packed in three thousand worshippers on Sundays. I counted the grand total of sixty heads in the old oak pews.

The pastor was a graying, distinguished-looking man named Rev. James Booker, and I wondered if I was related to him. My question was answered when he asked for any visitors to rise.

Asha and I were the only ones to stand. Every head in the congregation swiveled to us.

"I sure thought that was you, Cousin Danny," the pastor said. He flashed a grin. "Family, that there is Cousin Danny and his beautiful wife. They came all the way from Hotlanta to share in the Lord with us this morning. Won't you please welcome them?"

"His beautiful wife," Asha whispered in my ear, smirking, and then we were mobbed with handshakes and hugs. Everyone there, I realized, was a relative of mine. It was surreal, like discovering you'd been born into a tribe that you hadn't known existed.

Amid the onslaught of warm greetings, I noticed that even the elderly kinfolk were spry and bright-eyed, like Aunt Lillie. None wore glasses or hearing aids, or used canes or walkers. They zipped about the pews as agilely as school children.

Once everyone was seated again and my head was full of more names and faces than I could possibly remember, the pastor launched into his sermon.

As I followed along with the cited scriptures in my Bible, I noticed that Rev. Booker wore a ruby ring. In fact, I had seen many of my relatives, mostly those who looked to be in their thirties and older, wearing the same piece of jewelry, just like Cousin Tee, Aunt Lillie, and my grandma.

For no reason at all, I started thinking about the shotgun house and the red door, and I couldn't wait to get into the woods again.

Chapter Fourteen

But after church service concluded—almost three hours later—we were ushered to a dinner at Uncle Lee's place. Uncle Lee, Aunt Lillie's kid brother, was in his early eighties, tall and sinewy, with the straight-backed posture of a young athlete. He lived on family-owned land, too, down the road from Aunt Lillie, in a well-kept home with creaking wood floors. About fifty of us gathered inside, where the rooms were redolent with the mouth-watering smells of fried chicken, macaroni and cheese, greens, cornbread, sweet potatoes, baked beans, and peach cobbler.

All of us held hands as my cousin the pastor said the blessing, and then it was time to eat.

"With all this incredible food we've been getting, I'm going to be as wide as a barn," Asha said, as we shuffled down the makeshift buffet line in the hallway.

"Orca whale or not, I'll still love you," I said. She rolled her eyes.

But her remark made me notice something: none of my blood relatives were obese, though some of those who'd married into the family were on the hefty side. Some of my blood kinfolk were slim, others were athletically built, many were of average build, but none carried excessive poundage. Yet from what I'd seen, they didn't follow particularly low-fat diets.

I reflected that I'd never faced a weight problem, either, and I basically ate whatever I wanted, and exercised maybe three times a week. The same was true of my mother and grandmother.

Good genes? It had to be. Although the explanation failed to entirely please me.

Laden with plates and glasses of sweet tea and lemonade, folks were sitting on every available seat throughout the house, but Asha and I were given chairs of honor at the dining room table. Aunt Lillie was already seated there, along with several cousins whose names I'd been told earlier but couldn't remember; all of the faces and names of the people I'd met had become a cheerful blur.

"Y'all hear 'bout what happened to Miss Eunice last night?" one of the cousins said.

A chill gripped me; I knew what she was going to say. "Was it another home invasion?"

The cousin nodded, eyes downcast. "Poor Miss Eunice. They kicked her door in. She had a shotgun but I hear they took it from her and beat her with it—"

"Lord have mercy," Aunt Lillie said.

"Broke her ribs, her arm, and her jaw," the cousin said. "And they took everything. Her money she kept in there, her jewelry, her TV set . . . I hear she's in a bad, bad way up in the hospital. You know Miss Eunice got a heart condition . . ."

"Are the police doing anything about the rash of crimes?" Asha asked. "This is the fourth break-in."

Asha's question provoked scattered, bitter laughter around the table.

"Honey, this ain't Atlanta," another cousin said. "Police here ain't used to nothin' like this. I hear Chief Williams said he thinks it's a crew from Memphis behind it, but . . ." She shrugged. "He said he doin' the best he can to catch 'em."

"Thank God no one in the family's been victimized yet," I said.

"Yet," one of the cousins said. "Somebody need to put an end to things 'fore that happens."

There was murmured agreement around the table. My cousin's emphasis on the word *somebody* made me suspect she was speaking of an actual person, and I remembered what Cousin Tee had said at breakfast yesterday: *"If it keeps up . . . somebody 'round here gonna have to go 'head and take care of it on his own."*

Who was this somebody? Was there a family vigilante I'd yet to meet who ensured the safety of the clan? Some country crusader for justice, some backwater Charles Bronson?

The conversation abruptly switched gears, to Asha. My cousins remarked that it would be wonderful to have a doctor in the family, that she would be the first. Basking in their attention, Asha winked at me.

As dinner wound down and people began to drift outdoors, I cornered Aunt Lillie in the living room.

"How you doin', child?" she asked. "You enjoyin' meetin' all your kinfolk?"

"It's been great," I said. "I wanted to ask you about something I saw in the woods last night. The woods behind the house?"

"Hmm?" Her eyes gave up nothing.

"I saw a house back there, Aunt Lillie. One of those little shotgun houses."

"A house?" Blank eyes.

"Someone was living in there. There were candles burning inside."

"You sure you wasn't dreamin', child?"

"I was wide awake, Aunt Lillie."

"Child says he seen a shotgun house back in the woods," she said, in that manner she had, as if she were addressing an invisible presence. "That's news to me, sugar. Somebody livin' on ancestor land without us knowing . . . hmph."

"You know all about it, don't you?" I said. "Who lives there? Tell me, please."

But she only said, "Cousin Bert wanna meet you this afternoon. She ain't make it over here 'cause she had to up to Memphis this morning, but she wanted me to bring you by her place after dinner."

"Cousin Bert," I said glumly.

"She 'bout two years younger than me, she know a lot of family history, too," Aunt Lillie said. She tapped my arm. "Be good for that book you writin' 'bout us."

"Knowing who's living in that shotgun house might be good for my book, too," I said.

Her smile vanished. "Good to know, but not good for no book," she said, and squeezed my wrist firmly. I winced at her unexpected strength, tried to pull my wrist away, but her grip was iron. "Everybody don't need to know everything 'bout the family roots," she said.

"But this book is exclusively for the family, it's not for the whole world to read."

Her eyes were steady. "Everybody in the *family* don't need to know 'bout the family roots, neither. Don't you never forget that, child."

She released me then, smiled sweetly, and wandered away. I massaged my wrist, my head spinning.

I wanted to dismiss what she'd said as the meaningless blather of a feeble-minded old woman, but I knew there was nothing feeble about Aunt Lillie. She had as much clarity of thought as anyone I'd ever met, and she'd meant exactly what she'd said, as crazy as it sounded.

Everybody in the family don't need to know 'bout the family roots, neither.

What the hell was she talking about?

Chapter Fifteen

After our visit with Cousin Bert—she lived on family land, too, and was much like Aunt Lillie, with a sharp-eyed gaze, a hearty laugh, and an infallible memory that defied her age—we finally returned to Aunt Lillie's. I was eager to venture back into the woods, but Cousin Tee had offered to take us to the casinos in Tunica, about a half hour's drive away, and of course, Asha wanted to go. Not wanting to be a wet blanket, I went along and tried to act interested.

Asha and Cousin Tee loved the slots. While Cousin Tee steadily pulled the arm of one of the machines, the gleaming lights glinted off her ruby ring.

"Where'd you get that from?" I pointed at the gemstone.

She touched the ruby. "This? This here's the family stone."

"The family stone?"

"You know, how like some families have crests or whatever. We got us a stone."

"I've noticed a lot of our relatives wearing it," I said. "Can I get one?"

She shrugged. "I ain't the one who gives 'em out, Cousin Danny."

"Who does?"

"The family elder," she said.

"The family elder? You mean Aunt Lillie?"

"Oh, my goodness." Suddenly, Cousin Tee's eyes grew huge. "Oh, my goodness, I won!"

My question was lost in the ensuing excitement, and I didn't bother to bring it up again. I figured that Aunt Lillie, the eldest surviving member of the Booker family, had given Cousin Tee the ruby. Who else could it have been?

We didn't get back to the home place until almost nine o'clock that evening. Darkness had settled like a shroud over the land, the velvet sky bright with stars.

So much for exploring the woods by daylight, I thought. But I was not going to let the pitch-blackness keep me from going out there again. I wasn't going to let anything keep from me from going out there again.

We sat up for a while with Aunt Lillie, drinking chamomile tea spiced with honey and talking about family, and then Aunt Lillie retired to bed, and so did we. Asha and I made love, our hunger for each other as intense and urgent as it had ever been, and then I lay in my twin bed and waited for her to drift asleep.

As soon as I heard her breathing heavily, I silently dressed, and tiptoed out of the house.

Chapter Sixteen

One Monday morning in May, my literary agent, Sandy Clark, called with a shocking request from my publisher: could I turn in my next novel early? Like, within two weeks?

I hadn't even started writing the book yet. The contractual deadline was two months away. I paced across the kitchen, feeling as if I'd been sucker-punched in the jaw.

"Why?" I finally said, when I could speak again.

"An opportunity has come up with Wal-Mart," Sandy said. "They're launching a new promotional program where they're going to highlight three new mystery titles each month in all of their stores nationwide, and they've specifically asked about your new book, Daniel. They want to include it in the program during this year's holiday season, if it's available."

Prime placement at Wal-Mart during the holidays? Authors would have sold their firstborn for a chance like that.

"That's really exciting," I said. "But two weeks?"

"It could be a big boost to your numbers," Sandy said. "I wouldn't present this to you if I didn't think it was worth the effort, and you've

always been a relatively fast writer. You said you wrote your last novel in six weeks, if I recall."

"That's true . . . but I haven't even started on the book yet, Sandy."

"Oh, dear," she said, in a small voice.

"And my girlfriend and I are going out of town on Wednesday," I said. "We're going to Hawaii for ten days. Everything's already been booked, and Asha made me swear that I wouldn't do any work during the vacation, can't even bring my laptop."

"They aren't going to budge on the deadline—I've already asked." Sandy sighed. "I suppose I'll have to tell them to pass you over for this one. With us wanting a new contract in the fall, though, it would've been nice to have this feather in our cap when I go to bat for you."

I wandered into my home office and looked at the big calendar on the wall. It was Monday; in two days, we'd leave for Hawaii, and when we returned, the two-week deadline would be expiring in a couple of days, and I'd be seriously jetlagged and useless to work, anyway.

But . . . could I write the entire novel before my vacation? In two days?

Call me nuts, but I felt a twinge of excitement at the challenge. I'd heard of stories in which authors had written a complete novel over a weekend, and I'd long wondered if I were capable of such a feat. The only reason I'd never attempted it was because I'd never had a reason to try.

"Let me see what I can do," I said to Sandy. "I'll be in touch."

I hung up the phone, and as soon as I did, I sat in front of my laptop, opened Microsoft Word, and started writing. I didn't have any notes, an outline, or even a clear idea of what the novel would be about. My original plan had been to spend our vacation mulling over various plot ideas so that when we returned, I could get to work and wrap up the book in a few leisurely weeks.

It was around nine-thirty in the morning when I started working. When Asha arrived home at six that evening, I'd already written a hundred pages.

I'd never written so rapidly, or with such intense focus. I couldn't explain it. It was as though I'd discovered some hidden ability to immerse myself in a prolonged, creative trance.

Asha and I had dinner together. After dinner, I returned to the computer. I worked through the entire night; when Asha left for work the next morning, I was on page two hundred and forty.

The words were simply flowing out of me, as if funneled through my fingers from some pent-up reservoir of creativity that I'd managed to burst wide open. I couldn't stop, and though I hadn't slept at all in over twenty-four hours, I worked throughout the day, too.

At three o'clock that afternoon, I called Sandy.

"Check your e-mail, Sandy," I said.

"Okay," she said, and about thirty seconds later, I heard her gasp. "This is a new book?"

"Hot off the press," I said. "I think my laptop is still smoking."

She was quiet for a moment. Then: "You actually wrote all three hundred and eighty-two pages of this manuscript after we talked yesterday morning? You didn't already have this finished?"

"Wish I had," I said. "I would've gotten some sleep last night."

"Oh, wow," Sandy said softly. "I've never heard of anyone writing a book of this length at such an incredible speed, Daniel, and I've been in the business for twenty years. This is unbelievable."

"I only hope it's good." I wiped my eyes, which felt grainy and sore. "Now if you'll excuse me, I'm going to take a nap, and then start packing for our trip."

Six days later, when Asha and I were at the resort on Maui, we came back to our room to find a bottle of Moët champagne and a type-written note.

Book is not good—it's great! Publisher so excited they want to talk new contract. Call when you get a free moment.

Congrats,
Sandy

Chapter Seventeen

This time, the trio of canines did not escort me through the woods, but their guidance wasn't necessary. I knew exactly where I was headed.

And in case I didn't, the continuous droning drew me forward. It seemed louder than last night, deeper somehow. My entire body vibrated.

I glimpsed candlelight ahead, reflected flames licking the leaves. I was ready to plunge out of the thicket of greenery and into the clearing—but stopped when I heard voices ahead.

Men in a heated conversation. Two of them, it sounded like.

I took cover behind an oak tree at the edge of the clearing, and peeked around the trunk.

Through the interlacing leaves and branches of surrounding shrubbery, I had a view of the house. A very tall, slender silhouette paced back and forth across one of the front windows; the window was open, the warm night air carrying the men's dialogue to me.

I cocked my head, listening.

"You *must* choose a side, Oringo," a voice said, which I believed came from the pacing figure. The man had an accent that I took to be French. "Remaining neutral is not a viable choice. It is too important!"

"Neutrality has long been my preferred choice, Kyle," Oringo answered. He spoke in a resonant baritone, thoroughly American but with the eloquent air of an aristocrat. "Surely your dear mother has explained that to you. In fact, I am certain that she agrees with my stance."

"Leave Mother out of this conversation," Kyle said. "This is between us. You are either with me, or against me."

"Such moral absolutes . . . you remind me of your father," Oringo said.

"My father understood the true purpose of our kind," Kyle said. "It is not to live isolated in the shadows, away from the dwellings of men. It is to hold dominion over men! They are cattle to us, Oringo."

Sweat trickled down my temple. Was I dreaming again? What on earth were these men talking about?

They are cattle to us . . .

Were they even men?

"I respectfully disagree, my friend," Oringo said. "Peaceful coexistence benefits us all. It has been our way since time immemorial. I see no reason to break with tradition so that you may wage your selfish vendetta."

My feet tingled from standing in place. I shifted my stance slightly. The movement disturbed a nearby branch, a faintly perceptible noise.

But Kyle's head jerked in my direction, and he stepped toward the window, his face an ink blot. "I hear someone."

Heart in my throat, I ducked behind the tree. *Please, don't let them come looking for me.*

A huge, cold hand fell across my neck like a steel clamp. I screamed.

"Silence, you sniveling, sneaking little mongrel," Kyle said.

Incredibly, he was beside me. Just like that. From the house to the woods in a nanosecond.

I felt faint.

As if I were a tiny lion cub being carried by its mother by the nape of its neck, Kyle plucked me off the ground and brought me into the clearing. I was so terrified and stunned that my screams died in my lungs. I feebly kicked my legs, flailed my arms.

Kyle laughed. Holding me away from him, he examined me. Shadows danced across his face, and reflections of candle flames flickered in his eyes . . . eyes that were darker and deeper than any I had ever seen . . . like twin portals of oblivion.

Not human, a voice whispered in the back of my shell-shocked mind. *Whatever he is, he definitely isn't a man . . .*

"I should destroy you for eavesdropping on us." Kyle's lips parted in a cruel smile, and I saw the gleam of teeth. Sharp incisors. *Fangs.*

My stomach churned sickeningly. An impossible idea careened around my mind. *Could this be a . . . no . . . no . . . no . . . it's not possible . . . don't even think it . . .*

Behind us, a door banged open. Kyle glanced away from me.

"Is this one of yours, Oringo?" Kyle asked, as if I were a house pet.

"You know he is," Oringo said. "Leave him be."

"I should have noticed the resemblance." Kyle's bottomless gaze shifted back to me. He sneered. "You and your mongrel litter."

With a grunt, he flung me to the ground. My tailbone hit the grass, but in my dazed state, I was barely aware of the pain.

Oringo strolled off the porch steps and came to me. The three nameless dogs that I had seen yesterday flanked him, protectively.

I wanted to get up and run away, but as I looked at Oringo, I suddenly didn't trust my legs to work.

Oringo was the man whose portrait I had seen in the family photo album. The man with whom I shared a strong likeness. The man Aunt Lillie had called Grandpa Orin.

It can't be.

Although his photo was sepia-toned and tattered, this man looked to be no older than forty. He wore a dark button-down shirt, dark slacks, gleaming black boots.

A ruby glimmered on his finger. *The family stone . . .*

"Rise, my son," he said.

He took me by my elbow and brought me to my feet. His touch was paternal, and his calm, dark eyes held the wisdom of ages; I intuitively understood that I was looking at someone ancient, far older than I could comprehend.

Kyle clucked his tongue. "Your ways abhor me."

Oringo's nostrils flared. "Leave us, Kyle."

"We will resume this conversation," Kyle said. "But know that I will proceed—with or without your assistance."

"As you wish." Oringo shrugged.

In a blink, Kyle vanished. One second, he was there, decked out in his black ensemble. The next second, there was only empty space where he had stood, as if he had been absorbed into the night.

Dizziness spun through me, and my knees buckled. Oringo put his arm around my shoulder and kept me from falling, and the dogs closed ranks around me, too, seeming to sense my distress.

I dimly realized that the buzzing noise had finally ceased.

"What . . . what's going on?" I asked, in a wafer-thin voice. "Who are you?"

"Come inside, my son," Oringo said. "We have much to discuss. I have been waiting for you, and I believe you have been waiting for me, too."

Chapter Eighteen

In my dream, stepping through the red door had plunged me into an abyss of fathomless depths. In actuality, when I crossed the threshold the hardwood floor was completely intact—it was only inside my own mind that I was falling.

Falling into a bizarre new reality that turned my beliefs upside down. A reality where strange beings could teleport in a heartbeat, where those same beings spoke of men as cattle, where someone who looked like me lived without showing any signs of aging since his photo had been taken decades ago.

The thoughts made me weak, feverish. Oringo led me to a chair in the front room. He placed a ceramic mug of a steaming beverage in my hands.

It had a spicy aroma that aroused my thirst, but I hesitated to drink it. Everything was unknown, a threat, until proven otherwise.

"It's only tea, Daniel," Oringo said. "Drink. It will give you strength."

Using both hands to hold the mug—in my shaky condition, the only way I could keep it balanced without dropping it—I tilted the cup to my lips. The tea was hot and bitter, but I immediately felt the haze lifting from my thoughts.

I cast a quick look around. The room was narrow, lit by three white candles on an unadorned oak cocktail table. It was furnished with a fabric-covered sofa, two matching chairs. A collection of black-and-white photographs lined the burgundy walls; I recognized some of them as copies of pictures I had seen in Aunt Lillie's photo album.

On an end table beside my chair, there was a photo of me. A shot my mother had snapped when I was five years old: Grinning, I wore a floppy straw hat and denim overalls as I petted a puppy in my lap.

It felt so weird to find a photo of myself in this mysterious man's house that I felt as though I were looking at a picture of someone else.

"You were a good-looking child," Oringo said. He settled into a chair across from me, and the canines came to rest near his feet. A smile touched his lips. "You've grown into quite a man, as well."

"Who are you?" I asked.

"You may call me Grandpa Orin," he said. Another faint smile. "While not quite technically accurate, it will make things easier."

"I saw your picture in Aunt Lillie's photo album." I didn't know what else to say. Normally, I found it easy to conjure words, but my brain was sputtering like a faulty light bulb. "She wouldn't tell me where you fit into the family tree . . . if you do."

He released a hearty, good-natured laugh. "I'm the root of the family tree, Daniel. I'm the patriarch of the clan, the founder of the family."

I was shaking my head. "God, I must be dreaming."

"It would make it easier to believe if you were, eh?" He chuckled. "In 1734, I immigrated to America from Ghana. I was disgusted with the exportation of Africans as New World slaves, and fascinated by the notion of setting down roots in a fresh land. After taking many years to survey various territories, I took a human as my wife, and acquired the land on which my descendants reside to this day. I protected my children from the indignities of the slave trade. Know this, Daniel—on your mother's branch of your family, at least, your people have always been free."

His words swirled over me, but there was one piece that I couldn't dislodge from my mind.

"You said you moved here in 1734," I said.

He nodded matter-of-factly. "In August of that year, to be precise. A tedious, month-long voyage by sea. It would have been nice to have air travel then." He laughed.

"That was almost two hundred and seventy-five years ago," I said, numbly.

He nodded again. "Indeed. Time passes quickly."

I gazed into the cup. The tea had initially warmed me, but now I felt cold and shivery all over again.

"You're telling yourself that it's not possible," he said. "You are correct—the tremendous lifespan to which I lay claim is not possible for a man. While I immigrated to America in 1734, I've lived in countless countries before—Ghana, Egypt, Senegal, Rome, Greece, Brazil. I've seen empires rise and fall, great nations of which you've read in your history books. I've seen the fortunes of man go boom and bust and boom again. I've seen the entire course of human history, Daniel, thousands of years, and it is but a day to me."

Slowly, I looked up at him. My head felt heavy, as if a lead weight lay on the back of my neck. "What are you?"

"You pose the question to which you've already found an answer," he said. "You overheard my conversation with Kyle. You saw his teeth . . ."

He opened his mouth. I saw the gleam of saliva on sharp incisors. My heart clutched. It took all of my courage to keep from bolting out of the room.

"Ask yourself, Daniel," he said. "Have you ever suffered the common cold, or the flu, or any disease whatsoever? Have you ever broken a bone? Sustained a bruise for longer than an hour or two?"

My mind raced, searching for answers to his questions, and in every instance, finding the answer to be no. *No, no, no, never.*

"Do you understand the origin of your unusual agility and quickness?" he asked. "Has it not arisen to aid you when you needed it?"

I thought about dodging the blows of Bruno Jackson, the school bully.

"You make your living writing books," he said. "I've read them all, and I've read about your work habits in interviews. You say that you write your books in a mere few weeks—but you and I both know that you could write an entire book in a day, for you possess an extraordinary ability to focus your energies, as we all do."

He knows everything about me. He knows my entire life.

He leaned forward in his chair, dark eyes glimmering. "You've seen your blood relatives. You've seen how even the oldest among them walk easily without the aid of a cane, see clearly without eyewear, and possess a singular nimbleness of mind and overall robust health . . . many passing on from this world only after they surpass the glorious age of one hundred."

I envisioned Aunt Lillie, ninety-two, moving about with the energy of a woman thirty years younger.

He said, "You came here, to your family home, because you knew there was something in your family's history, a secret to which you had not been privy, hidden knowledge about yourself. I summoned you into these woods, for I believe the time has come for you to learn the truth of your ancestry."

He rose, and crossed the room. He placed a firm hand on my shoulder.

I didn't move. I was afraid to move.

"I am a vampire, Daniel," he said. "And you have my blood."

Chapter Nineteen

I am a vampire . . .

Head lowered, I pulled in a deep breath.

A vampire.

I swallowed.

Vampire.

I squeezed my eyes shut.

I had always known there was something different about me. I remembered how everyone in my second-grade class came down with chickenpox, and I was the only one who avoided the illness. Remembered how I'd been struck by a car, an accident that should have landed me in the hospital with serious injury, and how I'd gotten up with only minor bruises that had faded an hour later. Remembered how throughout school, I always managed to ace exams without studying much at all, how term papers and essays flowed out of me as if channeled once I settled down and focused. Remembered that odd sense I'd had so long I must have been born with it, that there was something unique about me, but unable to put my finger on what it was.

Those differences always had made me feel isolated. Alone in way that I couldn't describe with words, but which I'd long felt poignantly, like a burr under the collar.

"Come," Oringo said. "There is more."

He took my arm and lifted me to my feet.

As I shuffled through the house behind Oringo, I noticed that he and I shared the same posture, the same manner of walking, and that casual observation both fascinated and frightened me.

The dogs trailed behind us, herding me along.

Like in most shotgun houses, there was no hallway; each room led directly into the next. Beyond the living room in which we'd been sitting, there was a bedroom; beyond the bedroom, a kitchen.

There was a wooden door with a shiny brass knob set flush in the floor between the kitchen and bedroom. Oringo bent, lifted it open.

A candle on a nearby table revealed a stone staircase beneath the doorway that appeared to descend into the darkest bowels of the earth.

"The rabbit hole goes deeper, Daniel," Oringo said with a flickering smile.

He ushered me through the door, and closed it above us. The dogs did not follow, and intuition suggested that they would stand guard over the house until our return.

It was a narrow spiral stairway with a sturdy wooden railing, illuminated at several junctures by candles in sconces bolted to the faded stone walls. The air was cool, and I thought I detected the smell of paper, books. The bottom was so far below, however, that I couldn't see it.

"Almost there," Oringo said, as if anticipating my question.

We finally emerged in a vast, candle-lit, circular chamber that reminded me of a university library. The area was full of over a dozen bookcases that must have been twenty feet high, and the shelves were packed with books. A ladder on wheels leaned against the far wall.

"I'm something of a librarian, as you can see," Oringo said. "These are texts I've collected over the millennia, volumes valuable to humans and vampire alike."

"Books about vampires," I said.

"Genuine vampires, not the creations of over-imaginative novelists and filmmakers," he said. He strolled to the center of the room, a wide-open space furnished with a couple of immense oak desks, and leather armchairs. "Much of what you think you know about vampires is a fabrication. Myth, not fact."

My legs were quivering again. I lowered myself into a chair.

Oringo sauntered around the room, arms crossed over his chest, like a college professor ready to deliver a lecture.

"Vampires are not the poor, damned members of humanity, or some wicked spawn of Satan," Oringo said. "Vampires walked the earth long before the dawn of man. We are a species unto ourselves—we were living civilized lives while humans were hunting buffalo with spears and stones and living in mud huts. We've watched humans evolve, and aided the evolutionary process in instances when it suited our needs."

"Did you feed on humans?" I asked. The question had just popped into my head, and I spoke without thinking that maybe I really didn't want to know the answer.

He looked at me. "Yes. We preyed on them. That is one thing about vampires in fiction that is actually true—we do subsist on blood."

Nausea twisted my stomach. But I found myself thinking about those times when I had tasted my own blood—when getting a paper cut, for instance, or a bruise that broke the skin. I found myself recalling the jittery excitement that coursed through me when the coppery taste touched my tongue.

"You have inherited an affinity for the taste of blood," Oringo said.

"Sunlight doesn't bother me," I said, eager to change the topic.

"You are human enough that it would not. I can venture outdoors during daylight as well, if I take precautions to protect myself. While exposure to ultraviolet rays does not cause vampires to shrivel and explode as you see in popular films, it does irritate our skin and cause rather unsightly wrinkles."

I laughed sourly. "Sounds like what happens when someone sunbathes too much."

"As for garlic cloves, holy water, the Christian crucifix?" Oringo grunted with disdain. "They affect me no more than they would you."

"Mirrors?" I asked.

"A most absurd legend. Of course I would see my image captured in a mirror!"

"Sleeping in coffins?"

"I prefer my Tempur-Pedic mattress," Oringo said.

"Do you have to be invited into someone's house before you, ah . . ."

"No," he said. "Furthermore, I've not laid my lips on human flesh in over a hundred years. The advent of blood banks has been a boon to vampires, and we've brokered confidential arrangements with suppliers throughout the world. I receive a monthly shipment and keep the stock in my refrigerator."

I'm sitting here talking to a vampire who's telling me he gets a monthly shipment of blood by freakin' FedEx. Jesus.

I slumped in the chair. I was beginning to feel dizzy again.

"Each vampire does have particular talents, however," Oringo continued. "Kyle, the one you met earlier? He has the gift of telekinesis—he can move objects from one location to another, a rather useful skill. Others, such as his late father, could influence weather patterns."

"What can you do?" I asked. "Fly?"

Oringo didn't laugh. "I can procreate with humans, produce children that share traits of both species. Few vampires possess the gift—most of us who want to take on human partners must change the human's blood chemistry to a close approximation of ours, a painful and lengthy transfusion process."

"But not you?" My voice was slurred; I felt intoxicated.

"It's a humble gift, perhaps, but one with which I long ago made peace. I have no interest in waging wars with humanity. Why would I—when I count among them so many of my own children?"

"Right, makes perfect sense," I said.

Oringo came to me. "You must not share what I've told you with anyone. You cannot tell the woman you intend to marry. This is a secret that must remain within the blood circle of the family. Do I have your word?"

"Yeah," I whispered. I tried to nod, but my head drooped, and when I looked up, the room was spinning, as if I'd had way too much to drink.

"This is too much for you to digest," Oringo said. "You should rest now. I'm afraid a task awaits us, and you must be prepared when I call on you . . ."

He might have said something else, but I'm not sure what it was, because I passed out.

Chapter Twenty

When I came to, I was lying in bed in a dark room. Blinking groggily, I grappled for the edges of the mattress, hoping to discover I was sleeping in our king-size bed back in Atlanta—and felt the narrow width of the twin.

No. I was still in Mississippi.

Then, I felt a cool metallic chain around my neck, and a hard lump lying against the base of my throat. I closed my fingers around it.

It was too dark in the room to see, but I knew what it was: a ruby ring. The family stone. Given to me by the family elder.

You may call me Grandpa Orin . . .

I wanted to believe that my encounter with him had been only a dream, something I could dismiss and forget. But the feel of the gemstone in my hand brought everything back in an undeniable, delirious rush.

I am a vampire . . . you have my blood . . . much of what you think you know about vampires is a fabrication . . . you have inherited an affinity for the taste of blood . . . this is a secret that must remain within the blood circle of the family . . .

I looked across the room. Asha was a shadowy shape on the bed, sound asleep. The crimson digits on the clock read 3:28 AM.

I'm afraid a task awaits us, and you must be prepared when I call on you.

Before I realized what I was doing, I had pushed off the mattress and snatched my car keys off the nightstand. I was still fully dressed, from my earlier jaunt to the woods.

I hurried out of the house. Opened the door to my Expedition and got behind the wheel.

I didn't know what I was doing, or where I was going. I was driven by an impulse I didn't understand, and I was powerless to resist it, much as I'd been powerless to resist the humming that had drawn me to the forest like a pin to a magnet.

I fired up the engine and roared out of the driveway, gravel spinning from the tires. I swerved onto the adjacent country road.

I'd forgotten to switch on the headlamps. I started to reach for the lever, and that weird impulse told me not to, ordered me to drive in darkness.

This is crazy. But whatever's going on, I can't stop it.

After about half a mile, a three-way intersection came up. I didn't know these twisty roads in daylight, much less at night, but without a second's hesitation, I hung a left.

I found myself on a two-lane road with a blown-out streetlamp, and old small houses standing on big, sloping parcels of land.

I saw a dark Oldsmobile sedan ahead, idling on the shoulder. Tension plucked my nerves. Something about the scene struck me as wrong.

As I drew closer, I realized what it was: a man sat behind the wheel, smoking a cigarette. Who would be sitting in a car taking a smoke at three-thirty in the morning?

I looked toward the house beyond the Oldsmobile, saw the front door yawning open, and light beams bouncing around inside, like flashlights.

I suddenly understood what was going on. Although I had no idea how I was going to handle it, I slowed to a halt and shifted into Park.

The driver sprang from behind the wheel like an angry snake out of a sack. He scrambled around the front end of his car. He wore a dark T-shirt, jeans, and a black bandana knotted around his head.

He also had a pistol, and he was aiming it at me.

"Get the fuck out of the car, ma'fucker." He flicked his cigarette to the ground, but didn't take his gaze off me for a second. "You five-oh? Huh?"

A calmness that I could not logically explain had settled over me. Holding his gaze, I slowly shook my head. "I was only driving through," I said.

"Creepin' with yo ma'fuckin lights off? Huh? I said, get out the damn car! And put yo ma'fuckin hands up!"

I took my hands off the wheel.

Then, moving very slowly, I got out of the car.

Chapter Twenty-One

Once I climbed out of the car, things happened quickly.

The gunman stepped toward me, pistol tilted sideways and pointed at my face. "Turn the fuck 'round."

"Okay, no problem, man," I said. "It's cool."

He grinned fiercely, showing a mouthful of shining metal fronts. Beginning my turn, I did something he probably never expected.

I swiped at the gun.

He let out a soft sound of surprise as the weapon spun out of his grasp and landed on the gravel.

Do you understand the origin of your unusual agility and quickness? Has it not arisen to aid you when you needed it?

He cursed, and charged me. I launched a punch that connected squarely with his jaw, and his head snapped back, fronts clicking in his mouth. He sagged to the ground, KO'd.

I pushed out a heavy breath. The entire altercation had lasted maybe five seconds.

I picked up the gun and stashed it against the waistband of my jeans, and then flipped over the guy's body and found a cell phone riding his belt.

I called 9-1-1 and reported a robbery-in-progress, reading the address off the wrought-iron mailbox at the end of the driveway. The operator cautioned me to wait for the police to arrive, but I hung up on her.

I crept toward the house. The flashlights were in motion—the others hadn't seen me drop their lookout man.

Drawing the gun, I carefully entered the doorway. My shoe crunched across a broken vase.

"Who the fuck is that?" a man's voice asked nearby.

Two light beams swung toward me. I dove behind a sofa.

"I've called the police!" I said.

They responded with gunfire. Pistols boomed, and rounds tore into the sofa and the walls. I hugged the carpet.

From a back room, I heard a woman's muffled scream.

I had to do something, had to help her.

Risking a bullet in the head, I crawled like a crab around the end of the sofa. A bullet smacked into a floor lamp nearby, and glass shards rained over me.

I pushed myself to my feet and dashed for the hallway.

Gunfire, and a pain tearing through my shoulder. I crashed against the wall, sending a collection of framed photographs clattering to the floor.

I've been shot.

I looked behind me, fearful that one of the gunmen was coming to finish me off. But they were fleeing to the door to escape. One of them let out a sudden bleat of pain, and I wondered if the police had already arrived.

A familiar silhouette darkened the doorway. *Oringo.*

My shoulder burning, I scooted against the wall and watched.

Oringo had knocked the first gunman flat on his back. The second one raised his gun to fire on him, and Oringo took the weapon away from the man as easily as if the guy were a child. The gunman swung a fist. Oringo took the punch without slowing at all, grabbed the guy by his shirt and casually tossed him across the room.

He unhooked two sets of metal handcuffs from the loops of his slacks, and restrained the men. And then he came to me.

"How're you feeling, Daniel?" he asked.

"A bullet grazed my shoulder, but I'll live," I said. "There's a lady in the back . . ."

"Miss Etta, yes," he said. "I'll go to her."

He went down the hall, and returned about a minute later with an old, heavyset black woman in a tattered house robe and rollers bouncing in her hair. She was crying and thanking him profusely, and the way she leaned on him, I guessed that she had met him before.

"Daniel here is the one you should be thanking, my dear," he said. "He was the first one to arrive to help."

Her tearful eyes brightened when she looked at me. "God bless you, sugar, oh, bless you . . ."

I awkwardly accepted her gratitude. Oringo—by then, I'd decided to call him Grandpa Orin—winked at me.

"Thank you for heeding my call, Daniel," he said. "This is the land of our ancestors, and we must keep it safe, always."

A few minutes later, the police and an ambulance arrived. Paramedics, learning that I had been shot, wanted to check me out, but I politely declined medical care.

After all, by then, my gunshot wound had stopped bleeding.

Chapter Twenty-Two

A month after our visit to Mississippi, I proposed to Asha. She was thrilled, of course, and so was I. We set the wedding date for the following June, and she and her mother and girlfriends began planning for the big day, with me dropping in my two cents whenever I was asked.

Some nights, I dreamed of the house on ancestor land in the Mississippi woods. I dreamed of walking inside through the red door, taking a chair, and chatting with the patriarch.

There are many, many others like you, he told me during these dream conversations. *You are not the only one—I am the father of numberless generations, the grand ancestor of countless children.*

One autumn afternoon, I was at a bookstore and went to the café to get a coffee. The barista, tall and slender and slightly older than I, took my order.

A ruby ring adorned his finger.

He glanced at the matching ring I wore. We exchanged nods and a knowing look, and though he was a complete stranger, I felt such a bond with him we might have grown up as brothers.

I finally knew my place in the world.

I was no longer alone.

Ghost Summer

Tananarive Due

Davie Stephens was sure he must be dreaming when he heard his mother singing softly in his ear. It was an old call-and-response song she used to sing to him in Swahili when he was young: "*Kye Kye Kule . . . Kye Kye Kofisa . . . Kofisa Langa . . . Kaka Shilanga . . . Kum Adem Nde . . .*"

The sound nearly made him clap his hands in rhythm to the song, reminding him of the game they had played. His first name was Kofi, just like in the song, from his mother's homeland. But he had used his middle name since first grade because other kids called him Coffee and tried to pick fights. It was like a stranger's name. He preferred to be All-American David, like his father.

"*Kye Kye Kule . . .*"

When Davie felt a cold fingertip against his ear, he jumped up with a gasp.

He wasn't sleeping! A shadow sat beside him on the bed, washed in darkness. Davie's heart thumped. He opened his mouth to yell, but the shadow planted a firm palm across his lips.

"Don't be loud. You'll wake your sister," his mother said.

Only Mommy! He smelled the smoky scent of her shea butter as she flicked on his light. She was wearing her "home clothes," as she called them; green and gold and red and blue woven into her dress from Ghana. Davie looked at his Transformers clock radio, confused. Four AM.

"I thought you left," he said.

"I'm leaving now. One last goodbye," she said, and kissed his forehead. Davie thought he saw tears shimmering, but Mommy was always emotional about trips and airplanes. She thought it was every airplane's destiny to crash from the sky, and the pilots had to fight for their lives the whole way. For months, she had talked about nothing but her visit to Ghana to see her family, and now she seemed sad to be leaving. "I'll pack you in my bag, I think."

"You'll be back soon, Mommy," I said.

Mommy didn't answer, except to sigh. Suddenly, Davie was *sure* he saw tears.

"Saida?" Dad called from the hallway, his voice hushed in the dark. "Van's here."

Davie was glad Mommy had lost the argument, but he felt sorry for her. She wanted to take them all to Ghana with her, but this was time to go to Grandma and Grandpa Walter's in Graceville, Florida. The summer trip had been planned since Christmas, but Mommy wanted them to go with her instead. Mommy had said they should take a vote, and Davie had felt guilty raising his hand to choose Dad's parents over hers. Of course, Neema raised her hand to side with him too, because she mimicked his every movement.

Graceville won, even though their older sister, Imani, had refused to vote because she was going away to Northwestern for the summer anyway. The relief Davie felt only had a little bit to do with the farmer in Graceville who let them ride his tractor and horses whenever they wanted to, or Grandma's fried chicken and sweet potato pie. Mommy and Dad knew exactly why he and Neema wanted to go to Graceville instead.

It was never the same at Christmas. The best time to go was in summer.

"Hope you see your ghosts," Mommy said, and kissed his forehead. She was smiling; a sad, empty smile, but still a smile. Mommy's smile made Davie's heart leap. Maybe she wasn't mad about his vote against her, or how he had led Neema to his side. The injured look on her face when he'd raised his hand had pierced him in a strange new way, as if she was his child—and he a parent who had made a terrible, unthinkable choice.

"I'll get video this time," Davie said. "Proof. You'll see."

Mommy made a *tssk* sound. "You think I never saw ghosts? In my village, they lived in the acacia trees. They sang us to sleep! We never saw it as a special thing. Not like you. Take care of your sister. I'll miss you, Kofi."

"I'll miss you too, Mommy."

Her hug lasted so long that Dad called for her twice more. The last time, he came to the doorway and stood there as if to block her way. "You'll be late. Come on." His voice was clipped, like he was mad. But he was only tired. That was what Davie told himself then.

It would be a month and two days before he would see Mommy again. He had never been away from her so long, so he didn't move from her arms even after Dad huffed out an annoyed sigh. More than annoyed, actually. Later, Davie would wonder why he hadn't realized right then that something was very, very wrong.

He'd known, maybe, but he hadn't wanted to.

That summer wasn't going to be like the rest. Not one tiny little bit.

Davie heard the shuttle drive off beneath his window, taking his mother far away from them. But as he tried to go back to sleep, twisting and turning beneath his sheets until they bound his legs, ghosts were the only thing on Davie's mind.

The weeks in summer usually fly by, but the two days before they would leave Los Angeles for Florida passed as slowly as the last two days of school. The day of the trip passed even more slowly. First, the flight itself was endless. One plane to Atlanta took forever, landing at the airport that was more like a city, with a transit system and far-flung terminals. The next plane was so teeny that they climbed up metal stairs from the tarmac in the rain, and Dad had to stow his computer case because the attendants said there wouldn't be room.

Neema, of course, complained the whole way. She always complained more when Mommy wasn't around, because Dad would cluck and tug her braids gently and try to make her smile as if she was still a baby instead of eight already. She really played it up when Mom was gone, carrying around her brown-skinned Raggedy Ann doll and batting her eyelashes. Pathetic.

Maybe Mommy is right about planes, Davie thought when the second plane landed with a terrible shaking and squealing. But then they were on the ground and everyone clapped with relief, and Mommy's fears seemed silly again.

Not *Mommy*, he reminded himself. He was twelve years old now. He was going to middle school in the fall, and he'd heard enough nightmarish stories about middle school to know that if any of the other kids heard him call his mother Mommy, he'd come home with a bloody nose every day. He'd already seen evidence of it: A hard glare from a teenager watching him play with Neema on the playground equipment at the McDonald's Playland had been Davie's first hint that the Punk Police were watching him now. He wasn't a kid anymore; he was a target. His mother was *Mom* now. Nothing so hard about that. Like Dad told him, she would keep him a baby forever if it were up to her. He had to be stronger than that.

As if in confirmation, when the plane rocked to a halt Dad patted Davie's knee the way he patted his business partner's knee when he came over for dinner. (His father was a movie producer, except not the rich kind.) That pat made Davie feel grown, even important.

"Well . . . we're here now," Dad said. He didn't look happy the way he usually did when he visited his parents. He said it as if flying to Tallahassee to drive to Graceville was like being flown to the moon against their will, held prisoner for ransom by space pirates camping on moon rocks. Dad sounded like he wished he could go anywhere else.

There was no rain during the long drive past acres of thin, scraggly pine trees on I-10 west of Tallahassee, and Davie was disappointed to realize how much daylight was left even after such a long trip. Maybe two whole hours. He was ready to go to bed right now, even if it was only two o'clock in Los Angeles, not even time for *SpongeBob*. He was a little old for *SpongeBob*, but it was better than CNN.

But the ghosts never came until after dark. And to Davie, the ghosts were the point of visiting Grandma and Grandpa Walter in Graceville during the summer.

The ghosts were why he put up with having to share a room with Neema, and the excruciating fact that Grandpa Walter and Grandma only had a huge old satellite dish, and every time they came to visit the number of channels had shrunk because all the networks were bailing to cable and DishNet or DirecTV or something invented in this millennium, so unless he was going to watch CNN or the History Channel or Lifetime—*get real!*—there was hardly anything on

TV all summer long. And ghosts were definitely the reason he put up with mosquito-infested, broiling North Florida in the middle of hurricane season—yes, sometimes it rained every day—instead of just holding out for Christmastime.

In summer, it was *all* about the ghosts.

Large trucks carried away load after load of fallen pine trees, but the woods were still thick. *You see how they're cutting it all down?* Grandma always said on her way to this or that meeting to try to stop a new construction project. But while Graceville had a shortage of virtually everything else—particularly in the movie theater department—there was no visible shortage of trees whatsoever. *Welcome to Graceville—We've Got Trees!*

Grandma and Grandpa Walter had lived in Miami most of his life, but they had retired to Graceville four years ago, on six acres of land shaped like a slice of pie—well, not a perfect piece, but it tapered to nothing at the V at the far fence. The single-story house was fenced in and set back from a two-lane road where traffic raced past on its way to more interesting places.

It didn't look anything like Davie would have imagined a haunted house should look—old and decrepit, or with an interesting feature like a balcony, or at least a verandah. Graceville was full of plantation-style houses that looked like a reminder of the slavery Davie had seen with his own eyes when Dad showed him *Roots*, but Grandma and Grandpa Walter's house looked like they had ordered it over the Internet from Houses-R-Us. Just like any other house, except painted bright peach, a splash of Miami in the middle of the woods.

Grandma and Grandpa Walter were waiting for them in the yard when they drove up. The gravel driveway was a million miles long, so his grandparents needed plenty of notice to walk down to unlock the gate. Locking the gate was a Miami habit Grandma never gave up. Sometimes Grandpa Walter drove his car instead of walking because of his arthritis.

When Davie and his sister got out of the rental car, his grandparents fussed over them as if they'd been gone half a lifetime, like they always did. Tight hugs from Grandma. Playful punches from Grandpa Walter, who liked to remind Davie that he used to box when he was in the army in the 1950s. Promises of special outings and homemade sweets.

But it was different this time, too. Usually Dad just stood in the background and grinned, watching his parents. Davie's father had told him that when he was a kid, a psychic at a booth at a county fair told him that his parents would die when he was young—and he'd lived in fear of losing them since. Dad had never expected Grandma and Grandpa Walter to see him grow up, or to know his children. Dad said he finally figured out that the psychic wanted to scare him.

"But why would a psychic want to scare a little kid like that?" Davie had asked.

Dad had looked at him like it was the dumbest question in the world. "That was in 1976, Davie," Dad said. He waited a moment, as if the answer was hidden in the year, a code. Davie's blank face made him sigh. "Racist, that's all. What do you think?"

Dad's explanation for everything.

This time, Dad went straight to Grandma and hugged her almost as if he was too tired to stand, and she hugged him back with her eyes closed tight. *Did somebody die?* Davie thought.

The moment didn't last long—and Neema didn't even notice, because Grandpa was distracting her by pointing out a woodpecker in the oak tree—but Davie saw. Watching, Davie remembered that Dad hadn't always been a grown man. He'd been a little boy once, just like him, and he looked like a boy again, clinging to his mother in a way he always warned Davie not to cling to Mommy. *Mom.* Their faces captivated Davie, full of weary pain. Davie hadn't seen either of them look that tired before.

Then Grandpa Walter came over to pat Dad's shoulder, two solid taps, and the moment passed. Dad pulled away from his mother, and she turned her face toward the house, but not before Davie saw her wipe her eye.

Yep. Someone must have kicked the bucket. *Another one bites the dust*, he thought.

"Let's get the bags in," Grandpa said, even though Davie knew he couldn't lift heavy bags anymore because his joints hurt. He'd said it so Dad and Grandma would erase that hurting from their faces before Davie and Neema could see. Sometimes Davie wondered if he was psychic, too—a *real* psychic, not a county fair jerk who tried to scare little kids and maybe, just *maybe*, was a little bit racist. Davie could see things he couldn't see before.

Neema was in full whine, telling Grandma she wanted a nap, not even getting excited when they told her she would have *her own room* this time, and Davie couldn't bring himself to go inside yet to hear her complaining like a princess. There was a little sunlight left, and there was nothing to watch in the house, nothing to do. Not until after dark, anyway.

"Can I play outside?" Davie asked his father, an inspiration. They were in the foyer, walking carefully on the long rug so they wouldn't scratch Grandma's wood floor. There were a lot of rules in his grandparents' house, and sometimes it was easier just to sit and do nothing.

But outside! Outside was a whole different universe.

"Just watch for snakes," Grandma said. "And stay in the gate."

"Don't be silly, Mom," Dad said. "He's twelve now. Just don't go too far, Davie."

"Yessir."

Grandpa Walter always smiled when he called Dad "sir," so it was the quickest way to make sure Grandpa stayed in a good mood.

". . . the way those drivers race past that fence," Grandma was saying, but the front door closed behind Davie and he flew down the steps, momentarily saved from having to answer yet more questions about how school was going.

If he was lucky, Ricardo might be around. Ricardo was a Mexican kid he met at Christmas, whose parents were migrants. Ricardo said he never stayed one place long, but he might get lucky. Or he could hang out with the Reed kids at the end of the street. The Reed twins were two years younger and obnoxious rednecks, but their older brother had Rock Band for PlayStation 3, so they were the most valuable friends Davie had, period. Rock Band was simply the coolest game ever invented, bar none.

The dirt in the area where his grandparents lived was called "red," but to Davie it looked more like a deep shade of orange. It was still called "Georgia clay," even though the Georgia border was a half hour's drive—which Davie knew because the closest movie theater was in Bainbridge, Georgia, not to mention the awesome Golden Corral buffet. The dirt didn't care which side of the border it was on, Georgia or Florida. The orange dirt was everywhere, right beneath the grass.

The orange dirt and gravel path ran through the center of the yard, presenting Davie with a clear choice—the gate and the road were on one side of the path, and the fence and the woods were on the other. Davie noticed that Grandpa still hadn't repaired the broken logs in one section of the ranch-style fence that separated his property from the woods. The same fence had been broken six months before. Tell-tale hoof prints gathered around Grandma's fake deer near the driveway were evidence that woodland creatures were trespassing at night. *Dumb-butts can't tell the difference between what's real and what's not*, Davie thought.

Decision time: Hunting for snakes in the woods, or Rock Band?

Davie was about to take the path down to the road and head for the Reed house when he saw something move in the woods, beyond the broken fence. He heard dead leaves marking footsteps as it ran away, fast. Whatever it was, it was big. A deer? Another kid playing?

Davie's decision was made. He searched the castoffs from his grandparents' own personal forest of pine and oak trees until he found a sturdy dead branch as his walking stick. The stick was almost as tall as he was, and Davie liked the way it fit in his hand. He stripped away the smaller branches until it looked more like Mad-Eye Moody's staff from *Harry Potter*. He tapped the thick stick on the ground to make sure it would hold instead of rotting at the center. Satisfied, he headed into the woods.

Davie leaned on his stick for support when he climbed over the broken fence.

The woods behind his grandparents' house weren't shady like the woods in movies. Most of the trees had thin trunks and not much shade to spare, but they were growing as far as he could see. While it might not be much to look at, Davie knew there were snakes, because Grandpa had told him he killed a rattler in the driveway only two weeks before. At the very least, he would probably go home with a story to tell.

Davie liked running in the underbrush, with obstacles every which way and snap decisions to be made. There—jump on the stone! There—watch out for the hole! There were stumbles now and then, mostly just harmless scrapes. Acts of coordination and fearlessness were necessary for any ghost-hunter. Most ghosts were friendly, but how lame would it be to leave himself helpless if he met a hostile? Plan B was filed under R for Run.

Davie didn't have to run far. He'd gone only about thirty yards when he saw three boys huddled in a circle in a clearing. None of them were wearing shirts, only ragged-looking shorts of varying lengths. The three of them looked like brothers, each one younger than the next. The eldest could be Davie's age.

Davie's feet made a racket crackling in the dead leaves, but none of the boys turned around to look at him. When the boys held hands, Davie understood why: They were praying over a huge hole someone had dug in the ground. As he got closer, Davie saw a large German shepherd sleeping beside the hole.

Not SLEEPING, crap-for-brains, Davie told himself. The big dog was dead. Its face and muzzle were matted with orange-brown mud.

He'd interrupted a funeral! Davie backed up a step and halfway hid himself behind a rare wide-trunked tree of pale, peeling bark, thin as paper. Davie had never had a dog—Mom thought keeping a dog inside the house was a disgrace, as did her whole family in Ghana, where dogs apparently were not considered man's best friend by a long shot—but he understood how sad it was when a pet died. He'd had a rat once, Roddy, like in the movie *Flushed Away*.

Roddy was an awesome rat. Lay across Davie's shoulder while he walked around, no problem. Rats were as smart as dogs, people said, but rats definitely got screwed in the life-span department. His rat had lived only two years. When Roddy died, Davie had cried himself to sleep for two nights, and hadn't wanted a pet of any kind ever since. He, Dad, Mom, and Neema had buried Roddy in the backyard, just like these boys.

But Roddy's hole in the ground hadn't been nearly so big, like a tunnel. The mountain of Georgia clay dirt beside the hole was as tall as the oldest boy. Someone had done some serious digging, Davie realized. Maybe their dad helped, or someone with a jack. It would have taken him all day to dig a hole like that. Or longer. Davie noticed that all of the boys were caked in red clay dust just as the setting sun intensified in a bright red-orange burst the color of a mango, turning the boys into shadowed silhouettes. Watching their vigil, Davie made up an epitaph: *Here lies Smoky, a Hell of a Dog / Crossed McCormack Road in the Midnight Fog—*

Suddenly, the youngest boy turned and stared him in the eye, whipping his head around so fast that Davie's rhyme left his mind. The boy was standing only ten yards from him, but his eyes were his most visible feature. The whites were, anyway. That was all Davie could see, a white-eyed stare, vivid against dark skin.

"Sorry about your dog," Davie said. No need to be rude. The oldest boy looked about twelve, too. Maybe he knew somewhere to play basketball. This clan could be a valuable find.

None of the others looked at Davie. The youngest, who looked Neema's age, turned away again.

It seemed best to leave them alone. Davie had never been to a funeral, thank goodness—Mom couldn't afford to bring him and Neema when her father in Ghana died, so she and Imani went alone—but he figured funerals weren't a good place to make friends. If the boys lived nearby, he'd find them later. If not, whatever. Kids in Graceville weren't always nice to him, as if he didn't meet their standards. He talked funny and liked weird things, from a Graceville point of view, so he never knew what kind of reception to expect.

Davie left and turned for home, digging his stick into pockets of soft soil as he walked. He didn't run, this time. It was getting dark, harder to see, and there was no reason to take a chance on breaking his leg. It would be ghost time soon.

Davie didn't realize how relieved he was to leave the woods until he saw the welcoming broken fence in the shadow of his grandparents' huge oak tree, which was covered in moss like Silly String. Home! The underbrush had seemed unruly, and he was glad to find his shoes back on neatly cropped grass. He felt a strange wriggling sensation in his stomach. Until he climbed back over the fence, he hadn't let himself notice he was a little scared. Just a little.

But the real scare didn't come until he got to the house.

Davie decided to go to the back door instead of the front because his shoes might be muddy, and Grandma would have a fit if he tracked dirt on her hardwood floors. As he was climbing the concrete steps to the back door, he glimpsed through the kitchen window.

What he saw there made his stomach drop out of him.

Grandpa Walter stood by the fridge, arms crossed and head hanging; he might have been studying his shoes, except that his eyes were closed. Grandma was clearing away dishes from the table, where Dad was sitting alone. Muted through the window, Davie heard Grandma saying, ". . . It's all right, baby. It's all gonna work out. No court in the country will let her take them all the way over there, I don't care if she's the mother or not. What's she gonna do, steal them? If she wants a fight, well, she's got one. We have money put away. You'll get a good lawyer, and that's that. Don't you worry."

His father sat at the table, forehead resting against the tabletop, his arms wrapped around his ears. His father was crying.

All night, Davie lay in bed trying to unhear and unsee it. Every time he saw the snapshot of that kitchen window, remembering Grandma's words and Dad's grieving pose, his stomach ate him. Now he knew what people meant when they said Too Much Information: It wasn't about stuff being too gross, or none of your business. Some information was too big for a single brain. Each time

Davie remembered what he'd seen and heard, the enormity grew exponentially, with new and more terrible realizations.

His parents were definitely getting a divorce. Check. Hadn't seen *that* coming, since they never argued or raised their voices in front of him. They snapped at each other sometimes, but who didn't? Okay, so Mom thought Dad worked too much. She'd never made that a secret. And Dad definitely liked spending time alone. There was no denying it. And Mom's bad moods probably got on his nerves. So now, after twenty years, they were getting a divorce?

Divorce. That nuclear bomb should have been enough for one night—hell, one *lifetime*—but there was layer after layer, and it unspooled slowly as Davie stared at his grandparents' popcorn-textured ceiling, seeing only visions of the kitchen window.

As if the D-word wasn't enough, Mom wanted to take them to Ghana. Dad didn't want them to go. Grandma and Grandpa were Dad's war-chiefs, and they were about to go to war. Against Mommy. And Mommy against Daddy, Grandma and Grandpa. And no matter what happened, he and Neema and Imani were FUBAR. Effed Up Beyond All Recogition.

The only tiny morsel of comfort Davie could take from The Worst Moment of His Entire Life was the knowledge that Grandpa Walter, Grandma and—*Thank you, God*—Dad himself had not seen him at the window. He'd had the good sense to duck away before a wandering pair of eyes found him and waved him inside to take his seat at the Oh-Crap table.

"Davie, we're glad you finally know the truth . . . You'll need you to be a man now . . ."

The very thought of that conversation with Dad made Davie want to vomit. He kept his palm clamped across his mouth, just in case of a surprise puke attack. He felt it in his throat.

As long as he ignored their sad eyes, went on with his life and pretended he hadn't heard, they would have to keep pretending, too. All of them would be putting on a show for each other, like a reality TV show called *FUBAR,* but at least then Neema wouldn't find out. Or Imani, who couldn't possibly know, because she'd been in *way* too good a mood when she left for Evanston, Illinois, to meet her future as an incoming freshman in a minority summer program.

Let them have their lives a while longer, anyway. For the summer, anyway.

Ignorance was the only mercy he could still show them. He only wished his father had his S-H-I-T together and could have kept him out of the loop a little longer, too. How the hell would he get through the next month?

Davie was on the verge of crying himself to sleep the way he had after Roddy the rat died, but his unborn sob caught in his throat when he heard the footsteps padding against the hallway floorboards.

He thought he'd imagined it, so he sat up and didn't move, not even to get his flashlight. His ears were his most important tool: He listened.

Click-click-click. This time, he heard not only the footsteps, but clicking nails. Like a dog's paws. A heavy dog—about the size of the big German shepherd.

Davie had accidentally been holding his breath, and he needed to breathe. He took a long gasp of air, louder than he'd meant to, and stopped breathing again.

The dog's feet padded closer to his closed bedroom door. Davie stared toward the crack between the door and the frame in the moonlight, and he saw a shadow cross from one side to the other. About the size of a dog's nose.

Sffffff sfff ffffff. Sniffing at the door.

"Holy effing S-H-I-T," Davie said, but only after the sniffing noise stopped and the sound of footsteps had padded away to silence.

Davie's plan was to lie absolutely still and do everything in his power to convince the dog that there was no reason to try to get into his room. Good dog, bad dog, whatever, Davie didn't want a ghost encounter with a dog. His central plan in case of a hostile entity—Communication and Negotiation—wasn't worth crapola with a dog.

The first ghost he met up close should definitely be human.

But the ghosts were tracking *him* already.

The next morning, Neema was gone.

He heard her chattering to herself in her room through her closed door when he came to tell her breakfast was ready. Grandma had a thing about eating breakfast before nine, so there was no sleeping in at Grandma's house, not if you wanted to eat.

". . . And this one . . . and this one . . . and *this* one . . ." Neema was saying, probably for no particular reason. The eight-year-old girl's brain was truly the nonsense wonder of the world.

He knocked on her door twice. "Breakfast."

". . . and thi—"

Neema went completely silent, in mid-word. When Davie opened her door, the bed was empty. The covers were turned back as if she'd just gotten up, and Neema's Raggedy Ann doll lay in her place, her wild black thread pigtails fanned across the pillow. The doll's face was painted with a deformed triangle nose and a mental patient's smile. To Davie, dolls went from looking ridiculous to sinister in a blink. Davie took note: Weird.

"Neema?" he said.

Neema's room had been Grandma's doll room until this summer, since Grandma decided Davie was too old to share a room with her. Finally! Grandma had cleared out only enough space for the bed and a small desk. Other than that, the room was filled with shelf after shelf of brown and black and white dolls, most of them babies dressed like it was baptism day, frozen in infancy. There were dozens of sets of little eyes in the room—none of them Neema's.

Davie waited for her giggle, or a surprise lunge from behind, or a rustle as she tried to hide. Neema sucked at hide-and-seek.

Nothing. An empty bed. An empty room with too many dolls.

Definitely weird.

"Neema, you're not funny. Breakfast," he said. He glanced inside the open closet door, which was full of nothing but boxed dolls, collector's items, except for Neema's one Sunday dress and a wicker hamper with its lid piled with folded clothes.

Under her bed, Davie found nothing but dust.

The window was halfway open, Davie noticed, raised at least eight inches. Ten, maybe. Could a girl Neema's size have squeezed out of so small a space?

Davie ran to the window to peer outside. Neema's room overlooked the backyard, so he saw the bed of dried pine needles and pine cones that lay scattered across the grass. This side of the house was closer to the woods than the living room, shaded by the taller nearby trees.

The broken fence was only twenty strides from Neema's window. The fence mesmerized Davie, as if it were a key to a puzzle. Neema had been here one second, and now she was gone. But why the hell would Neema climb out of a window to go the woods? Since when? *Wouldn't.*

But this room was too small to hide in.

Davie scanned the doll shelves, almost expecting to find her there, as if she could have shrunk herself down to doll size. Row after row of unblinking brown, blue, and green eyes gazed back. And little taunting pink-lipped smiles.

"Neema, quit playing," he said, poking at her bedcovers to make sure she hadn't disguised her bulk somehow. The bed was empty.

Davie picked up Raggedy Ann—who truly *was* raggedy, since she'd belonged to their Aunt Evie when she was a little girl, special-made by a black dollmaker—and even looked under Neema's pillow, for no particular reason. "I mean it. Dang, you're such a baby."

Steely, eerie silence.

But I heard her. It was Neema. She was saying "And this one and this one . . ."

Just in case some law of physics or the space-time continuum had been violated, Davie checked the bathroom across the hall, too. And his own room. No Neema. There was always the front of the house, but how could she have gotten past him? No way.

You were standing right here in front of her door. YOU HEARD HER VOICE.

For the first time, Davie realized that the tears he thought he'd fought off right before he heard the ghost dog hadn't been banished very far. They were still there, just beneath his eyeballs, waiting for the slightest reason to peek out. Neema being gone made him want to cry.

How could he tell Dad?

"Please, Neema?" he said to her empty room, his voice small.

That did it—his appeal to her charity. Conceding his helplessness.

The closet rustled, and the lid to the clothes hamper opened, revealing Neema's round face inside. She grinned. "I tricked you! I kept the clothes on top."

Davie was so relieved to see her that he couldn't get as mad as he wanted to be. "Good one. Seriously," he said, and helped her climb out. "I'll get you back, though."

"Not-uh."

"You wish, freak-girl."

Just like that, life was normal again. Now there would be no exhaustive explanations ("*See, this ghost dog was here, and I think he dragged Neema into another realm . . .*"), no looks of disappointment, and then concern, and then yawning horror.

Reality check.

Yeah, the divorce would be bad. But not as bad as losing Neema.

In daylight, armed with his new glass-half-full outlook, Davie couldn't believe his luck: A ghost encounter his very first night! This house was like a river brimming with catfish. If he hadn't chickened out, he might have followed that dog to God-knew-what ghost rally, chock full of chances to capture the manifestation on video and audio for YouTube.

In daylight, Davie chastised himself for his loss of faith in the power of communication. If he could say, "I don't want to hurt you" to a human ghost, then "Good boy, good boy" should do for a dog. He'd let himself fall prey to species bigotry, and he'd lain there like a lump while his chance at ghost-hunting stardom had trotted down the hall.

He'd need to man up by nightfall. He was so determined that he walked to the Handi Mart at the corner and paid way too much for a bag of dog biscuits, just to be on the safe side.

"Yes, I'm sure it was a dog," he told Neema in his room while he made his preparations, when she demanded the full story of why he had dog biscuits alongside his ghost-hunting supplies out on his bed.

"How do you know?"

"Because I saw some kids bury a dog yesterday. Right outside the back fence."

He hoped he hadn't blown Neema's mind badly enough to give her nightmares.

"*Cool!*" she said. "I wanna see the dog too!"

"*Shhhhhh,*" he shushed her. That was the main problem with Neema: She couldn't keep quiet. With Neema tagging along, living room recon was a nightmare. She could wake up an entire house without trying. Between that and her inability to sit still longer than five minutes, Neema was pretty much useless. Stealth and patience were the only two qualities that mattered in ghost-tracking. So far, at least, his baby sister had neither.

But if she was going to get trained, he had to train her now.

Imani said she heard the ghosts the first year she came to the Graceville house in summer, but not after she was thirteen. She said it was as if the channel had changed, or she'd unplugged somehow. Grandma and Grandpa said they never noticed noises either except for occasional creaking, just like Mom and Dad. Maybe only kids could really hear the ghosts.

This might be his last chance. After this summer, Neema would be on her own.

"You have to take a nap so you won't be tired tonight, 'cuz we're gonna be up late," he said. "If I hear any whining—and I mean *any* whining about *anything*—I'm gonna go back to bed and do it alone some night when you're sleeping."

"No you won't. I'll stay awake every night too."

"I mean it, Neema. Either it's my rules or you don't play."

That shut her up quick. He didn't often have leverage over Neema, but he had big-time leverage now. She'd been begging him to let her track with him since she was three. Her face was longer every year, more like Mom's, and the thin cornrows Mom had slaved over for hours before she left still looked fresh and flawless on Neema's scalp, the ends anchored by a swarm of white barrettes shaped like tiny butterflies. She looked like a princess too.

"Why's Daddy sad?" Neema said. Changing the subject was her specialty.

He decided on the *nothing's-wrong-here* approach. "He's sad?"

She nodded, certain. "Yeah."

"I guess he misses Mommy."

"Yeah, me too," Neema said. Dad's sadness was contagious.

"We'll see her soon."

"Not-uh," she said. "A month's not soon. A month is a long time."

Neema often sounded certain of herself, but never more than now. She understood there was significance to it. She knew that Mom's time away meant something.

It might be harder to keep the secret than he'd thought.

At six o'clock, just when Davie thought he would lose his mind waiting for the sun to go down, Grandma excused herself from the Game of Life board game they were playing. She had a meeting, she said. The community was trying to stop another construction project. The "community" was busy.

"Why don't you want more houses, Grandma?" Neema said.

Davie wanted to kick her under the dining table. *Now* they were in for a whole tutorial on infrastructure and sewer lines. But instead, Grandma sighed and glanced at Dad, who shrugged. Dad barely listened to any of them; his conversations were in his head.

Grandma fixed her hair net, looking into an egg-shaped mirror on the wall. "I wasn't gonna say anything to you kids—but there's bodies buried over on that land across the street, out beyond Tobacco Road. McCormack's land. They found an old burial site, the bones of people who lived 'round here a hundred years ago. And not a cemetery neither—this has been McCormack land for generations. But the university folks say they were black. Nobody knows how many bones there are, or how far they're spread out . . . so if they keep building up these houses, we'll never learn the full story about who they were, or how many people died."

It was the coolest thing Grandma had ever said. Davie was captivated.

Grandpa Walter spoke up, half-limping from the kitchen. His joints hurt worse at night. "If it was Indians, see, there's special laws about that. It's a burial ground, so it's sacred. But not for *us*. Nothing that's got to do with *us* is sacred."

"Our family?" Neema asked. She hadn't figured out yet that whenever Dad and Grandpa said "us," they meant "black people."

"Everybody wants it buried," Grandma went on. "So I'm going to a meeting to try to stop the people from building more houses on top of the bones. In case there are more."

Neema looked at Davie with wide, gleeful eyes. Even Neema knew that the fresh unearthing of bones meant heightened ghost activity. What luck!

"How many skeletons did they find?" Davie said.

"Twelve," Grandma said.

"So far," Grandpa added. "Could've been a slaughter, like Rosewood. Hundreds of people hunted down like animals, a whole town."

Dad looked up at his parents, as if he'd just noticed the turn of conversation. "Thanks a whole hell of a lot. This is a great goddamn topic for my *eight-year-old*." He nearly roared Neema's age, and Neema jumped as if he was yelling at her. It was the maddest Davie had ever heard his father. Cussing at his parents! And blasphemy too, which Grandma couldn't stand.

Davie thought better of his next question, which was going to be: *Were there any dogs?*

Instead, they all stopped talking about the bodies. Grandma went to her meeting, and Grandpa kept coaxing Neema to spin the wheel and help him read the cards while Davie and his father only pretended to play the board game. (More like a *bored* game, Davie told himself.) He and Dad were both happy to miss their turns if they were forgotten. The Game of Life was not the product as advertised.

Bedtime was a relief beyond words.

Thanks to a consistent campaign at every birthday and holiday, Davie had decent ghost-hunting gear. No EMF or motion detectors yet—but he had a lantern-style flashlight, an old 8mm video camera with Night Vision (a hand-me-down from Dad), a mini-cassette recorder he wore around his neck, and the digital camera his mother had given him for Kwanzaa. He kept it all inside his old army-green knapsack, alongside the extras: protein bars, water bottle (Mountain Dew would spray him, alas), a small notebook. And now, dog biscuits.

Be Prepared, the Boy Scouts said.

Waiting for Grandma and Grandpa to go to bed was always a breeze—they were down by nine-thirty, tops. Dad was the problem, usually. Dad liked to stay up late on his computer or watching TV, but on this trip Dad was sleeping late and going to bed early, with naps in between. His laptop hadn't come out of its case once. "Are you sick, Daddy?" Neema had asked him after dinner. Dad hadn't even heard her.

Waiting for quiet was the hardest part. No TVs, no bathroom breaks, no refrigerator raids. Pure, uninterrupted quiet. Davie called it the Golden Hour, and it came at a different time every night. That night, the Golden Hour was ten-thirty. Quiet.

Davie leaped out of bed, unplugged his video camera (a dead video camera battery would be the difference between fame and obscurity), and strapped his ghost kit across his shoulder. Then he crossed the hall to Neema's room.

Neema's Raggedy Ann doll was propped up against Neema's closed door. The doll didn't look like it had been lain there gently, as Grandma would; Raggedy Ann looked thrown against the door, head lolling, legs akimbo. Her black-thread hair was wild, pulled out of its ponytails, or braids, or whatever she used to have. For the first time, Davie noticed the doll's faded red gingham dress, a relic. The doll looked a hundred years old, not just from the '70s.

What did girls *see* in dolls? After scooping up the doll, Davie opened Neema's door.

Neema was sitting at the foot of her bed, waiting for him. Still as a doll herself.

"What are you doing to her?" She said it as if Raggedy Ann was real.

He chuckled. "I'm not doing anything to your dumb doll." To put the doll in its place, he tossed Raggedy Ann to Neema, who caught the doll midair and clicked her teeth, irritated.

"Stop! Then why'd you take it?" Neema said.

"I have more important things to think about. It was outside the door, Brainiac."

"Liar."

"Whatever. Let's go."

Neema didn't get up. Instead, she hugged the Raggedy Ann to her chest, gazing across the room at the doll shelf. "I don't like all the dolls in here. It's like they're looking at me."

Davie glanced at the dolls' unblinking rows of eyes, and they gave him the creeps, too. But this wasn't the time to worry about a bunch of old dolls.

"If you're a scaredy-cat, stay in here," Davie said. "Ghosts aren't for scaredy-cats."

"I'm not a scaredy-cat."

"Then come on. And *no noise.*"

Davie had recorded ghost activity all over his grandparents' house: A salt shaker that fell down on the kitchen table by itself, a faucet dripping backward in the bathroom (hard to prove, but he had seen it), and the egg-shaped mirror skewed slightly to one side in the foyer. (Grandpa, seeing Davie's footage, had just said, "So the mirror's crooked—so what?")

But the living room was Davie's favorite place to camp. The living room was his grandparents' museum, the place for their old black-and-white photographs, old books, old paintings on the wall, old everything. Even the furniture had been in Grandma's family forever, shaky antique legs and upholstery that smelled like a dark closet. Ghosts liked the old and familiar. The living room was definitely the first place *he* would go.

"What now?" Neema whispered. She couldn't keep quiet to save her life.

"*Shhhh.* We camp out and we wait."

"I'm thirsty."

Davie closed his eyes and counted to five. Dad's trick to keep from getting too mad.

"Davie? I'm thirsty."

He reached inside his ghost kit and pulled out the water bottle. "Don't spill it on the wood, or Grandma'll freak out. Now just sit and be still. They won't come unless it's quiet."

Bringing Neema was a mistake, he decided. Fine: They'd camp out in the living room for an hour, she'd mess it up with her complaining and whining, and he'd go to bed. Tomorrow, he'd wait until she was sleep for sure. Tomorrow, he'd wait until midnight if he had to.

But Neema surprised Davie. After he chose their ideal camping spot behind Grandpa's recliner, right near the bookshelf full of musty-smelling books, Neema sat as still as a doll herself. Sometimes she hummed a little, but she caught herself and covered her mouth. Like him, she just stared into the darkness and cupped her ear to listen. Davie couldn't believe how much older Neema seemed since last summer, or even Christmas.

He'd tried ghost-tracking at Christmastime, but nothing happened, of course. Ghosts only came in summer.

It was amazing how much noise even a quiet house could produce. When he was younger, Davie used to think he heard ghosts in every creak of the ceiling, every whir of the central air-conditioning, and every cyclic hum from the refrigerator. He used to jump when the automatic sprinklers went on outside and sprayed the windows with water.

Now, of course, Davie was an expert listener. And since he'd already heard a ghost the night before, he knew what he was listening for: click-click-click. The dog's paws. He kept a dog biscuit in his hand, a ready peace offering. The sweat on his palm was making it gummy.

They sat and listened for a solid hour. No clicking.

Beside him, Neema was nodding to sleep with her head against the recliner. *Just as well,* Davie thought. With Neema asleep, he could wait another hour, no problem. After that, he'd take her back to bed.

Davie felt a cramp from sitting in the same position with his hip bone against the hard floor, so he shifted until he was sitting Indian-style. When he did, he felt something wet seep into the seat of his pajama pants. Wet and *cold.*

He touched his pajama pants, and they were soaked. His hand splashed into a shallow puddle of cold liquid. "*Hey,*" he said, nudging Neema. "You spilled your water."

Neema blinked her eyes open, alert, and held up her half-empty water bottle, tightly capped. The light through the window allowed him to see her in the moonlight. "Not-uh," she said. "The top's on."

But before Neema had said a word, Davie realized the water couldn't have come from Neema's water bottle. No way had Neema's water been this cold. And there was too much. Water was all around them.

"Crap-o-la," Davie whispered, and rushed to take off his pajama top. He started wiping the floor as fast as he could, because Grandma would have a serious meltdown if her floor got spotted with water. Who else would she blame but him?

Davie's pajama top soaked through as soon as it touched the floor. Davie suddenly saw a shimmering sheen of water across the entire living room, from the foyer all the way to the kitchen, all the way toward the back hall. *The floor was completely covered in water!*

A scent had been faint at first, but now he realized it filled up the entire room. The living room smelled like the water in the fish-tank where his third-grade teacher, Miss Richmond, kept the class's frogs and turtles. Sour. Like old, rotting plants and leaves.

Neema was sleepy, but she was getting the picture too. "My clothes are *wet*—" she said, raising her voice, but Davie clamped her mouth quiet.

"*Shhhhh*," he said. His heart was a jackhammer in his chest. "Ghosts, Neema. Ghosts."

"In the water?"

"Yes," Davie said, because he didn't have time to explain. The ghost *was* the water—that was why it was so cold. The water was real, but it wasn't. He hoped not, anyway, because it was getting deeper. Maybe an inch deep already.

Davie pulled Neema to her feet, and he stood at a crouch, pulling his ghost kit higher so it wouldn't get wet. The dog biscuit fell out of his hand, forgotten, as he flipped his tape recorder to ON and opened the video camera's eye. He switched on Night Vision.

Through the viewfinder, the room was almost too bright. The moonlight exaggerated the gleam in the mirror on the wall and the screen on the TV, washing them in whiteness. His hand slightly unsteady, Davie lowered the camera toward the floor. Toward the water.

SPLASH

He saw bands of ripples, as if he'd tossed a handful of pebbles into the water.

Neema made a whimpering sound, clinging to Davie's hand. Without moving the camera, he turned his head to look at her, and Neema's wide, delighted eyes met his.

Did You Hear That? Neema mouthed.

Davie nodded, grinning. Neema grinned back.

If Neema had been scared, or crying, he would have whisked her back into her room and locked the door. But Neema *wasn't* a scaredy-cat, just like she said. Good girl! Neema was a ghost-hunter after all. Starting this young, she might be one of the best.

SPLASH SPLASH

Davie saw the water ripple again, synchronized with the sound. The sound was retreating. Someone—or some *thing*, like a dog—was walking toward the kitchen.

Davie held tight to Neema's hand, kept his camera trained on the ripples, and carefully began walking to follow the splashing sound. Immediately, a sensation of cold water seeped up to Davie's ankles, startling him. Behind him, Neema only giggled.

Weird, Davie realized. *We feel the water, but it doesn't splash when we walk.*

The water only splashed for the ghosts.

SPLASH SPLASH SPLASHSPLASHSPLASH

The splashing sound was faster, from more than one direction. It sounded like several people, or dogs, splashing at once. It sounded like . . . running.

Suddenly, water spattered to Davie's chest from the splashing. He felt something bump against his arm, knocking him off-balance for a step, and it was gone. Not a dog, then. Too big for a dog. Something as tall as him.

"Who are you?" a stranger's adult-sounding voice said.

"I'm Davie Stephens."

It was only him. But his mouth was doing all the work, because Davie's mind was frozen shut. Sure, he'd seen a salt shaker fall, and he'd seen water dripping backward and a mirror suddenly askew, but he'd never *felt* a ghost touch him before. In movies, ghosts always walked through people, weightless.

But that one had pushed up against him. That one could have knocked him on his butt.

"*Run!*" a child's husky voice said in the dark, up ahead.

Not him. Not Neema. Someone else. A boy he didn't know.

From somewhere very far away, Davie thought he heard the sound of barking.

Davie realized only then that he was struggling to breathe, because fear and surprise had clotted his throat. Warm liquid seeped through his pajamas now; he had wet himself for the first time since he was Neema's age.

"He said, 'Run,'" Neema said.

Davie's lips only bobbed.

The boy's voice came again, from the kitchen doorway: *"Follow me!"*

"He said 'Follow me'!" Neema said, an urgent whisper.

Davie's body had forgotten how to move. Neema tugged on his hand, pulling him ahead toward the kitchen. One or two steps were enough to freeze Davie again, because the water felt higher now, up to his shins.

From his new vantage point in the center of the living room, Davie saw that the back door was wide open in the kitchen. Grandma and Grandpa Walter would never leave their back door open, especially with the mosquitoes in summer. The door definitely had not been open before.

Davie remembered his camera. Somehow, he had let it drop to his side, but he raised it. In Night Vision, the doorway looked like it was bathed in a spotlight.

And Davie saw a silhouette framed there—a boy turning to look at Davie over his shoulder. He was wiry, like Davie. He reminded Davie of the oldest boy he'd seen burying the dog. The fuzzy black silhouette in the light motioned his hand toward Davie.

"*Hurry*!" His voice was more faint.

"I heard something else," Neema said. "Something . . ."

Davie raised his eyes to peek at the doorway—but it was empty, dark. He could only see the ghostly figure when he raised the camera to his eye again. Still there!

Davie's instincts were at war. One part of him wanted to run back to his bedroom as fast as he could. The other part of him wanted to follow the boy calling to him from the doorway. Neema tugged on his hand, toward the kitchen. Neema wasn't just a ghost-hunter—Neema, it turned out, was a kamikaze.

Davie allowed himself to be pulled for two more steps, but then they both stopped.

Davie felt water above his knees now, and to Neema it had to be higher. He took a startled step back. Walking in ghost water was one thing—but swimming was something else. Neema was a good swimmer because Mom made her take lessons at the Y every summer, but Davie's lessons hadn't stuck. Davie never liked water above his knees, and the way this water deepened, it would be above his *waist* soon.

"No," Davie told Neema, holding fast. "Stay here."

The dark image framed against the doorway's light hesitated. Turned his head to look outside, then back toward Davie. Then back outside again.

Then, he ran. And he was gone. As the boy ran, the splashing sound faded to nothing.

It took Davie a minute to realize there were tears running down his face.

It would take Davie Stephens several hours, until almost daylight, to realize *why* he had cried in that moment, standing with Neema in the living room. He wasn't crying because the ghost had sounded so scared—even though he surely had, and the ghost was just a kid, like him. And Davie wasn't crying because he knew that only his fear had held him back from following, and maybe the water *wouldn't* have gotten any deeper.

No, Davie was crying for one simple reason: For all the summers he had come to Grandma and Grandpa's house, with the strange noises in the hall and objects falling down, he had never actually *seen* a ghost. He had never seen a human being who had come to visit from somewhere far away; actual proof that dying wasn't forever.

That ghost was the most beautiful sight of his life.

When a sight like that crosses your eyes, Davie learned, there is nothing to do but cry.

"Yeah, I see the dark spot, Davie. What I *don't* see is a little boy." From Dad's voice, Davie knew that was the last time he would look into the viewfinder to see last night's footage. "And I've told you about staying up late. Look at you: Did you get any sleep?" Dad swiped at the camera as if to knock it from the kitchen table. Davie pulled it out of his reach just in time.

"What you got there, Davie?" Grandpa said. "Show me."

Neema was bouncing in her seat, dying to say what she'd seen, but Davie had made her *promise* that she wouldn't tell anyone she'd been up late with him. If Dad knew that, Davie would be locked in his room all night the rest of the summer.

The water didn't show in the camera, of course. Davie hadn't expected it to. Anyone knew that even infrared cameras couldn't pick up manifestations with any reliability; the energy field was too fragile. But he'd lucked out and captured actual evidence—the image in the doorway, silhouetted by the light. He *could* see it! There was no denying the shadow.

Davie leaned close to Grandpa while he gazed into the tiny viewfinder. Grandpa smelled like aftershave. Old Spice. An old man's smell.

"So . . . that's your ghost?" Grandpa said.

"I heard him, Grandpa. He said 'Run!' and 'Come on!' There was a splashing sound when he ran across the floor."

"*Lots* of splashing," Neema broke in. "And water up to here." She motioned up to her belly button. Then she caught herself, remembering her promise. "Davie told me."

"Well, that's a strange story, all right," Grandpa said, and turned his attention to his coffee cup. At least Grandpa pretended to be interested, which was more than Dad had done, but who wants to drink coffee when they believe they've seen a ghost?

What was wrong with grown-up eyes? *Will I go blind like them too?*

From the stove, Grandma looked at Davie over her shoulder. "Well, there's no sign of water now, thank goodness. One time the

AC broke, and our bedroom was flooded. Those floorboards warped and cracked—"

"But it wasn't *real* water, Grandma. It's like . . . old. Like ghosts."

Grandpa chuckled. "Well . . . you know what, Doris?"

Grandma shook her head. "Don't encourage him, Walt. He needs his rest at night."

"What's the harm?" Grandpa put his coffee cup back down and leaned over to look Davie in the eye. What he said sent a bolt of lightning through Davie's spine: "You know . . . all this land out here, before the developers came, it was nothing but swamp. Water all around."

Davie's heart was pounding as hard as when the ghost called out to him, beckoning.

Dad got up from the table and walked out of the kitchen. Probably to take a nap, Davie guessed, even though he'd just gotten out of bed.

"Swamp?" Davie said, remembering the smell of the water; almost a living smell.

"Shoot, yeah. They had to drain it. There's still some swampy patches out back, probably a hundred yards 'yond the gate."

Grandma set a plate of pancakes down in front of Davie loudly enough to stop the conversation. "All these crazy stories about Graceville in summer. You ought to be ashamed of yourself, Walt," she said. Then she took up the conversation in her own way: "They're trying to build back there now. You can bet they wouldn't tell anyone who buys those houses it's only swampland underneath. Just like they won't tell them there's no hospital for thirty miles. The land's not fit! And where's the sewage gonna go?"

Grandma could have gone on, but luckily the phone rang then. It was Imani, so her call was a big production. Everyone wanted their turn to talk to her. Even Dad came back to grab the portable kitchen phone to say hello.

Davie waited last to take his turn. Talking to Imani might mean lying, and he didn't like to start out any day with a lie. If she asked *How is everything?,* he'd be lying right from the start.

When it was Davie's turn on the phone, he took it in his own room to tell her about his adventure with the ghost. For a while, Imani seemed interested, especially the part about the water. She talked to him like a real person, not her little brother, for a change. She didn't try to rush him off the phone to be with her friends or to watch her favorite anime, *Death Note*, or to do her work. She said things like "Wow" and "Cool!" She said she couldn't wait to see his video. *Couldn't wait*, she said.

But then she asked a question that had nothing to do with ghosts: "How's Dad?"

Davie's stomach, suddenly, was a knot.

"Sleeps a lot," Davie said. "All the time."

"People sleep when they're depressed," Imani said.

She knows, Davie realized. *She wants to know if I know too.*

"Well," Davie said, heart pounding again—but this time from a deeper place, a more dangerous place—"I guess he's got a lot to be depressed about."

For a long time, neither of them said anything.

Then Imani said, "Did he tell you?"

And Davie said, "I heard him talking to Grandma."

And they were quiet for a while again. Davie's hand with the phone was trembling.

"It may not be for sure," Imani said finally. "You know how Mom is. Dramatic. She calls me every other day. I'm trying to talk her out of it. And Dad's stubborn, as usual. I know you don't want to live in Ghana. Neema either."

"No." Davie could barely speak over the lump in his throat. He'd been to Ghana once, when he was little, and all he remembered about that trip was heat and a man with no teeth his grandmother had haggled with at an open-air market. Africa didn't feel familiar to him, with too many differences—and it would be too far away from Dad. Too far away from his whole world.

"But if you do end up in Ghana, it wouldn't be all the time," Imani went on. "You'd go back and forth. And remember: Her dad worked for the government, so they have a nice house with a swimming pool. And there's an American school nearby, like where diplomats and people send their kids. You wouldn't be out in some village somewhere. You can't blame Mom, Davie. Yeah, she's dramatic, but look at Dad too. He works all the time. Mom says he used to laugh and have more faith in life. She feels isolated. When they got married, he promised her they could live in Ghana for a while—and it's been almost twenty years. He always says no. What's she supposed to do?"

Davie had no idea what Imani was talking about, but the details of his life had already been decided. All he knew was that it felt wrong for Mom to talk to Imani like one of her girlfriends, not like her mother. Imani was on Mom's side, Davie realized. So that was how it would line up: Mom and Imani against Dad, Grandma, Grandpa Walter, him, and Neema. Those would be the camps.

Davie blinked. His eyes stung, but they were dry. Tears weren't enough for the feeling. He suddenly hated his sister for her breeziness and her dorm room that felt safe to her, a haven she had claimed for herself. No wonder she'd been in such a good mood at the airport—she was escaping just in time, and she knew it. She had left him and Neema to fend for themselves.

"Anyway . . ." Imani went on, "like I said, I'm trying to talk her out of it. A month's a good break for them. It'll all be okay. Don't worry. You'll see."

A sudden, loud knock on Davie's door ended their conversation.

"Davie—unlock this door!" It was Dad.

Davie hadn't realized he'd locked his door, thereby breaking the number-one house rule. He told Imani he had to go, clicked off the phone, and bounded from his bed to let Dad in. He hoped his unshed tears wouldn't show too much. He didn't want Dad to start talking to him about Mom and how dramatic she was ("*Don't you agree, ol' buddy?*"), patting Davie's knee and asking him to see things from his side. Davie already felt like he might puke.

Dad looked like he had aged ten years in two days. He hadn't shaven, and his stubble was more white than black.

"Did you leave this in my room?" Dad said. "Under my pillow?"

Davie looked at the object in his father's palm for at least five seconds before his brain allowed him to understand what he was seeing: A gummy-looking dog biscuit.

Gnawed at both ends.

Davie wanted to go outside to the woods and find the place where the kids had buried the dog. That was his whole afternoon's plan, a no-brainer. But as soon as he got outside, he saw his father standing at the back fence, near the broken log, almost like he was guarding it. Dad's foot rested on the surviving lower log rail as he stared into the woods.

Davie walked beside him and stared, too, wondering if he would see the boys from there. He would enjoy a long conversation with them, all right. At first, Dad didn't hear Davie beside him. There were too many crickets and bugs of endless varieties singing up a storm. But when Davie's foot snapped a twig with a sharp crack, Dad turned around.

"I should fix this," Dad said, squeezing the broken log, which crossed the next fencepost like an X instead of lying down flat. The break was a tangle of wire and splinters.

"Why?" Davie said. "It lets the deer come in."

And maybe the ghosts too. Davie didn't know why he thought so, but he did.

Besides, if the fence was fixed, he'd have to find another way to get back there. He couldn't let the opportunity pass him by.

But if he couldn't find the kids, or the place they buried their dog, he could cross the street to look for the construction site where the bodies had been found. He didn't know if it was marked or anything—Grandma said the bodies had been dug up for weeks already—but it might be. There might be yellow tape strung up, like a police crime scene.

Dad sighed. "They expect me to fix it." He was probably talking about the fence, but his voice had sounded so faraway that suddenly David wasn't sure.

"Do you know how?" Davie said. He could answer that question either way. Dad could organize a whole documentary crew, but at home he could barely change a light bulb. That's what Mom said.

Dad's face snapped to look down at Davie, surprise in his eyes. Maybe he'd sounded too much like Mom. Or maybe he wondered what they were talking about, too.

"Neema's shopping with Grandma," Dad said. "We should go somewhere. Us two."

Davie didn't want to go anywhere with his father, but Dad needed him.

"How 'bout the library?" Davie said.

That time, his father even smiled.

* * *

"Kid, you're a genius," Dad whispered, setting up his laptop on the long library table. "I'm a week behind on this grant proposal, but there's something about a library, right? Makes you want to work. You gonna be all right?"

To Dad, "doing something together" meant being in the same room at the same time. Davie had figured he would be able to peel off on his own if he brought Dad to a library, so he could kill two birds with one stone. The library in Graceville was hardly bigger than the library in Davie's elementary school, without the fun posters on the walls.

Dad was way too excited to be in a library. His knees bounced beneath the table, his eyes flitting around like every shelf was sprinkled with fairy dust. Davie wanted to ask his father if *he* was all right, but what was the point? Of course he wasn't.

"I'll go see what's in the sci fi section," Davie said.

Dad winked at him. "Good man." He clapped his hands, ready to work. "Good man."

Davie made an appearance in Science Fiction/Fantasy/Horror, noting that the entire Harry Potter series was checked out except for *Chamber of Secrets.* Lame. A quick peek at Dad, who was typing like a fiend, and Davie hustled over to the research desk. The woman who sat there was old, of course, but weren't all librarians old? Maybe it was a job requirement. She was a black woman with silver hair she had cut very short, and her face was dotted with what looked like freckles from a distance, but were really big moles. If the woman's eyes weren't so bright, it would have been hard not to stare at her moles.

"Help you, young man?" she said.

"Uh . . ." Davie tried to think about the best way to put it. He had learned that mentioning the word *ghost* was a sure way to lose an adult's attention. He didn't discuss his hunts with strangers. "I live near the place where those bodies were found."

"You do, huh?" She was instantly interested, taking off her reading glasses. Her eyes were suddenly intense. "How do you feel about that?"

Davie was confused by the question. "Okay . . . I guess."

"What I mean is . . . does it upset you that so many people were buried there?"

"Nah. It's kinda cool. I just wonder who they were. Did they live in the swamp?"

The librarian looked at him with a smile, as if he'd said the magic words. "So you want to know the history of the area?"

Davie nodded. "Right."

Apparently, librarians get excited when kids come up to them and ask about history. The librarian even called her boss over, a reedy white man, and he recommended a book too. Before Davie knew it, she had a stack in her hands.

"By the way," the librarian said, "my name is Mrs. Mabel Trawley. I'm from the Trawleys who live here in Graceville, out near Trawley Hill. My great-grandfather was born on a tobacco plantation not far from the Stephenses. Are you their grandson?"

Davie nodded, but what did that have to do with anything? Just because he'd asked about the land didn't mean he wanted to hear the history of the world. Or tell her his life story.

"Well, you just tell your grandmamma that Mabel Trawley said hello. That's how people like to do here in Graceville. We want to know how people's families turned out. See, it didn't start out so well for most of us. Our ancestors were slaves here. Did you know that?"

"Yeah. I know about slavery."

Davie was glad his father had shown him *Roots*, or he wouldn't have known what "slaves" really meant. Sure, he'd learned about Abraham Lincoln and the Civil War in school—and it had something to do with slaves—but only *Roots* had shown him how Kunta Kinte lost his foot trying to run for freedom. And how people's babies got sold away. The librarian pulled out a book called *Black Seminoles*. "There were lots of runaways who lived in the swamps. Met up with the Indians, all of them hiding out together."

"What about dogs?"

The librarian pursed her lips and flipped a book open to a drawing of a black man, woman and young boy dressed in tatters, running through a swamp—chased by barking dogs. The dogs looked like ferocious monsters, with coats of fur so thick at their necks that they seemed to have manes. "Most times, tracking was the only way a slave master could bring his runaways back. Pieces of them, anyway."

Davie's neck felt ice-cold when he remembered the splashing water in the living room. The photo of the tracking dogs cast a very different light on the past two nights. *Tracking.* As in looking for him. Would he and Neema end up in pieces if they kept hunting for the ghost dog?

"Can I check out those books?" Davie said.

"What's got you so interested?"

What the heck? "Ghosts," Davie said.

"Oh, so you're seeing spirits," she said. Her voice made it sound everyday, like *Oh, so you had chicken for dinner last night?*

"That's right," she went on. "Summer."

"What about summer?"

She pursed her lips. "Come on, now. You wouldn't be seeing them otherwise."

Aside from Mom, who talked about ghosts singing in trees,

Davie had never met another adult who would hold still and listen when he talked about ghosts. Even so, this woman's eyes were only half engaged; from time to time, she glanced down at a stain on her white blouse.

"What do you know about the ghosts?" he said.

"You tell me," she said. "I haven't seen any since I was your age."

Davie's heart fluttered. "It's true you don't see them when you're older?"

"Not in Graceville. Nope." She brushed at the stain.

That afternoon, while Davie's father worked on his computer to forget his problems, Mabel Trawley shelved books and told Davie the history of Graceville, Florida. Founded in 1845 by James Grace, who would later fight as a Confederate officer in the Civil War. The town started out prosperous because of tobacco farming, since people who smoked rarely quit the habit, and there were plenty of new people to take it up—and slaves to bring in the harvests. ("No tobacco, no Graceville. No slaves, no tobacco. Plain facts," she said.) The huge tobacco barns, where the leaves were hung out to dry, still stood up and down the roads. ("There's a tobacco barn out back there somewhere behind your grandmama's house, for a fact.")

There was one Really Bad Thing that happened right after the turn of the century, she said. The year was 1909.

"In summer?" Davie said.

"'Course it was summer."

Mabel Trawley told the story:

Most black folks in Graceville didn't have two dimes to rub together since slavery, but there were a handful of Negroes here and there who did all right. Men farmed and hired themselves out to the growers, or sharecropped, women took in wash, and babies made up of all their parents' hopes and dreams.

One such family was the Timmons family. Isaiah Timmons and his wife, Essie, had three sons. He'd planned to stay in Graceville only another year or so, just long enough to pay his debts and save enough money for train tickets to New York, where his brother could help them settle in a boarding house. He had it all planned out. Isaiah Timmons left behind his journal and notes. Otherwise, we might never have known about him at all.

Well, the Timmons family had to be mindful of all manner of trouble. All black folks back then lived under terrible rules with unthinkable consequences, so you best believe Isaiah Timmons was the most polite, gentle-mannered and kind-hearted Negro these white folks had ever seen. It was said he might have helped foil a riot or two in Graceville; depending on the point of view, he was peacemaker or race traitor, or maybe both.

Well, despite all of Isaiah Timmons' unending politeness, he gained powerful enemies in Graceville for the simple reason that he was doing all right. If white folks saw that Isaiah Timmons had a hog, why, their first thought was, "Well, how come that nigger's got a better hog than me?" ("Sorry to use that word, but that's how folks talked back then. Calling black folks nigger was the same as calling them by name.") *Instead of shaking their heads to marvel that a black man could put a roof over his family's heads, they begrudged him every tiny victory.*

If there was one man he hated most, and who was happy to return the sentiment, it was Virgil McCormack. He was a grower whose father had been a genuine slave-holder, and Old Virgil McCormack had never gotten used to the idea that the Negroes who worked for him weren't slaves. And that anyone with dark skin might have any rights to speak of.

Isaiah Timmons worked for Virgil McCormack from time to time—a task he hated more than any other—and they also had the misfortune of sharing a border, right out where Tobacco Road is right now. Come to think of it, your grandparents' house used to be Mc-Cormack land, of course, so you're living right by the very spot where Isaiah Timmons and Virgil McCormack argued over whose land was whose.

Well, the whole argument came to a head one summer when, in plain daylight, someone set fire to Isaiah Timmons' barn. The barn wasn't fifty yards from the house, and it burned straight to the ground. Well, that put the writing clear on the wall—Isaiah Timmons decided he and his family would head up north to New York whether they had train tickets or not. He packed up everything he could in a wagon, working the whole night through, and was ready to leave by dawn. Isaiah wasn't a coward, but he also wasn't a fool. Disputes with neighbors never ended well for black folks. Isaiah Timmons figured the sheriff would come next with an accusation of rape or some other charge to get rid of him—if he didn't string him up in a tree outright—and he wasn't going to wait around to see how creative his death would be.

The three boys, it was said, had been helping their father pack that wagon . . . but when it was time to go, Isaiah and Essie Timmons called up and down the road, but they couldn't find a sign of those boys anywhere. The way Essie Timmons would tell the story later, it was as if they vanished into the air itself! Friends and neighbors helped them search—even the white man who ran the general store, whose great-great-grandson is the mayor of Graceville today—and they searched through and through. But those boys never turned up.

Well, Isaiah Timmons was sick at heart and mad as hell, no doubt out of his mind with grief. It was one thing to try to hurt him, but what kind of people would hurt children? He took his shotgun and walked across the road to McCormack's land. Virgil McCormack lived in the same antebellum house where his family lives in today. Isaiah

Timmons found McCormack washing his automobile—the McCormacks were among the first in Graceville to have a car—and Timmons aimed that shotgun right at McCormack's head, demanding to know what happened to his boys.

I can tell you no white man in Graceville had ever been spoken to by a Negro that way; not one who lived, anyway. They say Isaiah Timmons fired a warning shot into the air and just about made McCormack jump out of his skin. Got him to crying and begging. McCormack swore to God's Heaven he didn't know where those boys were, and Isaiah Timmons let him live only because he was too heavy-hearted to pull the trigger.

You remember this: He could've killed him, but he didn't. And it wasn't about trying to save his own skin, 'cause confronting a white man with a shotgun was gonna look like a murder to white folks whether the white man lived or died. Isaiah Timmons' fate had been decided from the moment he walked up behind McCormack with a gun and too much manhood in his voice. But he lay that shotgun on his shoulder and walked away. That's the part everyone forgets.

Well, that night the fireworks went off in Graceville.

All those folks who'd been held off from rioting, and all those scared whites who were sure the blacks were planning to slit their throats, built a bonfire of hate and fear that night. "Did you hear what happened to the Timmons boys?" on one side, and "Did you hear a nigger tried to shoot McCormack?" on the other, and everybody all worked up in a frenzy.

There's always blood in a frenzy like that, and the side with the most manpower and the best weapons always wins. Isaiah Timmons was easy to find: McCormack and the police found him looking for his boys, and he probably didn't live long enough to tell his side. He died first. But lots of other black men in Graceville got held to account for

Isaiah Timmons and his shotgun. Anyone who looked like they were in a bad mood got rounded up, especially if they didn't have family in town. It's said a bunch of black men were rounded up and taken to McCormack's place and questioned. Somebody must not have liked their answers, because they got shot down right there in the muck. ("Are those the people the bones came from? The ones the builders are digging up?" Davie asked, and Mabel Trawley nodded slowly. "That's what we think. The bodies from the Graceville riot. It looks like they were dumped in the same plot.")

There's bad blood between the McCormacks and the Timmonses to this day—they say McCormack stole those three Timmons boys, probably killed them outright, and that's what started it all. They had a sister, and she wrote a book about those boys and the Graceville riot. Three Brothers, *I think she called it. I haven't seen a copy of it, but people mention it from time to time. Isaiah Timmons probably ended up in that mass grave with the bones from the construction site—but I hear his widow told the story until the day she died: "McCormack took my three boys. My three precious boys."*

"I saw them," Davie said, his heart banging in his chest. The library felt like a church chapel, as if they were talking about something holy.

"You saw who?"

"The boys. The three Timmons boys. They were burying a dog. I didn't know they were ghosts. I thought they were real, 'cuz it was still light outside. I forgot that . . ."

". . . sometimes you can see them at dusk," Mabel Trawley said, with a nod and a smile. "That used to fool me too."

Davie hadn't realized his father was listening from the next row until he and Mabel Trawley rounded the corner and almost ran into him. There was a thunderstorm on Dad's face.

"Are you the one who's been filling his head with these ghost stories?" Dad said to the librarian. Davie was so embarrassed by his father's anger, he wanted to melt into the floor.

"No, sir. I've just met this young man today. He's the one filling *my* head."

Dad's face softened. He shuffled his feet, unsure. "Sorry. I thought I heard you say . . ."

"You're Darryl Stephens, aren't you? Your father's the Stephens who enlisted in the Army, went to Korea, settled in Miami. You didn't grow up here in town at all, did you?"

Dad looked at the librarian as if he were almost afraid of her, like she was the psychic at the county fair of his youth. "How'd you know that?"

"Everyone knows everything in a small town. Bet you never even spent a summer here."

"Once. When I was about . . . fifteen."

"Too late," she said.

"Too late for what?"

Mabel Trawley looked at Davie and winked. "You and your son should have a talk, Mr. Stephens," she said. "He can show you what you missed. And while he's at it, Davie might be able to answer a question that's given a whole lot of folks in Graceville a whole lot of grief."

Summer, 1909

The Timmons boys were, in order of birth, Isaac, Scott, and Little Eddie. Isaac, the eldest, was twelve, and each brother was separated by almost two years to the day, ending with Little Eddie, who had just turned eight the day before the barn burned down.

Isaac had never been afraid of fire. He'd mastered fire when he was younger than Little Eddie, and he'd been using it ever since for cooking, heating water for bathing and washing clothes, melting lye, sharpening blades, and any number of other tasks for which fire came in handy. Fire, to Isaac, was just another tool. He had forgotten how destructive it could be.

The fire that burned down the barn had actually started *outside* of the barn, where the boys were roasting themselves yams while their father was out in McCormack's field and their mother was pounding clothes at the creek. Isaac had gotten some honey from his gal Livvy's mother, and yams with honey were his favorite treat. He and his brothers were roasting yams in secret because they were supposed to be hanging clothes up to dry, but the Timmons boys found ways to do what they wanted when no one was watching them.

One call from Mama waving in the distance was enough to get them on their feet and running. They didn't notice the change in the wind, and they didn't realize the barn wall's wood was so dry because it hadn't rained a drop all summer. They never actually *saw* the cloud of sparks from their cook fire that flew against the barn wall and came alight almost immediately. They were nowhere near the barn when it happened. What they did see an hour later, however, was roiling smoke carrying bad news. As soon as Isaac Timmons smelled smoke, he knew.

Their family's two horses and milking cow were safely clear of the barn when the fire broke out, but everything else was lost, charred and black. The barn was still standing, but two of its walls had burned clean away, and it was nothing but a big, ugly ruin. It was as if God was laughing at his father, telling him he would never have a farm of his own. He would be working for Old Man McCormack forever.

The older boys, in quick conference, tried to decide on the best way to tell Papa how they started the fire. Confession would mean consequences, of course. Their father had been raised on a razor strap *his* father had learned to wield like a long-dead overseer once wielded his cow-hide whip, so a confession would mean marks, welts, and blood for Isaac. But he was the eldest, and it was his fault anyway—he'd told Scotty to put out the fire, but he hadn't seen him put it out with his own eyes—so a man had to take a punishment like a man.

He planned out how he'd say it: *Papa, we didn't mean it, but we burned down the barn.* He said it over and over again, marching outside to where Papa was assessing the damage.

"Papa?" Isaac said.

"Goddamn crackers," Papa said.

The idea came from Papa's own mouth.

To Isaac, his stroke of luck was too good to be true: Papa thought white folks had burned down the barn—probably McCormack and his sons. From the conversations Isaac had overheard when his parents thought he was sleeping, Papa already had plenty of reasons to be mad at the McCormacks. They were cheats, one thing. Never wanted to pay Papa what he was owed, like Papa was too dumb to count. And if Mama worked her hands raw to make Isaac a new shirt, one of the McCormack boys would go and tattle, and Ole Mr. McCormack would tell Papa, "Well, your boy just got a new shirt, so I reckon y'all doin' better'n most niggers." And then he paid Papa even less. Mama hated Ole Missus McCormack so much that she could hardly make herself smile when she passed her on the road.

And McCormack, who had more land than he knew what to do with, was trying to say his plot bordering Papa's land was beyond the old oak, rather than just shy of it. He was planning on calling out surveyors and putting up a fence, since he knew Papa couldn't afford to pay anyone to say what *he* wanted them to say—not that any surveyor would side with him over McCormack. That McCormack was a thief to his bones, Mama always said.

And McCormack had the biggest, meanest dog in the county, trained to snap at black folks on sight. Papa had told him it was called a German shepherd dog, ordered special from up north, but Isaac was sure that big dog was part wolf. It had wolf eyes and wolf teeth. Sometimes Isaac had nightmares about being chased by that dog. He never went anywhere close to McCormack's place without a big, heavy stick in his hand.

All in all, Isaac Timmons figured the only reason Ole Mr. McCormack *hadn't* burned down the barn was because he hadn't thought of it first.

"It was McCormack, huh Papa?" Isaac said to his father, outside the charred barn.

Papa looked at him good and long. At first, Isaac was afraid his father had seen straight through his lie, but there was something new and terrible in his father's eyes—it wasn't there long, but Isaac would never forget how his father's face chilled the blood in his veins. Papa was *afraid!* Isaac wanted to tell the truth as soon as he saw how scared of McCormack his father was, but he couldn't make his mouth work.

And so the story was born.

After that, the truth just got harder and harder to utter. And by the time all of them had been up for hours loading the wagon, with Papa trying to cheer them up with stories about the north while Mama pretended she wasn't crying, he had almost forgotten what the truth was.

Little Eddie would have told on them for sure, but Little Eddie hadn't figured out that the barn burned down because their makeshift cook fire was too close to the wall where they were hiding from sight. Scott was usually the fastest tattle in town, but this time he kept the truth to himself, too—especially given his role in not putting out the fire properly. Scott was thinking about that razor strap and how Papa had promised that the next time he and his older brother messed up, Isaac wasn't the only one who would take the blame. So Isaac and Scott cast each other miserable looks by lamplight all night long, folding Mama's quilts and blankets neatly into crates, carting out cooking utensils, and packing up the few farming supplies that weren't burned beyond usefulness.

Maybe it wouldn't be so bad to move, they thought. Mama was always afraid someone would come burn their whole house down with everyone inside, not just the barn. It had happened to a family in Quincy just a month ago. Besides, Papa was always in a bad mood after a day's dealings with McCormack, and Mama was worried Papa might say something to get them all killed. Papa did have a mouth on him.

Maybe, in fact, the barn burning down was something like Rev. Crutcher had said in church on Sunday, about how *ad-ver-si-ty* is a blessing in disguise.

The secret weighed heavier with each passing moment.

But the Timmons boys carried it. They were stronger than anyone could have imagined.

"So . . . you heard a dog . . . and then a little boy?" Grandma said.

After a half-dozen repetitions, she finally had it right. At dinner, Davie had told the whole story, even admitting that Neema had been up with him. He'd started with the sniffing dog at his door and ended at the library. Mabel Trawley's information made his story seem that much more worth telling, so he had left nothing out.

"Right," Davie said. "A dog and a little boy."

"The boy said, 'Run! Follow me,'" Neema added.

"Pass the meat loaf," Grandpa Walter said. He was usually quick to play along, but not this time. Maybe his arthritis was hurting, Davie thought. He had noticed that because of pain, Grandpa Walter laughed less and less.

Dad, though, was suddenly so interested that he was resting his cheek on his elbow as he listened. His elbow was planted beside his plate on the table. *No elbows on the table*, Grandma always said, but she was probably so glad to see Dad talking for a change that she kept quiet.

"But slave-catchers with dogs were before their time," Dad said. "Those boys, I mean."

"You think tracking dogs went away after slave times?" Grandma said. "The point is, maybe we can find an argument to stop the construction in all this, since those Timmons boys were never found. There weren't any children's bones at that first dig. I'll need to talk to that librarian myself."

Davie knew that Grandma couldn't care less about ghosts—she was just happy to have new ammunition in her anti-construction arsenal. Grandma reminded Davie of the mother in *Mary Poppins*, Mrs. Banks, who only truly came to life when she talked about her protests.

Davie noticed that both Dad and Grandma had red plastic cups instead of regular water glasses. A quick glance over, and Davie saw foam in his father's cup. He smelled it then: Both Grandma and Dad were drinking beer. Davie had never even heard of, much less seen, his grandmother drinking beer—but Dad drank a lot of beer between projects. He drank more than Mom knew, because Dad took his bottles out for recycling late at night. Davie had seen him do it once and hadn't understood why until they were sitting at the dinner table a year later. Dad was used to hiding his drinking. It was a habit.

The mashed potatoes in Davie's mouth suddenly tasted like paste. He missed his mother so much he wanted to cry, maybe because he was thinking about the three missing boys. He only had a very tiny idea of what being lost from his parents might feel like, and already he could tell it might be a feeling that never got better.

"Tell me again what you saw out back," Dad said. "In the woods."

Dad's eyes were dancing like they had at the library, and Davie didn't like those eyes. Dad didn't believe in ghosts either; he was just trying to lose himself in something else. Davie felt like he was wearing X-ray glasses and could see down to his father's bones.

"I saw three boys burying a dog," Davie said. "There was a deep hole. *Really* deep."

Dad snapped his fingers. "Stop right there. Look at that image like a filmmaker would. You're looking at it too literally—it's a symbol. If these are ghosts, their appearance doesn't have to be some kind of literal recreation of an event from their lives. It might be more like a dream instead. That deep hole is a visual symbol for you. A message."

Grandma grinned, her eyes sparking. "Evidence in a town mystery buried right smack in the middle of Lot Sixty-five!" she said, giggling with glee. "You wait till I call Alice and tell her! What are those fat cat lawyers gonna say when we roll poor old Miss Timmons up in her wheelchair? Bet they won't be throwing up any more models after that."

"Who's Miss Timmons?" Davie said.

"She's ninety-some years old now," Grandma said. "She was kin to those boys, a sister born after they died. I think their mama was the only one who survived, and I guess she remarried. How she didn't lose her mind after her whole family died, I just don't know. And the geography checks out, doesn't it, Walt? We're right near the McCormack land."

Grandpa Walter grunted, fascinated by his cornbread. "Half the town's McCormack."

"You know what I mean. The plantation's still there."

"That really really big one?" Neema said. "The really really big white one?"

"Pass it by every day," Grandpa Walter said.

"I know which one," Dad said. "I see it through my bedroom window."

Maybe there *had* been fairy dust at the library, Davie realized. No one else in his family had cared about the ghosts he'd seen, and now everyone cared except Grandpa Walter. Neema grinned at Davie with rare admiration. She was wondering how he'd done it too.

Davie's father nudged his grandfather. "You sure you never saw ghosts, Dad?" Joking.

"I went through all that," Grandpa Walter said. "During the day, I watched my father catch hell from folks who couldn't stand the sight of a black man who wasn't stooping. At night, it was bumps and creaks. I loathed Graceville. I was glad to be through with all of it."

Loathed was a strong word, and Davie hadn't heard his grandfather say it before. Grandpa Walt *had* seen ghosts as a child! He just hadn't liked it.

But maybe it could be different now.

"Will you stay up with us and hunt for ghosts, Grandpa Walter?" Davie said. Across the table, Grandma only laughed and shook her head. He'd known better than to ask her, beer or no beer. Ghost-hunting wasn't Grandma's style.

"*Please*, Grandpa?" Neema said.

"I'll stay up," Dad said instead.

Grandpa Walter shrugged. That was how it was decided.

That night, all four of them sat huddled behind the easy chair, not just him and Neema. Davie heard Grandma watching TV in her bedroom, so it didn't feel like the Golden Hour, not exactly. But with Neema, Dad, *and* Grandpa Walt with them, Davie figured that whatever beacon he sent out to the ghost world was in overdrive tonight.

"I didn't know you felt that way about Graceville, Dad," Dad said in the quiet.

"Why do you think I didn't want to raise you here?" Grandpa said.

"Why'd you come back, then?"

"Times are different now," he said. "Mostly. And your mom wanted to go to the country. Home is home. Even if it doesn't always feel good, it's the only home you've got. You find a way to make it work."

"We're not talking about *that*," Dad said, voice clipped and low.

"We need to," Grandpa said.

Silently, Davie groaned. The real world couldn't intrude on their hunt! Davie had learned a long time ago that he never heard ghosts if he brought a book, or tried to do Sudoku puzzles. A ghost-hunter's mind had to be quiet, even on the verge of sleep. *That* was when they came. So Davie was afraid the spell would be broken. Dad would sigh and say they were being silly, or Grandpa would complain that his knees were aching. Neema might trigger the collapse by purring to Dad that she wanted something to drink. Davie could hear the foundation cracking.

But miraculously, for five minutes, they were quiet in the dark.

And then, just like that, the water was back.

Neema was so startled that she let out a little yelp, which scared Dad enough to jump.

"The floor's wet!" Neema shouted. Yes, *shouted.* (Ghosts, FYI, do not like shouting.)

"*Shhhhhhh,*" Davie whispered, shaking her arm. "You'll scare it off."

"Davie, let go of your sister," Dad said. "And I don't feel any water."

"Me neither," Grandpa said. "We were promised ghost water, and I expect ghost water."

"You have to be a kid," Neema and I said together.

Dad and Grandpa looked at each other, practically winking.

Even with all of the distractions, Davie's mind was on the hunt. In a flash, he'd switched on his video camera, and his eyes were armed with Night Vision. Seeing in the dark was like being a superhero. Tiny snakes of light wriggled across the living room floor.

"It's all shimmery, like in moonlight," Davie said.

Neema wrestled over his shoulder. "Let me see."

Neema had pointed out that she hadn't been allowed to look through the Night Vision even once the previous night, so he gave her the camera. He pointed the lens toward the coffee table; the light hitting the glass-top table made it easier to see the water underneath.

"Whoa," Neema said.

"Before, we heard splashing," I whispered to Dad and Grandpa. "I don't hear any splashing yet. We need to be still and listen."

"Yessir, yessir," Grandpa said, and saluted.

So, they sat. While they waited, the water felt deeper. And colder. Neema and Davie rose to their feet because the floor felt so wet. Dad and Grandpa watched with fascination while Davie and his sister shook invisible droplets of water from their fingers, patted down wet clothes. Both Dad and Grandpa looked like they could hardly keep a straight face.

Then, Davie heard barking.

It was distant, but very distinct. And getting closer. Moving fast.

"The dog . . ." Neema said.

"It's coming," Davie said.

The barking didn't sound friendly. It was jabbering, persistent. Angry.

"Is it a good dog or a bad dog?" Dad said.

Davie's hands shook as he reached into his ghost kit for his doggy biscuits, wishing he had a better plan.

"Wait a minute," Dad said. "You *did* put that biscuit in my bed, Davie."

"No I didn't," Davie said.

"The ghost did it," Neema said.

"That's not funny, Davie. Playing games is one thing, but I when I ask you a question, I expect a truthful answer."

"Relax, Darryl," Grandpa said, sounding tired. "Let's be ghost-hunters."

Most ghosts run off lickety split when there's too much talking. Davie had read countless stories about it on the ghost-hunter message boards on the Internet. But all in all, that angry dog scared him enough that maybe he hoped the dog would turn and run the other way. Maybe he wished the dog would do just that.

But the barking was louder. The dog was still coming.

Davie thought he'd been snapped into the dog's jaws when his father grabbed his arm and yanked him closer. It almost hurt. Maybe it did, a little. Dad's breath smelled like beer. "Davie, you promise me you had nothing to do with that doggy biscuit getting into my bed. You swear it wasn't you."

"Dad, I swear. It wasn't me."

"Me neither, Daddy," Neema said, although of course Dad would never get mad at her.

It was too dark for Davie to see his father's face, and Davie decided that using the Night Vision on Dad would get his camera broken. A painful instinct told him to expect a blow, maybe a slap. His father had never slapped him before, but there was always a first time. Dad was breathing fast, as if he had been running.

"You still hear a dog barking?" Dad said.

"Yessir," Davie said. He always called Dad "sir" if he was in trouble.

"And you and Neema feel water on the floor? Both of you?"

"Actually," Neema said, "it's up to my ankles."

"Shhhhh," I said.

Splashing!

Davie heard the chaotic sound of feet splashing in the water in uneven patterns, staggering. A boy shrieked like Davie had never heard anyone shriek, much less a child. The shriek wiped the grin off of Neema's face. It was the kind of shriek it was best to hear from a distance, because it might tear a hole in you up close.

But the shrieking was getting louder. Crying children were getting closer, splashing and stumbling. The three boys.

Davie's knees stopped working. His legs could barely support him.

"I'm scared," Neema said. She was crying too, joining their chorus.

When Grandpa turned the lights on, all the noises went away.

Grandma called a family meeting at breakfast. After she heard Neema's crying the night before, she was in a bad mood about the whole ghost business. Neema had been too scared to sleep in the room full of dolls, so she had slept with Daddy. While the eggs and bacon got cold, Grandma spent the morning telling everyone she thought it was foolish for two grown men to be feeding a children's fantasy about ghosts chased by a dog. And she had some choice words for Davie, too: He was too old—too *old*, she kept saying—to behave that way. He was supposed to be an example to Neema, and he needed to start acting his age.

"It was just some fun that went too far," Grandpa Walter said.

But that didn't satisfy Grandma. Dad tried next, telling her it was a valuable exercise in imagination, and how working through the scenario would help them understand the region's history—in fact, he said, the whole history of black America. Dad made it sound like something boring from a classroom, but that was Dad.

"It helps them process their history in terms they'll relate to," Dad finished.

Grandma gave him a dirty look.

Davie sighed, raising his hand. "Grandma . . ." he said. "If we don't listen to them, nobody else can. We can follow their voices. Maybe even find out if they died out back where I saw them with the dog. If their bones get dug up, you can stop the builders."

"Get an injunction . . ." Grandpa Walt cooed. He blew on his coffee to cool it.

But Grandma didn't fall for it right away. Not this time. "It's not good for Neema!"

"I won't cry this time," Neema said. "Davie told me to remember we're not hearing *real* screaming. It's old, so it's not really there. And they're not hurting anymore."

Well, that last part wasn't exactly true, Davie thought. If the three boys weren't hurting, they wouldn't be trying so hard to be heard. But Neema didn't need to have that spelled out. Like all ghosts, they just wanted their story known.

Grandma stared from face to face, shaking her head. "Everyone in this house has lost their doggone mind. That includes me."

And so it was decided. Again.

That night, Grandma made special ghost packs for everyone—extra flashlights, including the powerful hurricane flashlight that could light up the night like a spotlight. Packages of cheese and crackers. ("In case you're up late and get hungry.") Bengay for Grandpa. ("You know how your joints get, Walt.") Even boots and raincoats! ("Real water or not, I don't want you all getting wet.") For good measure, she handed Dad a shovel. ("Just in case you can get the digging started . . .") Then she wished them luck and went to her bedroom to watch TV, closing her door tight so Lifetime wouldn't be too loud.

That night, Davie felt more like a ghost soldier than a mere ghost-hunter. He had better supplies *and* reinforcements! And now that all of them knew what to expect, they wouldn't be surprised by the shrieking. The pain might not bother them so much.

He hoped not, anyway.

That night, the ghosts made them wait.

The excitement Davie had felt all day—really, every day since he'd first heard the dog sniffing at his door—burned into exhaustion. By nine o'clock, an hour after their vigil began, his eyelids were heavy and he was bothered by the hot raincoat. He felt a little silly wearing a raincoat inside the house. In the quiet, it was hard to remember the past few nights at all.

"Daddy?" Neema said in the hush.

"What's that, Pumpkin?"

Davie hoped they would keep their voices low.

"Are you and Mommy mad at each other?"

As scary as the barking and shrieking had been, Davie was more afraid to hear his father tell Neema a lie. Or worse, to tell her the truth.

"We shouldn't be talking now," Davie whispered.

"No, let's talk," Dad said. "It's all right."

But then Dad paused so long that Davie thought he'd changed his mind. After a few seconds, Dad took a deep breath. "Your mom and I love you very much . . ."

Oh crap, here it goes, Davie thought, his heart pounding. His hands trembled like they had when the ghost dog ran toward them with that angry bark. "And we love each other very much. God knows that's true. But Mommy misses her family in Ghana—her mother is sick—and she wants to live closer to them. But I have a job where I can't just pack up and move. I work in Hollywood. So right now we're having a disagreement about where we're going to live. And where you're going to live."

It didn't sound as terrible as it had seemed when Dad was crying at the kitchen table. It didn't even sound like a divorce, not for sure.

Neema squirmed, moving to her father's lap. He was sitting cross-legged in front of the bookshelf behind the big recliner. Their lucky spot.

"You mean . . . we can't all live together?" Neema said.

"Maybe not right now."

"But . . ." Neema fought to put it all together. ". . . where would *we* live? Me and Davie?"

"With Mommy," Dad said, and Davie heard his voice crack. "Probably."

Grandpa's sigh was the only sound in the silence.

Until the scream.

The scream sounded like it was from right across the room, as close as the living-room window. So loud that the window pane cracked. All of them jumped and gasped. Neema wrapped her arms around her father's neck.

Grandpa's flashlight switched on. He bobbed the light near the window. The curtain was open, revealing veins of broken glass. "What the . . . Who broke that?"

"*No light*," Davie whispered. "Shut it off, Grandpa. Ghosts like the dark."

Muttering and cursing to himself, Grandpa turned off his flashlight. When he did, the brightness in Davie's Night Vision dimmed enough for him to gaze through the lens without squinting. This time, he didn't see any shadowy figure framed against the light from the window. Whoever had screamed was gone.

But the water was back, creeping higher while he hadn't been paying attention. This time, he saw currents swirling in the water, tiny rapids. Cold water crept into his boots, numbing his toes. Davie switched on the tape recorder around his neck. Back-up evidence.

"Water!" Neema said.

"I know. Watch out—it's getting higher."

"I can't believe that damn window broke," Grandpa said. "That thing cost . . ."

"*Shhhhh*." This time, it was Davie's father. "Don't break the spell, Dad."

Sixty seconds passed. The scream sounded again, as if it was a movie that had been on Pause. Sounds crashed into the room: Splashing. Yelling. Barking and growling. Chaos.

"*Git 'im off! Git 'im off!*" a child's voice screamed.

Davie's mouth dropped open. His hands were unsteady, but he trained the camera back toward the window, toward the noise. This time, he saw several shadowy figures against the moonlight, arms flailing in a struggle. The tallest shadow—the oldest boy, Davie figured—was holding what looked like a giant stick. He raised it high and stabbed it like King Arthur's sword.

This time, the scream wasn't human. It was a dog's.

Another window cracked. Glass tinkled to the floor.

Grandpa Walt came to his feet. "*God*damn it," he said, sounding almost as scared as he was mad. He spoke to the darkness. "You stop breaking those windows!"

"The noise is doing it, Grandpa," Neema said. "Can't you hear it?"

Maybe Grandpa Walter was lucky he couldn't hear it. One, two, three boys were sobbing. One was outright wailing, as if he was in the worst pain of his life.

"*Is he dead*?" one of the boys said.

"*Ithurtsithurtsithurtsithurts . . .*"

"*Hurry up and help me grab 'im. Let's go!*"

In Davie's viewfinder, the shadowy figures were gone. But he heard the splashing of several sets of footsteps running toward the kitchen again. Where the water would be deeper.

"They're moving," Davie said.

"The kitchen," Neema said, on Davie's heels.

While the rest of them scrambled to grab their supplies and follow, Grandpa only shook his head. "I'm not chasing nobody nowhere," Grandpa said.

"You sure, Dad?" Davie's father said. "It may turn out to be something."

Davie barely heard them over the sloshing of water as he ran to the kitchen doorway. He ignored the terrible feeling of cold water rising as high as his thighs. The back door was wide open again, just like he'd known it would be. When Davie looked through the viewfinder, he saw the taller boy beckoning in the door frame.

Beckoning to them? To his brothers? Davie didn't know.

"We have to hurry!" Davie said, forgetting not to shout. "Before they're gone!"

The recliner hissed when Grandpa plopped himself down to sit. "My chasing days are over. But I'ma sit right here, and *nobody* better break no more of my damn windows."

Grandpa was talking to the ghosts.

"The water's too deep for me!" Neema said at Davie's side. "Over my waist!"

"Here, Pumpkin," Dad said, and hoisted her to his shoulders.

All three of them were breathing fast.

This was as far as Davie had ever followed the three boys. He didn't know what would come next. The dark kitchen suddenly looked strange and forbidding, full of shadowy hazard.

Still, Davie waded into deeper water, one step on the linoleum at a time.

Summer, 1909

It was an hour before dawn, and Isaac Timmons was supposed to be resting. That was what his mama had told him to do. She'd made all three of them curl up on the living room rug under the oak tree, where the grass was soft. Mama had moved her favorite rug out of the house to keep it from getting muddy tracks, and she was planning to roll it up to pack last. She said they'd worked hard all night, so they deserved some sleep. "There's a long journey ahead," she'd said. Then she'd given them each a kiss and said, "And then we'll be away from Graceville forever!" As if she'd come up with the plan to leave all on her own, and it had nothing to do with the barn. Mama had always considered Graceville cursed, especially for Negroes.

His brothers were asleep, but Isaac Timmons wasn't. He was

thinking about his best gal, Livvy, and how sad it was he would never see her again. Livvy's mom had just given him the honey he'd taken home to his brothers, which started the whole business with the barn, but Isaac couldn't blame Livvy for that. Hadn't Livvy said only last Sunday that she was *his* gal? And what kind of man would abandon his gal without so much as a goodbye?

No kind of man, Isaac thought. That's what Papa would say.

He would slip away and come right back. He'd be gone a half-hour at the most, if he ran. He couldn't ask Mama and Papa, because he knew what they would say. Livvy lived out McCormack's way, and he should never go that way. Not ever.

But Livvy was his gal. Once, she'd held his hand. Papa said he could expect to get married in three or four years, and Isaac decided he would come back for Livvy when he could. But for now, he had to tell his gal goodbye. *Had* to.

Isaac wasn't planning to wake his brothers, but each one nudged the next when he rolled off the rug. Even Little Eddie woke right up with bright eyes, ready to play.

"Where you goin'?" Scott said.

"Nowhere. Just stay here. I'll be back."

"*No*, Isaac," Scott said, sitting straight up. "He'll blame me."

"Pretend you're sleeping. Use your head." Papa used that phrase a lot.

"You going to Livvy's?" Scott said. "I wanna go too."

So all three of them snuck away from the rug, through the pines in back, beyond the creek and over to the McCormack side of the road, which had a fence. The long fence stretched as far as they could see. It was still half-dark, so it was quiet and still. Isaac took a long look at Graceville as he walked—the long grass, cotton patches and pine trees—and wondered what New York would look like. He had never even seen a picture in a book.

All of the lights were still off in the McCormack house, which stood on the hill. That house looked like a castle, which he *had* seen in a book. Isaac wondered if the McCormacks would ever find out his father thought they'd burned down the barn. Maybe they would never even know. Isaac hoped not. He didn't want to give Mr. McCormack the satisfaction.

"We gotta go faster," Isaac said, "or they'll see we're gone for sure."

"You think Livvy's mama's gonna give us more honey?" Little Eddie said.

"You think Livvy'll give you a big sloppy kiss?" Scott teased.

Instead of getting mad, Isaac enjoyed the quiet around him. McCormack's land was on one side, swampy land on the other. Walking with his brothers on the empty road toward Livvy's, it was hard to believe Mama and Papa were packing up everything they owned in a wagon to drive farther than Isaac's mind could imagine. Two days' journey was a long way away. If you married someone two days away, your parents might not see you for years. Papa had said New York was weeks away, by wagon. Papa didn't even think the wagon could make the trip.

A dead pine had toppled over and knocked out the logs to the McCormack fence. Most of the fence was intact, but one entire section had been crushed, and the fence was gaping open.

That was why he'd felt so peaceful, Isaac realized. Quiet. He should have known.

Isaac tugged on Little Eddie's shirt to keep him from walking ahead. He held up his hand to hush his brothers' tittering. The dawn was as silent as a tomb.

"Where's the dog?" Isaac whispered.

The boys looked up and down the road, dreading the sight of the dog sprinting toward them, freed from its prison. In their imaginations, the dog was three times its normal size, a monstrous beast. A Negro man in town missing three of his fingers told stories about McCormack's dog. McCormack trained his dog to bite niggers, the man said.

No dog was in sight. On McCormack's land, only a few chickens stirred. On the swamp side, there was no sound except from insects and reptiles; the swamp's constantly trilling song.

"We gotta go back," Isaac said. He held tight to Little Eddie's hand.

"What about the honey?" Little Eddie said.

"Mama say they treat that dog like family," Scott said. "Maybe it sleeps in the house."

It was a tempting thought, for a moment. Surely the dog was somewhere close to the house. The dog wouldn't be roaming on the road or the swamp, would it? Issac hated to lose his honor by leaving Livvy without a word of explanation. What would she think of him?

"Yeah . . . maybe," Isaac said. "Maybe."

Then they heard the barking.

"You hear that? Run!" the shadowy figure in the kitchen doorway said. He waved furiously, as if their lives depended on it.

"He's telling us follow him," Neema said from her perch on her father's shoulders.

"Then . . . let's follow," Dad said.

Davie waded farther into the kitchen, until he felt the water at his mid-chest. The sensation of fighting against the water to walk made it feel like he couldn't breathe. He was shaking all over. But the door was so close! The shadow was almost within his reach.

Water converged around the base of Davie's throat, a collar of ice. But the cold liquid didn't feel like clean water: it was heavier, more viscous, a slime of sweet-sour dead marine life and vegetation. The smell of the old, dead swamp made Davie want to vomit.

"I can't go anymore," Davie gasped. "The water's too high."

"Just to the door, Davie," Dad said. "If you can't after that, you can't."

"You can do it, Davie!" Neema said. Easy for *her* to say, Davie thought.

Davie gulped at the air. He didn't want to know what the water tasted like, but he wasn't going to turn back. With his next step, he held his breath in case he wouldn't touch bottom.

But he did.

The next thing Davie knew, he was standing outside on the back porch. Dad was one step below him, still carrying Neema. Staring toward the woods. The water had receded dramatically, only as high as Davie's ankles. Davie gasped two or three times at the clean air, remembering the awfulness of the water he'd waded through. He reeked of it.

"What now?" Dad said.

Neema pointed. "That way. I hear splashing."

His bearings returned, Davie raised the camera, using Night Vision to follow her finger. Whether she knew it or not, Neema was pointing straight toward the broken fence. With every step, Davie better heard the urgent whisper ahead in the darkness.

"*We'll lose 'im in the water! Run!*"

More splashing. Sets of feet in a hurry.

"Yeah, this way," Davie said.

They trotted off together, following Neema's finger and the splashing. They didn't run in a straight line, but they eventually ended up at the broken fence. Even with Night Vision, the woods were nearly pitch black through the viewfinder. His only clear view was of the broken fence post, a jagged log toppled down.

The sight of the broken fence in the frame scared Davie. Once they left the backyard, all of the light would be behind them. "Official ghost-hunting audio journal," Davie said in a shaky voice to his tape recorder, remembering his protocols. "We've reached the broken fence. We still hear the splashing on the other side."

"Hurry, Davie!" Neema said. "They're going too far."

"Hold on," Dad said. "I can't carry Neema on my back in the woods."

Thank goodness. Dad was predictable, and suddenly Davie was glad.

"How's the water?" Dad asked.

The water was like cold claws grasping his ankles, even with oversized boots on.

"Fine," Davie said. "It's lower now."

Dad grunted, lowering Neema to the ground. Then, Dad bent over to be closer to her eye-level. Neema giggled and danced when her feet touched the water.

"All right, listen, you two," Dad said. "We'll go to the woods. I'll allow this. But we'll have rules, and I'm only gonna say them once."

"Daddy, just say them *fast*," Neema said. The broken fence didn't scare her at all. She sounded like she was ready to wet herself from excitement.

"Stay close. Come when I call. *Watch* where you're walking," Dad said. "Davie?"

"Yessir." The splashing had veered right, up ahead. "The splashing is softer and softer," he said, speaking his audio journal. "But I still hear it."

Neema pointed again. "That way!" she said.

"Let's do it," Dad said, raising his shovel high.

As he stepped over the fallen log, Davie's heart pounded so hard that the blood rushing in his ears drowned out the splashing. He couldn't believe Dad was letting them do this! There were snakes in the woods. There were coyotes and bears too, not just deer, and there were ghosts for an absolute fact. And Neema was with them, the one he babied to death over nothing!

Something was different about Dad. Something had changed, and Davie didn't know if the change was good or bad. Davie wondered if *he* should be the reasonable one tonight, just in case Dad had forgotten how. Maybe Dad had snuck more than one beer after dinner.

Dad flicked on the hurricane flashlight, and a precious circle of the woods before them turned as bright as midday. Every twig, leaf and stump threw a shadow.

Behind them, in the dark, came the sound of barking. The dog's splashing was directed, more disciplined. Like a guided missile.

"The dog!" Davie said.

"Run!" the boy up ahead yelled.

They ran awkwardly, more like jogging, careful with their speed to avoid tripping. Up ahead, the splashing sounded more and more frantic. The younger boys were crying, or maybe all of them were. Their cries filled the woods.

"Faster," Davie huffed.

"No," Dad said. "Too dangerous."

"No, Dad, it's too dangerous *not* to." Davie ran ahead, just to set a good example.

"Get out your doggy biscuits," Dad said.

"That won't work!"

"How do you know?"

The dog was very large, and its bark sounded slobbery. Hungry.

"Because I can *hear* him! That. Won't. Work."

Neema wasn't saying anything by then. She could hear the dog's hunger too. She was proud she had made it past the first shrieks this time, but Neema was good and ready to go home. Lesson learned. She wasn't old enough to be a ghost-hunter. Like with Grandpa, the idea had lost all of its attraction.

Davie's father, who couldn't hear the barking, tugged on Davie's raincoat to slow him down. "Keep this up, Davie, and we'll go home."

"Yeah, Dad, we *should* go home, but now I don't know if we can." Maybe Dad would have understood if he'd waded through that muck. They had crossed to another side. It might not be easy to cross back. "Let's just go faster."

"Kofi David Stephens . . . *Slow down.* Someone could break a leg out here."

The barking and splashing behind them grew impossibly loud just before it fell silent. Davie held his breath.

Neema screamed.

For a blink, Davie's brain shut down: His baby sister was screaming?

Water thrashed as Neema writhed beside their father, still screaming. *"Something bit me!"* Neema cried, all childhood stripped out of her voice. "*It bit me, Daddy! My leg!*" And she screamed again, her horror renewed at the retelling.

There was more splashing when Dad bent over to pick her up. Vaguely, Davie wondered when their feet had started making the water splash, too. If the splashing water was real now, was the dog real now too? In his flashlight beam, Davie saw something wet glisten on Neema's leg. The dark wetness startled him so much that his hand shook, nearly dropping the flashlight, and the terrible image went away. Not water. Blood.

"Oh, babydoll, you're okay. *Shhhh.* You're okay." Even while Dad comforted Neema, he sounded petrified. Davie didn't have to wonder if he had imagined the blood. He knew the blood was there from the tremor in his father's voice. And he knew it was more than a little. Davie felt steaming water in his pants as he pissed on himself.

"Davie," Daddy said, in a soldier's voice Davie hadn't heard before. The tremor was gone, as if it hadn't been there at all. "Grab Neema."

Davie couldn't say anything. Couldn't move, at first.

"Davie, grab her. Something bit her, it's big, and it's still out here."

Davie grabbed Neema's hand, and Neema sobbed because she didn't want to be away from her father. Dad was the solver of all of Neema's problems, and now he had pushed her aside. Davie had to physically restrain her to keep her from clinging to their father. Using his muscles helped Davie shut off the panic ruling his mind.

Dad grabbed his shovel and picked it up, testing its weight in its hand.

Splashing came from behind them.

Davie gasped, diving away from the splashing, yanking Neema with him. Neema screamed, clinging to him with so much strength that Davie nearly staggered to his knees.

Dad whirled, his eyes following his flashlight beam. Nothing visible but brush. Davie tried to help with his own flashlight, but his beam kept zigging into the treetops because he couldn't hold his hand steady, especially with Neema pulling on him so hard.

"Can't see it . . ." Dad was whispering to himself. "I can't fucking see it . . ."

Davie remembered his audio journal: "Something just bit Neema," he said. Neema wailed, hearing the horror repeated.

"Davie, *be quiet*," Dad said.

But Davie couldn't be quiet. He was screaming too.

First, he felt a tug on the back of his raincoat. Then, something raked through clothes and skin on the back of his thigh, with the precision of knives. Davie had never known his body could feel so much pain. He fell to his knees, stunned by the fire in his nerves. As he fell, slimy water splashed his face.

Not cold anymore. Warm.

Inches in front of him, more water splashed, some of it stinging his eyes.

The dog was probably staring him dead in the face.

"*IN FRONT OF ME!*" Davie screamed, and Dad took a wild swing with his shovel at the air in front of Davie's face. Dad only threw himself off-balance.

But Dad's second swing hit something. There was a *ping* sound, a watery thud, and the sound of an animal's yelp. Dad stabbed the shovel down like a stake, and a shriek flew from the nothing under Dad's shovel. A beast, invisible.

"Is it dead?" Neema said.

Dad jabbed his shovel into the land around him, and water splashed.

"I hear that," Dad said, amazed. "Jesus. I hear it."

"Why can't-can't we-we see it?" Neema stuttered, wrapped so hard around Davie that he could barely breathe. He screamed out again. The pain was truly dazzling.

By then, all three of them might have been crying.

"Okay," Dad said, trying to find a place for it in his mind. "Okay. Okay. I know it's here, but we can't see the dog. We can't see it. Okay."

"Is it dead?" Neema said again.

Dad jabbed at the ground. More splashing. "I don't know. I don't know where it is. I don't know if it's dead. It's not here. It's not here." Dad's voice sounded far away, from California. Dad was fading too.

Davie felt his father's hands patting him, examining his injury. His father's touch made him cry out again.

"Davie? Listen to me."

Davie tried to listen, but Dad's voice kept melting. Slipping under the world.

Water splashed on Davie's cheeks, and his eyes jolted open. Dad's nose was nearly touching him. "Davie, I know you're hurt, but you need to listen to me. Can you walk?"

Davie tried to stand up, and the pain made him vomit. Dad patted his shoulder.

"Davie, I can't carry both of you. Do you hear me?" Dad said. His voice was shaky, almost pleading. "Neema's ankle's hurt, so she can't walk. But I think you can."

"I can't!" he said. The back of his thigh was on fire. "Dad, it *hurts*."

"I can't leave you here. So that means we all have to go—*now*," Dad said, breathing in his face. This time, Davie didn't smell beer; he smelled his father's perspiration, the smell of horsey rides and swinging from Dad's arms in the back yard. The memories made Davie cry out, worse than the pain from his bite. Dad was panting. "This one time, Davie, I need you to grow up very fucking fast."

Davie gasped out a sob, but then he lost interest in crying. He was in pain in every way, but the pain wasn't as bad as knowing the dog was still out there. They were in big trouble, and crying wasn't going to change it.

"I need a stick," Davie said. He sniffed, and snot churned in his nose. "A weapon."

"Good boy." Dad's flashlight swept the forest floor, and the stick appeared as if by miracle. "Grab that one, fast. Then we'll go back the way we came. Did you get enough for YouTube?" Dad picked Neema up again.

Davie tried to laugh, but it only came out like crying. He grabbed the fallen branch, which was thick, but not too thick for his palm. A perfect fit. It reminded him of the same stick he'd used when he saw the boys in the woods, already free of excess twigs and dead leaves. But it couldn't be way out here. Could it? *My magic staff*, Davie thought, hopeful. Desperate.

When Davie shifted his weight to his good leg, his injured leg screamed at him. He didn't know how much he was bleeding, but he could feel the fabric of his jeans knotted up in his bloodied parts. Every movement was agony. Panic tangled his breaths in his lungs. Suddenly he was gasping.

"Stay calm. We're gonna get out of here, Davie. I promise. I'll get you a doctor."

"Me too?" Neema whispered from the safety of Dad's arms.

"You too, Pumpkin. You ready, Davie?"

Davie nodded, catching his breath, but his lips were shaking. He gripped his stick tightly with one hand, trained his flashlight ahead with the other. He couldn't use Night Vision now—it limited his scope too much. He would have to trust his own eyes for the walk back to the fence.

"Let's go," Dad said, just before they heard the barking behind them again.

Angry barking. *SPLASHSPLASH*

Davie just kept thinking *No*. It wasn't possible. It couldn't be. It wasn't fair.

"I heard that," Dad said, amazed and frightened. "I hear something coming."

"*Run!*" said a boy's voice from ahead of them.

"I heard that," Dad said. His voice was dazed.

They had no choice but to run; the boy's urgent voice only confirmed their instincts. Dad's feet made heavy splashes as he staggered under Neema's extra weight. Tree trunks appeared suddenly in the beams from their flashlights, almost too late to avoid colliding with them, so running took all of Davie's concentration—at first. Then he realized they were following the voices, keeping ahead of the dog's splashing behind them, running the wrong way. The fence back to his grandparents' house was *behind* them.

Where were the ghosts taking them?

Davie ventured a quick glance through Night Vision for a long view—and he saw a huge, looming structure up ahead and toward the right, blocking the moonlight.

"A tobacco barn," Davie said.

He had never seen it in daylight. He doubted that it was real, but it was there. At the edge of the swamp. *The Timmons boys crossed a swamp to lose the dog,* Davie realized. He thought he said it aloud for his audio journal, but he was only whispering.

"*Come on, we'll close the barn door,*" the boy's husky voice ahead said, full of reason.

"The barn door!" Dad said. "We'll close the door."

Consensus.

The barking was getting closer again.

Davie and his father must have caught up to the others, because the splashing of the ghost boys blended with theirs. He heard their sobs and whispers close to his ear. They were running together, all of them. Combined, their feet sounded like an army, and Davie hoped they were.

Like Davie, they were crying and in pain. They understood. But still they ran.

Davie thought his lungs would burst. The meat of his back thigh hurt so much that he was convinced it was falling apart, unfurling flesh with every twig he brushed against. He couldn't tell the difference between his sobs and his hitching breaths, but he checked his Night Vision lens again. Part of his head was still working.

Were they moving at all? The tobacco barn was too far. Too far.

They wouldn't make it, he realized. The barking behind them was gaining too fast. The dog was too loud, too close.

They needed another plan.

"We can't . . . we can't . . ." Davie wheezed.

A shriek sounded, to Davie's left. The bottom fell out of his world until he saw that neither Dad nor Neema was shrieking. Dad froze in his tracks, lowering Neema to the ground so he could wield his shovel as a weapon. Neema sobbed, clinging to their father's legs, staring wide-eyed toward the place where the shrieking had come. Dad was wide-eyed too.

Beside them, there was a frenzy of splashing in the water.

"*Ithurtsithurtsithurtsithurtsithurts!*"

Davie didn't know whose voice it was. It could be any of them.

"Where is it?" Dad said, ready with his shovel.

Davie looked through Night Vision and saw the whorls of water dancing about ten yards ahead of them. There was a great commotion. "There! By that stump!"

Dad had only lunged ahead one step when a beast let out a terrible sound. For an instant, right before he blinked, Davie thought he saw water splash as if a boulder had just been tossed inside, framing the dead dog like a chalk drawing. The dog was big. He could have killed them.

"*I got it!*" the oldest boy said.

"Is it dead?"

"It's not dead!" Davie said. He had heard the dog felled three times and counting, but the dog always came back. Davie had learned that much. As soon as his legs started pumping again, he heard a splash behind him—and a sound like a shower as the dog shook off water.

The barking started right away.

"Run!"

Davie no longer knew whose voice he heard. Dad scooped Neema up into his arms and followed Davie's lead, racing toward the barn. Neema clung to Dad so she wouldn't hit her head on tree branches, but Dad still had to run slowly with her in his arms. Too slow!

The dog would catch them again. The dog always caught them.

"Run!" the voice said ahead.

Then, even worse, an urgent scream: "*STOP!*"

But Davie couldn't stop his legs in time. Suddenly, there was no ground beneath Davie's feet. His feet plunged downward to nothingness, like stepping off of a sand bar at the beach.

He was drowning in soft earth. Mud.

Even before Davie fully realized he had fallen into some kind of hole—and a large one, since the earth yawning around him—he began scrabbling to try to pull himself out. His slide was slow, a taking-its-time kind of terror, and Davie screamed, grasping for a twig or a rock, anything to hold him above ground.

"Be still!" Dad said. Davie had heard that same terror in Dad's voice when Neema screamed, except now Dad's voice was more hollowed out, like he was witnessing a death. He had dropped Neema just short of the hole, or they all might have fallen. "Davie, don't move! Please don't move, Davie."

As Dad reached for him—his hand still a good six inches off—something cracked beneath Davie, old damp wood aged beyond its time, and Davie plunged downward again. Suddenly, Dad's hand was gone.

Dad and Neema both yelled his name, as if they could will his fall to stop.

Davie screamed and sobbed, panicked by the bitter taste of mud in his mouth. His legs jerked, kicking, and there was nothing but air beneath him. Below, there was a long fall. As mud slid down around him, gathering speed and resolve, Davie couldn't understand why mud had risen to his chin and no farther. Or why he hadn't fallen yet.

He felt his clothes pinching at the nape of his neck, as if he was dangling on a hook. Something was holding him up from behind.

The ghost?

His jaw trembling, Davie turned around to see with his own eyes.

A stubborn tree branch had snagged his raincoat, he saw from the corner of his eye. Grandma's raincoat had saved him from falling.

"I said *be still*," Dad said, grabbing his arm. "It's like a . . . well . . . or something. It's a long drop down, Davie."

Davie last brave act that night was to train his Night Vision down to the hole below his dangling feet. He thought he saw the flare from the whites of a small boy's eyes. No, two! Terrified eyes. Davie heard three boys yelling beneath him, and then only a horrible silence.

They had fallen. All three boys had fallen, just like he, Neema, and Dad almost had.

Davie could only breathe again once Dad had pulled him far clear of the hole, when he was sure all four limbs were on solid ground. He was afraid to walk anywhere, afraid of falling again. "You're okay," Dad said, stroking Davie with one arm and Neema with the other. Davie could hear his father's heart thundering in his chest. "You're okay. It's all okay."

"Is it gone?" Neema said.

Davie wondered if she was talking about the dog or the hole, or both. No barking, but it could be hiding. Waiting.

"I don't know," Dad said. "We're going to the barn. Where is it, Davie?"

"What if it's not real?" Davie said.

"It's real enough."

They were only forty yards away from the barn, but it was a long forty yards. Davie realized he didn't hear splashing when he walked anymore. The barn was on dry land.

By the time they got to the barn door, Davie's body was drenched in perspiration. He felt like he was swimming in his clothes. But he helped Dad pry the barn door loose from its mooring, and they slammed the heavy door shut behind them. Dad used his shovel to lock it in place, since there was no other way to secure it.

By then, Davie was lying on the barn floor, his face pressed against the scratchy wood. The barn smelled of sweet tobacco leaves, a smell that burned his throat. "The dogs chased them to the swamp," Davie said. "They killed the dog. But they fell in a hole."

Dad barely heard him, too consumed with comforting Neema. As much as Davie craved comfort himself, he didn't mind. He would have died to keep Neema safe. He still might.

"Maybe a . . . storm cellar," his father panted. "Maybe a well. Probably no way out."

Maybe they had fallen and broken their necks right away. Or been buried alive. Maybe they had died waiting for someone to find them. And all the while, the town was going to hell because they were gone. Davie could only cry about the whole sad mess.

The Timmons brothers never made it to the barn. They fell when the barn was just within sight. It wasn't fair, after what they'd been through. It wasn't fair.

While Davie cried, Dad undressed him and Neema, examining their wounds by flashlight, washing them with bottled water. He looked relieved. There was blood, but the bleeding had already stopped. He divided the packet of Extra Strength Tylenol he kept in his wallet between them. The pain was still at a roar, but having a pill to take made him feel better.

"You're fine," Dad promised them, and they hoped he wasn't lying.

The tobacco barn was cavernous. When Dad walked to the other side of the barn to make sure there were no other doors to lock, his absence seemed eternal. Davie thought he would faint waiting for his father to come back to their corner, where Dad had spread out their coats to make a cushion for them to rest. If Davie hadn't been stroking Neema's hair and telling her everything was fine, just like Dad, he might have started crying again.

But his father did come back, and he brought good news.

"We're locked tight as a drum," he said. "I checked every corner. Nothing's getting in."

And that was that. By silent agreement, they knew they weren't going to open the door until morning. Ghosts don't like the light.

They ate cheese and crackers and drank bottled water. They talked about favorite characters from television, movies, and books to keep from thinking about their world.

That was when Davie heard it from the slats in the wooden wall, a foot from his ear:

Snnnnffffff snnfff snnfffffff

The dog was sniffing at the door.

A loud bark woke Davie, a roaring in his ear. Daylight blinded him when he opened his eyes. He blinked, his limbs frozen by a sight so improbable that he forgot his pulsing pain: The towering tobacco barn around him was no more than a shell, most of the wall planks stripped away, its rooftop lost among the pines, its floor overgrown with generations of underbrush.

A German shepherd's face lunged toward Davie, pink tongue caressing sharp teeth.

He's followed us to daytime, Davie thought. That thought blanked out anything else that tried to come into his mind, until he couldn't remember where he was. Or who.

Neema's scream pulled Davie out of his trance.

Davie let out his own yell, pinwheeling his arms as his only weapon against the dog.

"Calm down, Davie!"

"Son, it's all right. Whoa there. Whoa."

"Neema, it's Grandma! It's all right."

"Can't you see, Sheriff? They're scared of the *dogs*."

Once the police tracking dogs were well out of sight, the world came back to Davie in slow bits and pieces. But it took a while.

Davie's next fully formed memory was sitting on a yellow police blanket slurping apple juice from a juice box; the best apple juice he'd ever tasted. Neema, slurping her own juice box across from him, was sharing the exact same feeling as she gazed at him. Both of them almost smiled. That was the first hint Davie felt that maybe they were all right. Maybe.

Davie couldn't hear what his father was saying to the sheriff over the hood of the sheriff's huge SUV, the sheriff nodding and taking notes. Davie couldn't imagine what kind of story Dad could tell someone who hadn't been there.

Davie gasped. He patted his side for this gear, but everything except his shirt had been stripped off by the paramedics. "My camera!" he said. More like a croak.

Grandpa held his ghost kit high up in the air. "Got everything here, Davie. Just relax." Grandpa was using his cane, Davie noticed. He had never seen him use his cane outside before.

"Grandpa, it *bit* us," Davie said. "Even though we couldn't see it."

Grandpa nodded, gesturing for him to hush. "*Shhhh.* You just relax right now. No need to get excited. It's gone now."

Grandma's eyes were tired. Davie realized they both must have been up all night, worried sick when they never came back from the woods. Davie didn't know how far they had traveled, but it had taken a long time to find them. Davie felt terrible for causing his grandparents the same awful suffering Isaiah and Essie Timmons had, even for a night.

When Grandma stroked Davie's head, he held her wrist tightly. "Grandma, I know what happened to the Timmons boys," he whispered.

"Hush, Davie," Grandma said. "Walt's right. Forget about that, baby."

"There's a hole—over there! A dog was chasing them, and they fell in. I know it. I almost fell in, too!"

Grandma sent a withering look Dad's way. She was so mad at Dad for taking them out into the woods at night, she probably could barely think of anything else.

"Somebody has to find the bodies," Davie said. "Or it's all for nothing. Just tell them to dig. Tell Miss Timmons her brothers are here. If she wants to find them, she's got to dig."

The particulars are unnecessary. All three Timmons boys eventually died, though not at once. Isaiah Timmons died never knowing that his sons lay trapped in the abandoned cellar of a house knocked over in a twister in '02. That house had crumbled like toothpicks, but the barn beyond it hadn't had a scratch. Such is the way with twisters.

The boys' mother, Essie, would walk the ground within a stone's throw of her sons' burial place on three separate occasions in the fifty years before she died. She never knew, not even a hunch.

All Old Man McCormack ever knew was that someone had killed his dog.

The dog was found, at least.

There was no justice in it. All four of the deceased thought so.

After Davie and Neema were released from their night's stay at Tallahassee Memorial, Dad moved them to the new Quality Inn that had just opened off of the 10, only ten minutes from Davie's grandparents but safely across Graceville's boundary. Technically, out of town.

Neema wouldn't hear about sleeping at the house another night, even when Grandma promised to put the dolls away. But Davie wasn't ready to go home to California yet.

Not until he *knew*.

Grandpa Walter and Grandma were sweetness and spice around Davie, but Davie knew they were furious with Dad for taking his two children into the dark woods. *What were you thinking?* Mom was on her way, too. Dad had tried to sound happy when he told Davie she was coming, but the dread on Dad's face had been hard to ignore.

So Davie knew there was really nothing in the way of it now. So much for their month apart. So much for Imani's plans to change Mom's mind. The future was here, a month early.

To take his mind off of the impending disaster, Davie checked his video footage.

The footage of the living room only showed the broken windows—not the *breaking* windows, a key distinction—and conversations between him, Neema, Dad, and Grandpa Walter. No splashing or shrieking on the video. Same old same old. Nothing new. Even the shadow of the Timmons boy in the kitchen doorway wasn't as distinct as it had been the first time, and the first time it had been pretty sucky.

The footage got better in the woods, but Davie had to stop the tape when he heard Neema scream. Out of nowhere, he suddenly heard all of it: Barking. Voices. Water. Not as loud as it had been, but undeniably there—true ghost phenomena, when he was ready to show it. He just wasn't sure when. Maybe soon, maybe not. Maybe tomorrow. Maybe never.

Davie found that it was hard to know anything anymore.

Dad quietly let himself into the hotel room and motioned Davie over. Grandma had dozed off in the hotel room's recliner and Neema was curled up sleeping at the foot of the bed, where she'd been watching the Disney Channel at a low volume. Hopping with his crutch, Davie followed Dad into the hotel room's bathroom. The bright lights made Dad look older.

"So . . . they're digging," Dad said, out of the blue.

"Right now?"

"Started this morning. Mom and Dad didn't think I should say anything, but I thought you deserved to know, Davie."

Dad said it as if it was something to think about.

"I have to go," Davie said.

Dad's face flinched, a tic that almost closed his right eye. "How's your leg?"

Davie's back thigh radiated pain, flaring with every step, but that was irrelevant. "Painkillers," Davie said. "It's fine."

"Davie, they might not find anything. Or, maybe they will. Either way, it'll be hard."

If Dad hadn't been there . . .

The thought began as a constant refrain in his mind, but it never finished itself. That thought didn't need finishing, because he would be dead if his father hadn't been there. Davie knew that as well as he knew his name. But they hadn't talked about it yet. Dad had never told Davie what he thought had happened in the woods. Maybe he didn't need to.

"Is Mom coming to take us now?" Davie said.

Dad didn't blink. "Looks that way." He made a fist before slowly fanning his fingers.

They stood in the bathroom, quiet. Dad's fingers drummed on the sink's fake marble counter. Dad didn't seem like the man who had been crying in the kitchen anymore.

"I'll tell her it's not your fault," Davie said.

"It has nothing to do with that. Or you. That's the truth, Davie."

Davie believed him, but he also remembered the animal terror and loathing on his father's face when he was swinging his shovel at the invisible thing chasing him and Neema. He wondered if Dad would feel that about Mom one day, or if maybe even *he* would. He wished a fight wasn't coming. He would have to choose sides.

"What time is Mom getting here?"

"Late. Seven."

There was still time for things to stay the same. Just for a while.

"Don't you want to see the bones too, Dad?"

"I just . . . want to be careful about it. I'm on thin ice around here, Davie."

Davie hoped Dad wasn't convinced there had never been a dog, that maybe they had been attacked by a hungry bear in the dark. He hoped Dad wouldn't start forgetting.

"But you want to, don't you?" Davie said. "Don't you want to see?"

Dad bit his lip and nodded.

So, they left a note for Grandma on Quality Inn stationery—and they went.

The dig for the bones of Isaac, Scott, and Little Eddie Timmons had begun quietly, without fanfare. The attorneys for the warring parties—the developer, Stellar Properties Inc., and a group of residents calling themselves the Graceville Citizens Action Council, of which Miss Essie Timmons was an honorary chair—exchanged phone calls and reached a compromise.

The digging had begun only a day after the missing family told its ghost story.

At dawn.

Despite the instability at the surface, much of the old abandoned cellar had filled with debris and soil over time, so it wasn't as easy as finding a ready tunnel. The dig took time.

As the day wore on, a bulldozer and small scooper wound their way down the newly worn path to the abandoned tobacco barn that developers would have razed the week before, if town politics hadn't hung them up. They would have found the hole themselves the hard way, so it was best it was found before someone got killed.

The company CEO, who'd approved the dig personally, thought it was a win-win: His company could demonstrate goodwill to the superstitious, rustic locals and symbolically lay the whole issue of corpses to rest. ("You see?" he could say. "This proves it for once and for all: No more bodies here!" It wasn't exactly the ideal slogan for a housing development, but it was an improvement over their current PR standing.)

Neighborhood Watch, which had transformed into a satellite of the Graceville Citizens Action Council, had volunteers up and down McCormack Road who called multiple numbers on their phone trees when they saw construction trucks on the move. The movement of workers and equipment to Lot Sixty-five gained more attention on a Saturday than one might think.

By midmorning, a good crowd had gathered at the edge of the dig.

In fairness to the Timmons family, the excavation was eight feet by eight feet, which Stellar had argued was more than enough of a safety margin for finding the bones. A square block of the soil would be dug up, bit by bit, and the dig wouldn't end until it was twenty yards down. Almost like digging for oil, some onlookers thought.

While one set of workers hauled up the soil, another sifted through it looking for bone fragments, with help from students from the anthropology department at the college. Adults shooed children away from the sifters, and police officers shooed adults and children alike away from the growing hole, which looked more deadly as the day wore on.

Before noon, there were three occasions of great excitement at the dig on Lot Sixty-five.

The first was when a green van from Graceville Glen Retirement Home came bouncing along the path, and two uniformed workers wheeled out ninety-one-year-old Essie Timmons, named for her mother, who had spent her lifetime drowning in her mother's grief about her three lost sons. Essie Timmons had been raised in the shadow of her dead brothers, and her mother's obsession with finding out the exact how and why of their vanishing had been bequeathed to her. In the 1940s, she had written a book on the subject, *Three Brothers: The Timmons Family and the Graceville Riots*. (She owned the only three remaining copies, and she never allowed anyone to touch their pages.) She had always given talks at the elementary school on the subject until her stroke a decade before. But while her body was diminished, her mind was sharp.

Essie Timmons' dark face was deeply webbed by her age lines, but her cheekbones were still a carbon copy of her dead brother Isaac's. She wore a mound of white hair so vivid that it was visible from a distance. She never left her wheelchair and had trouble holding her head upright, so she looked more dead than alive. But no matter. While a uniformed worker stood over her with an umbrella, Essie Timmons sat out in the sun and watched the workmen dig.

Every once in a while, a well-meaning citizen came up to the old woman to offer her a cold drink, or to ask her if she was hungry. Essie Timmons just raised her hand to motion them away. Her eyes were an eagle's, never distracted from the rising clumps of Georgia clay soil.

Watching and waiting.

The second event of great excitement was heralded by a murmuring through the onlookers that spread from one end of the gathering to the next: *McCormack's here.*

Frank McCormack was a slightly built man of seventy-two, whose face looked much older. He owned the land where the first bodies had been found, and his grand old house on the hill was visible from the Stephenses' windows.

In the wake of that ill-fated dig on his property, nearly two miles from this one, word had spread that his great-great grandfather sanctioned the burial—on his own land—of twelve black men killed in the Graceville riots. A different reporter called him about it every other week, the latest from as far as California. As if that wasn't enough to make his stomach ache at night, Frank McCormack had lost millions of dollars when the construction on his lots came to a halt, and much of that money had been lost because of Essie Timmons.

Although they technically weren't in sight of each other yet, it was rare to see Frank McCormack and Essie Timmons in the same company. Their families hadn't spoken for generations. And there they both were, at the dig.

The third unexpected thing was when the boy and his father came.

By that time, the number of onlookers at the dig had swelled to at least sixty, maybe more, with yet more planning to come watch the spectacle on their lunch breaks. No one had wondered before why the Stephens children weren't there, given their ordeal, so the boy's arrival was that much more a surprise. He was so small! And so brave.

A crutch was the only visible sign of whatever had happened to the boy in the woods. Both the father and son had the haunted look of war veterans, and they stayed close to each other, but far from everyone else, standing in the shade of a live oak as old as the tobacco barn. Their shyness was understandable, after what they'd been through. (And the Stephens clan could be stand-offish, so it was to be expected.)

Some of the onlookers speculated that Davie Stephens had dreamed it, and he'd found the burial site sleepwalking. Others were sure that the ghost of the Timmons boys had taken him by the hand and led him to the collapsed cellar. As for the reports of a wild animal attack, no one gave that much credence. ("That's just crazy talk.")

In any case, the Stephens boy's presence made the dig seem even more significant—perhaps, in a way, even historic. A few people grumbled about poor taste when Hal Lipcomb showed up selling roasted ears of corn and bags of pecans from a basket, but he sold plenty. If it felt more like a town fair, so be it. This wasn't something that happened every day.

"Don't you get your hopes up, Miss Essie," said the man holding the old woman's umbrella. His name was Lee, and he loved his work; every old woman reminded him of his grandmother, who had raised him and whom he missed every day. He didn't want any more heartaches for Essie Timmons. He had warned her not to come. Not being from Graceville, he didn't understand all the excitement about somebody claiming they'd seen a ghost.

Essie Timmons nodded, barely hearing him. Her eyes on the clods of falling dirt. "The boy said so," she said.

One of Frank McCormack's sons, Sam, who had driven to the dig from his tax attorney's office in Tallahassee, sighed and ran his fingers through his sandy hair. Tobacco squirted from his teeth to the soil below. He noticed that he and his father were only two of a handful of white people at the gathering; his wife said that noticing such things made him a racist, but he noticed all the same. Lately, race was all anyone wanted to talk about, and Sam McCormack was so sick to death of it that he didn't care if he was racist or not.

"Reckon they'll find anything?" Sam McCormack asked.

Old Man McCormack shielded his eyes from the sun with his palm. He ventured a quick glance at Davie Stephens before his eyes went back to the dig. "He's the right age," he said. "For seeing 'em."

"Yeah, just right," his son said. "And it's summer."

Essie Timmons, far across the plot, whispered to her attendant: "He saw them. They're down there. He says they fell."

Davie hadn't realized how much he was considered a celebrity until he and his father arrived at the dig and people stepped aside to make way for them. He'd never experienced so many eyes on him, like a movie star. The hush following his every step felt as dreamlike as the shouts and screams he'd heard in the night.

Davie took his father's hand as he walked, like Neema would have. He felt eight years old again. Davie hadn't expected so *many* people either, like someone had sold tickets.

What if everyone ended up thinking he was a fool?

A hydraulic shovel was set up over a gaping hole, which reminded Davie of the hole he thought the Timmons boys had dug, with the dead dog lying beside it.

Thoughts of the dog made Davie shiver. He blocked the memory by watching the people picking through clumps of soil, and his heart caught when a young woman in a white T-shirt with a university logo pulled up something big enough to be a leg bone.

But it was just a heavy stick.

Davie's heart pummeled him. Maybe it hadn't been a good idea to come.

"We're here in Graceville, Florida, at a most unusual community event," Dad said. Davie thought his father was talking to him, but when he looked up he saw that his father was shooting the video camera, panning across the crowd. "Three young boys have been missing for nearly one hundred years, and these Graceville residents believe the bones of those boys will be found. Here. Today. And they believe it because of ghosts."

"Hope you're not recording over mine," Davie said. Part of him knew he wouldn't care, in some ways. The video of that night only showed part of what had happened.

"Fresh tape. Yours is safely labeled, in the drawer."

Davie smiled. Dad was right: It felt safer to look at everything through a lens. Like someone else. His eyes followed his father's camera to the shell of a tobacco barn, nearly hidden within the trees. Next, two young boys buying roasted corn from a vendor. Girls climbing a tree. An old black woman sitting in a wheelchair under a caretaker's umbrella.

Dad put the camera down. "That's Essie Timmons, Davie," Dad said. "Those boys were her brothers. Do you want to go over and . . . ?"

Davie shook his head, mortified. He wouldn't be able to talk to her about the boys.

"That's okay," Dad said. "I only said it in case you wanted to. You've done plenty."

"Are you making a documentary?" Davie said.

Dad nodded. "Actually, *we* are, if that's okay with you. Forget a grant—we can get investors. A ghost story. Then I could take some time off."

"What for?" Davie said. He hoped Dad wasn't going to go off to hide in his work.

"To go to Ghana."

Davie was afraid he had heard wrong. "I thought you didn't want to go."

"Shouldn't we all be in one place?"

Davie nodded, blinking to keep his tears away. "Does Mom want you to come?"

"I think so," Dad said. The tic squinted his eye again. "We'll see."

That answer was a kick in the stomach, far from the assurances Davie had hoped for. But that was growing up, Davie figured. Gloves off. The bites are real.

The truth would have to do.

A workman wearing a red helmet popped up above ground to wave his flashlight frantically. "*Hold up!*" he said. His voice tremored with excitement. "Look at this!"

By then, in the middle of lunchtime, the crowd numbered more than a hundred.

The woods went silent as the machinery stopped. Miss Essie Timmons sat up straighter in her wheelchair than she had in years. Old Man McCormack began reciting the Lord's Prayer. Both of them were begging God for relief.

A far-away dog was barking, mostly yapping, but Davie and his father were probably the only two who noticed the sound. The barking raked across Davie's memories, sharp as teeth. Davie closed his eyes, feeling a lightheadedness he knew might make him faint.

That's not him. He's not real. He won't come out in daylight.

Slowly, Davie's heart slowed. His breath melted in his throat so he could swallow.

A sound Davie would never forget traveled through the crowd. A chorus of gasps first, almost one collective breath, then a continuous hum from one throat and chest to the next, some high, some low, a sound of depthless grief and boundless wonder. Davie felt his father's hands squeeze his shoulders hard, clenching so tight it hurt.

"God," his father said.

Davie opened his eyes to see what the people of Graceville had found.

The workman climbed to the surface gingerly, cradling a calcified child's frame. The corpse was curled in rigor mortis, but intact. Muddied bones dangled, but didn't break. He was small. Maybe the youngest.

"Little Eddie!" Essie Timmons said, rising to her feet. Two miracles, side by side.

An old white man wearing a suit and tie walked to the old woman's wheelchair and leaned close to her ear. She nodded. He put his hand on her shoulder, and she patted it. Then the man walked away, toward a younger man who might be his son.

Dad kept his camera trained on Essie Timmons for a long time. When the worker brought the bones to her and she wiped away a tear, Davie heard his father suck in his breath.

It took two more hours to find the other two sets of bones, and they weren't intact like the smallest child's had been. Instead, they came up in pieces.

All Davie ever saw of Issac was his skull, every tooth in place. Smiling, in a horrible way.

By that time, Davie was almost sorry he'd come. He would rather remember the Timmons boys as living. Running. Trying to save each other.

Davie's thigh was killing him. He needed more pills. Besides, he noticed, it was three o'clock. Three was a long way from dusk, but he didn't want to take any chances. No way did he want to be in these woods anytime even close to dark.

"I'm ready," he told his father.

"You okay?"

"Yeah, just tired," Davie said, but that was a lie. He didn't know yet if he was okay. That would depend on whether Neema would ever again sleep through the night without screaming and crying. Or if either of them would ever pet a dog. Being okay depended on Dad. Or Mom. Or maybe all of them.

When he and his father started walking toward Dad's rental car parked at the edge of the orange Georgia clay road, everyone stopped what they were saying and doing, even the workers. Someone started clapping, and soon everyone was, a few of them hooting. Their applause rose into treetops that had been filled with screams so shortly before. The prettiest girl Davie had ever seen—tall and dark, about thirteen, with a face like a girl from TV—grinned at him as if she had met him in her daydreams. Davie felt his face blush for the first time in his life.

His heart almost didn't give a cold shudder when he heard the faraway sound of the yappy dog's barking. He almost didn't wonder how he would ever sleep again.

Enjoy the following excerpt of
Brandon Massey's thrilling new novel,
DON'T EVER TELL,
on sale now wherever books are sold.

Prologue

On the morning of the day he would taste freedom again for the first time in four years, Dexter Bates lay on his bunk in the dimly lit cell, fingers interlaced behind his head, waiting for the arrival of the guards.

He did not tap his feet, hum a song, or count the cracks in the shadowed cement ceiling to pass the time. He was so still and silent that save for the rhythmic rising and falling of his chest, he might have been dead.

Incarceration taught a man many lessons, and chief among them was patience. You either learned how to befriend time, or the rambling passage of monotonous days eventually broke your spirit.

He had long ago vowed that he would not be broken. That he would use time to his advantage. The day ahead promised to reveal the value of his patient efforts.

Resting peacefully, he thought, as ever, about her. About her supple body, and how easily he bent it to his will. Her soft skin, and how it bruised beneath his fists. Her throaty voice, and how he urged it toward raw screams of terror. . . .

Pleasant thoughts to dribble away the last grains of time he had left in this hellhole.

Soon, the metal cell door clanged open. Two correctional officers as tall and wide as NFL linemen entered the cell.

"Let's go, Bates," Steele said, the lead guard. Sandy-haired, with a severe crew cut, he had a wide, boyish face that always appeared sunburned. He had a green parka with a fur-lined hood draped over his arm. "Hurry up or you'll miss your last ride outta here."

Dexter rose off the narrow cot. He was nude—he had stripped out of the prison jumpsuit before their arrival. He spread his long, muscular arms and legs.

"All right, open that big-assed cum-catcher of yours," Jackson said. He was a stern-faced black man with a jagged scar on his chin that he tried to hide with a goatee. He clicked on a pen-sized flashlight.

Dexter opened wide. Jackson panned the flashlight beam inside his mouth, and checked his nostrils and ears, too.

"Now bend over," Jackson said.

"But we hardly know each other," Dexter said.

"Don't test me this morning. I ain't in the mood for your bullshit."

Dexter turned around and bent over from the waist. Jackson shone the light up his rectum.

"He's clear," Jackson said.

"How about one last blow for the road, Jacky?" Dexter grabbed his length and swung it toward Jackson. "You know I'm gonna miss that sweet tongue action you got."

"Fuck you," Jackson said.

During Dexter's first month in the joint, Jackson had tried to bully him. Word of Dexter's background had spread quickly, and there were a number of guards and inmates who wanted a crack at him. A shot at glory.

Dexter had repeatedly slammed Jackson's face against a cinder-block wall, fracturing his jaw and scarring his chin. Although assaulting a guard would normally have resulted in a stint in the hole and additional time tacked onto his ten-year sentence, Jackson had never reported the incident. He had his pride.

Jackson searched Dexter's jumpsuit and boots for weapons, found nothing, and then Dexter dressed, shrugging on the parka that Steele gave him. Jackson cuffed his hands in front of him and attached the ankle restraints.

The guards marched him down the cell block. None of the inmates taunted Dexter, as was typical when an inmate departed. There were a few softly uttered words of support—"Peace, brother," "Take care of yourself, man"—but mostly, a widespread silence that approached reverence.

"These guys are really gonna miss you, Bates," Steele said.

"They can always write me," Dexter said.

They took him to inmate processing, where the final transfer paperwork was completed. He was being sent to Centralia Correctional Center, another medium security prison, to serve out the balance of his sentence. He had put in for the transfer purportedly to take advantage of the inmate work programs offered at that facility, and it had taken almost two years for the approval to come through.

The administrator, a frizzy haired lady with a wart on her nose, expressed surprise that Dexter was not taking any personal items with him. Most transferring inmates left with boxes of belongings in tow, as if they were kids going away to summer camp. Dexter assured Wart Nose that he would get everything he needed once he was settled in his new home.

Paperwork complete, they walked Dexter outside to the boarding area, where an idling white van was parked, exhaust fumes billowing from the pipe. "Illinois Department of Corrections" was painted on the side in large black letters. Steel bars protected the frosted windows.

It was a cold, overcast December morning, a fresh layer of snow covering the flat countryside. An icy gust shrieked across the parking lot and sliced at Dexter's face.

He wondered about the weather in Chicago, and felt a warm tingle in his chest.

Steele slid open the van's side door, and Dexter climbed in, air pluming from his lips. Two beefy correctional officers from Centralia waited inside, both sitting in the front seat. A wire mesh screen separated the front from the rear bench rows.

"Sit your ass down so we can get moving," the guard in the passenger seat said. "It's cold as fuck out here."

Steele lifted the heavy chain off the vehicle's floor and clamped it to Dexter's ankle restraints. He nodded at Dexter, his blue-eyed gaze communicating a subtle message, and then he slammed the door.

As in police vehicles, there were no interior door handles. Packed inside and bolted in place, a prisoner bound for another concrete home could only sit still and enjoy the ride.

"Headed to our home in Centralia, eh?" the driver asked. He glanced in the rearview mirror at Dexter. "Just so you know, brother man, whoever you were outside won't mean shit there, got it? You'll be everyone's bitch, especially ours."

"Spoken like a man who's always wanted to be a cop," Dexter said. "Did you fail the exam? Or wash out of the academy?"

"What a piece of work," the passenger guard said, shaking his head. "You must want deluxe 'commodations in the hole soon as you get there."

At the manned booth, a guard waved the van through the tall prison gates. Dexter looked out the window. The snowy plains surrounded them, so vast and featureless they nearly blended into the overcast horizon.

By design, many state correctional centers had been erected in barren wastelands, to make it almost impossible for an escaping inmate to progress far before recapture. Dexter had heard rumors of inmates who managed to get away being tracked down within three miles of the joint, upon which they were brought back, weeping like babies, to an increased sentence and a long stay in solitary.

The two-lane road was crusted with dirty slush and riddled with potholes. It wound through nothingness for close to five miles before it fed into a major artery, which eventually intersected the highway.

At that time of morning, there was no traffic, and there wouldn't be much at all, anyway. The road dead ended at the prison, a place most normal people preferred to avoid.

The guards switched on the radio to a country-western station. The singer crooned about seeing his lady again after being away for so long.

Dexter wasn't a fan of country western, but he could dig the song's message.

"What time is it?" Dexter asked.

"You got somewhere to be, asshole?" the driver said.

"I want to make sure we're on time. I've got a hot date with my new warden."

"Whatever. It's a quarter after nine, numb nuts."

Nodding to the music, Dexter dug his bound hands into the right front pocket of the parka.

A key was secreted inside, courtesy of his good man Steele. Correctional officers were even more receptive to bribes than cops, and that was saying something.

"I'm really feeling this song," Dexter said. "Turn it up, will you, man?"

"That's the smartest thing you've said yet," the passenger guard said, and cranked up the volume.

Dexter used the key to disengage the handcuffs, the loud music drowning out the tinkle of the chains. Leaning forward slightly, he stretched his long arm downward and unlocked the ankle restraints, too.

Then he sat back in the seat, and waited. He crooned along with the song, his intentionally bad voice making the guards laugh.

"You sure ain't got no future in music," the driver said. "Jesus Christ, you're terrible."

Dexter shrugged. "A man's got to know his limitations, I guess."

After they had driven for about three miles, they came around a bend. There was a gray Dodge Charger stalled on the shoulder of the road. A blond woman in a shearling coat and jeans was at the trunk, apparently trying to lift out a spare tire. Her long hair flowed from underneath a yellow cap, blowing like a siren's mane in the chill wind.

"Would ya lookit that?" The passenger guard leered at the woman. "Pull over, Max. Let's help her out."

A green Chevy Tahoe approached from the opposite direction.

"You know we're not supposed to stop, Cade," Max said.

"You better not stop," Dexter said. "You're going to screw up my schedule."

"Shut up," Cade said. He turned to Max. "Look, it'll take ten minutes. That young broad can't change the goddamn tire by herself."

"You just wanna get laid," Max said.

"Hey, I'm a Good Samaritan. I gotta do my charitable deed for the day."

"To get laid," Max said. But he slowed the van and nosed behind the Dodge. "You got ten minutes. No word of this to anyone."

"I'll snitch on you," Dexter said.

"The hell you will," Cade said. He licked his fingers, patted down his eyebrows, and then climbed out of the van. Strutting like a rooster, he approached the blonde.

The oncoming Tahoe suddenly slashed across the road, snow spraying from the tires, and blocked off the van. Tinted windows concealed the occupants.

"Holy shit," Max said. "What the hell's this?"

On the shoulder of the road, the other guard noticed the Tahoe, and froze.

Dexter dug his hand in the coat's left front pocket and clutched the grip of the loaded .38, also compliments of Steele.

A gunman wearing a ski mask and a black jacket sprang out of the Dodge's trunk. The masked man shot Cade twice in the head with a pistol, and the guard dropped to the pavement like a discarded puppet.

Cursing, Max fumbled for his radio.

"Hey, Max," Dexter said. "Look, buddy, no chains."

When Max spun around, Dexter had the gun pressed to the wire mesh screen. He shot the guard at the base of the throat, just below the collar.

The guard's eyes widened with surprise, and he slid against the seat, a bloody hole unfurling like a blooming flower in his windpipe.

The passenger-side door of the Tahoe swung open. A refrigerator-wide black man attired like a correctional officer scrambled out and ran to the driver's side of the van.

The ski-masked shooter bounded out of the trunk. The blonde took the ring of keys from Cade's belt, and unlocked the van's side door.

"Morning, Dex." She smiled brightly.

"Hey, Christy."

Moving fast, Dexter and the ski-masked man lifted the guard's corpse off the ground and laid it across the floor of the van. In front, the guy dressed like a guard had gotten behind the wheel and was propping up the wounded guard in the seat to look like a passenger if one gave him a casual glance.

The dying guard was moaning entreaties to God in a blood-choked gurgle.

"Someone shut him up." Dexter slammed the side panel door. "Fuck it, I'll do it myself."

Opening the passenger door, Dexter shot the guard twice in the chest, permanently dousing the struggling light in the man's eyes. Except for the splash of blood on his coat, he appeared to be sleeping off a hangover.

"Good to see you, man," the new driver said.

"Same here." Dexter nodded, closed the door. "Let's roll out."

The ski-masked gunner scrambled behind the wheel of the Dodge, the blonde got in on the passenger side, and Dexter hustled in the back.

Beside them, the Tahoe backed up and executed a swift U-turn, maneuvering behind the prison van, which had begun to rumble forward.

Both the SUV and the van were driven by longtime colleagues, upstanding members of the Windy City's finest.

"How long?" Dexter asked.

"Two minutes and fourteen seconds," Javier, his former partner said. He had peeled away his ski mask. A native of the Dominican Republic who had moved to the States when he was five, Javier was a lean, bronze-skinned man with dark, wavy hair and a pencil-thin mustache.

Javier flashed a lopsided grin that reminded Dexter of their wild days working together.

"We kicked ass, Dex."

"Like old times," Dexter said.

"How's it feel to be out?" Christy asked. Unlike every other member of the operation, she wasn't a cop—she was Javier's wife, and as trustworthy as any brother of the badge.

"Like being born again," Dexter said. "Hallelujah."

Christy passed him a brown paper bag that contained a bottle of iced tea and two roast beef-and-cheddar sandwiches wrapped in plastic. Dexter ate greedily. After four years of bland prison food, the simple meal was like a spread at a four-star restaurant.

A bag from Target lay on the seat beside him. He opened it, found a pair of overalls and a plaid shirt.

"The rest of the stuff?" Dexter asked.

"The duffel with all your things is in the trunk," Javier said. "But you need to get out of that ape suit pronto, man. Who would I look like giving a prisoner a taxi ride?"

Dexter peeled out of the prison jumpsuit and dressed in the civilian clothes.

When they reached the main artery that ran through town, Javier made a turn that would take them to the highway. The prison van, followed by the Tahoe, went in the opposite direction.

They would drive the van over a hundred miles away and abandon it, and its cargo of dead guards, in a pond. With luck, it would be at least several days before the cops would discover it.

Dexter settled back in the seat and dozed. He dreamed, as usual, of her. She was weeping, screaming, and pleading for her life.

It was a good dream.

When he awoke over two hours later, they were bumping across a long, narrow lane, freshly plowed of snow. Tall pines and oaks lined the road, ice clinging to their boughs.

Javier turned into a long driveway that led to a small A-frame house surrounded by dense forest.

"My mother's crib," Javier said, and Christy laughed.

Dexter laughed, too. The house was no more inhabited by Javier's mother than it was by the Queen of England. Javier had bought it in his mother's name to conceal his ownership, a ploy that many of them had used at one time or another to hide their connection to various properties and valuables they purchased—things decidedly *not* paid for with their regular cop salaries.

A car, covered by a gray tarp, sat beside the house.

"What's that?" Dexter asked.

"Something special for you," Javier said.

They parked. Dexter got out of the car and walked to the covered vehicle, snow and ice crunching under his shoes. He peeked under the tarp.

It was a ten-year-old black Chevy Caprice, a model that was once the ubiquitous police cruiser.

Dexter laughed. "You kill me."

"Glad the joint hasn't taken away your sense of humor," Javier said. He opened the Dodge's trunk and handed a big, olive green duffel bag to Dexter. *"Feliz Navidad, amigo."*

Dexter placed the bag on the ground and unzipped it. It contained a Glock 9mm, five magazines of ammo, a switchblade, a concealable body armor vest, a prepaid cell phone, clothing, keys to the Chevy and the house, a manila envelope, and five thick, bundled packets of cash in denominations of twenties, fifties and hundreds, totaling approximately ten thousand dollars.

It wasn't a lot of money, but more waited in Chicago. Substantially more.

"Santa brought you everything on your wish list," Javier said. "In spite of how naughty you've been."

Dexter grinned. In the manila envelope, he found an Illinois driver's license, U.S. passport, and a Social Security card, all listed under the alias of Alonzo Washington.

"Alonzo Washington?" Dexter asked.

Javier smiled. "Sound familiar?"

"The flick about the narc—*Training Day,* right? Denzel's character was named Alonzo something."

"I thought you'd appreciate it."

"You're a regular fucking comedian, aren't you?" Dexter tapped the IDs. "These solid?"

"As a rock," Javier said. "The finest money could buy."

In the ID snapshots, Dexter's face had been digitally altered to depict him as clean shaven. Dexter rubbed the thick, woolen beard he had grown in prison.

"We threw some Magic Shave and a couple razors in the bag, too," Javier said.

"I've had hair on my chin since I was fifteen. I'll hardly recognize myself."

He turned to the house. Although it offered perhaps fifteen hundred square feet, a decent amount of space but nothing spectacular, to a man who had lived in a seven-by-twelve cell it would be like having the run of the Biltmore Estate all to himself.

"Utilities are on," Javier said. "Christy went grocery shopping this morning, packed the refrigerator with everything a growing boy needs."

"Your loyalty," Dexter said. "That means more to me than anything. Thanks."

"Speaking of loyalty, we tried to track down your ex-wife," Christy said.

"Wife," Dexter said.

"Right. Anyway, she's dropped off the grid, like you thought. We got nothing."

"That's good," Dexter said.

"How the hell is that good, after how she screwed you?" Javier asked.

"Because," Dexter said, a grin curving across his face. "I get to find her myself."

SUBSCRIBE TO BRANDON MASSEY'S *TALESPINNER*

Readers of Brandon Massey now can subscribe to his free *Talespinner* newsletter by visiting his website at www.brandonmassey.com. *Talespinner* subscribers get a quarterly e-mail newsletter, opportunities to win prizes in exclusive contests, and advance information about forthcoming publications. Go online today at *www.brandonmassey.com* and sign up. Membership is free!